Summer of
GOLD
and
WATER

Summer of GOLD and WATER

KATHLEEN DANIELCZYK

TATE PUBLISHING
AND ENTERPRISES, LLC

Summer of Gold and Water
Copyright © 2012 by Kathleen Danielczyk. All rights reserved.

No part of this publication may be reproduced, stored in a retrieval system or transmitted in any way by any means, electronic, mechanical, photocopy, recording or otherwise without the prior permission of the author except as provided by USA copyright law.

The opinions expressed by the author are not necessarily those of Tate Publishing, LLC.

Published by Tate Publishing & Enterprises, LLC

127 E. Trade Center Terrace | Mustang, Oklahoma 73064 USA
1.888.361.9473 | www.tatepublishing.com

Tate Publishing is committed to excellence in the publishing industry. The company reflects the philosophy established by the founders, based on Psalm 68:11,

"The Lord gave the word and great was the company of those who published it."

Book design copyright © 2012 by Tate Publishing, LLC. All rights reserved.
Cover design by Nicole McDaniel
Interior design by Rodrigo Adolfo

Published in the United States of America

ISBN: 978-1-62024-665-8
FICTION / Historical
FICTION / Romance / Historical
12.07.19

Dedication

This book is dedicated to
My husband, Michael.
Without his support and encouragement,
this book would never have been written.

Prologue

The muddy water was churning, swirling above Sarah's head. She struggled to get a breath of the night air. As she thrashed her arms and legs, desperately trying to swim to the surface, she was bumped and banged by tree limbs, logs, rocks, and pieces of furniture. Unable to decide whether the darkness above or below her was the night sky, Sarah realized she was going to die. A sudden peace overcame her, and she stopped moving.

Fortunately, the rest of the debris had not stopped, and a large log hit Sarah in the stomach, knocking the air from her lungs and thrusting her toward the surface. When her face emerged, she greedily gulped the night air. Pelting rain filled her open mouth with water. The fast-moving current pushed Sarah farther down the river. She reached for the large log that had thrust her to the surface and hung on for dear life as it bucked in the swirling river.

All she saw was rain and muddy water swirling around her. Occasionally she would see outlines of what she thought were trees and logs, some with people clinging to them. Sarah tumbled in the turbulent water as she raced toward some unknown destination. She looked for something more substantial to hold on to in her vicinity, but the only other passengers on this wet ride were small branches, shards of wood, and…dead bodies. Shocked by the surprised looks on their faces as they drifted by, she gripped onto the log tighter, more determined than ever not to go under. Rooftops and sides of houses or barns also floated by, some with people holding on for dear life as they were tossed around in the current. A rooftop came very close to where Sarah was clinging to the log. The men on the rooftop reached for her and tried to pull her to its relative safety. She stretched one hand, her fingertips brusher theirs, when a wave pushed her out of reach. She let out a sob as the rooftop was pushed in another direction and she watched as the men faded in the veil of rain.

Sarah's grip on the log was weakening; she had been in the water for what seemed like hours, holding on, hoping for a miracle. Up ahead, she saw a gray outline that looked in the haze like a large tree at the edge of the churning water in an eddy by the shore. Hoping she could make it, she kicked her feet, pushing the log toward the tree. In the branches she thought she saw a person and hoped that person would share their sanctuary. As she neared the tree, she saw that the person was Walter. How could her husband be in the tree?

Confused but even more determined to make the tree, she kicked harder. Slowly the log moved toward her goal. As the eddy pulled her from the main current, she realized she was heading straight for the tree, and hope flared in her breast that she would be safe. The log plunged into the lower limbs beneath Walter's waiting hands. She reached for him, her wet hands sliding along his cold fingers.

"Walter! You're going to have to reach farther and pull me up."

There was no response. He didn't reach for her. Shielding her eyes from the rain with a hand, she peered up at her husband. It was a corpse, arms dangling, reaching for the water.

Sarah pulled her hand back and in the same moment lost her grip on the log. She slipped under the murky water and this time did not struggle. The churning of the water pushed Sarah to the surface once again. She reached for the log that had been her raft and her hand closed on something soft. She instinctively pulled her hand back, fearing it was one of the dead bodies floating by and then felt as though she was being shaken.

Still struggling against the waves, she could hear her name being called. She looked around and saw Walter. Thinking it was the corpse talking to her, she pulled back and cried out.

"Sarah! Sarah! Wake up, honey! It's only a dream! Sarah!"

Drenched in sweat, she finally stopped struggling as relief flooded through her. She opened her eyes to see she was in her bed in Pittsburgh and Walter was alive and next to her.

She collapsed in Walter's arms, sobbing hysterically.

"It was horrible, just like the rest of the nightmares. When will they go away?"

Walter covered Sarah with the blankets she had knocked off with her thrashing and held her close to him. Her sobs subsided as she rested her head on Walter's shoulder, taking comfort in his strength and warmth as she moved as close as possible into his arms.

"Soon, very soon. They aren't as frequent as they were. Maybe it was the thunderstorm last night. It got pretty nasty there for a while."

Walter held Sarah for a long time, stroking her hair and making sure she felt safe once again. When he thought Sarah had gone back to sleep, he closed his eyes and prayed for her nightmares to end. A few minutes later, Sarah started to get up.

"Go back to sleep, Walter. I am going to go sit up. I couldn't possibly go back to sleep now. I have to get up soon anyway. I will be all right." Sarah kissed her husband and got out of bed. She got her robe and slippers and made her way to the living room.

The fire in the stove had burned down to smoldering embers. Sarah grabbed a few sticks of wood, laid them on the embers, and watched as they caught fire. Closing the door to the stove, she moved to the window. The sun would be coming up over the horizon, and Sarah knew that it would chase away the bad dreams. Today was the big day, and she needed to have all her wits about her. Maybe after today, the nightmares would go away completely. She focused on that hope as she watched the sun color the sky with red and pink streaks. It seemed that the world was new again, the rain having washed away all the dirt, and the world was clean, ready for a new start. The red and pink streaks gave way to the clear, blue sky as the sun rose higher over the horizon.

She sat on the couch and covered her feet with a coverlet that her mother had made for her fifth birthday. She always felt a sense of loss when she remembered how her parents had died many years before, and today was no different. She wished they could be here to be a part of the day, but she knew in her heart they were watching from heaven and would always be with her. As she sat in the early morning quiet, she thought about the road that she had traveled to be where she was today. She thought about the people that were no longer in her life and of all the good things that were a part of her life. She loved this time of the morning. She settled back on the sofa and let her mind drift to the past.

Chapter One

Dinner was a pleasant affair, as it usually was when Walter's parents came. Shirley loved her grandparents. It was July 25, 1875, and she turned six that day. After dinner she was allowed to open her birthday presents. Her grandparents brought her a new book, and her parents gave her a new dress and bonnet. Sarah's grandparents had dropped by earlier and given Sarah a gift to give to Shirley that evening, as they were unable to come to dinner. Shirley loved her gifts and ran to the bedroom to try on her new dress. She burst back into the dining room and twirled around.

"That dress is just lovely!" Walter's mother said.

"Beautiful princess!" Walter exclaimed.

Shirley ran over and gave her parents a hug and a kiss. Sarah smiled.

As Sarah watched Shirley walk to her chair and open the book, she smiled. Her daughter would be occupied for at least an hour, giving the adults time to talk. Sarah turned back to the table. "Have you seen the ad? For hired help, for the Danverses?

"If they are looking for a maid, why, I can do that. I can cook and clean. I do it here. And with my skill as a seamstress, oh, Walter, do you think that it is possible that I could apply and, oh, the possibilities are endless!" Sarah smiled at Walter. After a moment's reflection, the smile slipped from Sarah's face, and she shook her head slowly.

"Sarah, what is wrong?" Walter's mother asked.

"Nothing. It is just a pipe dream. Why would she pick me? And even if she did, it is so far away, how would I get to work? We have no horse and buggy to get me there."

Walter's father smiled and patted Sarah's hand. "Well, let me tell you what I know about the Danverses, and we can see if we can figure something out. It is good to have dreams and hopes, let's see if we can make them come true."

Sarah looked up and smiled at Walter's father. With a hint of doubt still on her face, she leaned back in her chair, lifted her coffee, and settled in to listen. After years of working as a seamstress for the miserly Mrs. Hill, the news that the Danverses, one of Pittsburgh's richest families, were finally hiring help came as a glimmer of hope.

Mr. Wesley Danvers was the president of the largest bank in Pittsburgh, Pittsburgh Federal Savings. It was rumored that he started out as a mail clerk and worked at every position in the bank until he became the right-hand assistant of the former president, Mr. Kendall Miller. Walter's father banked there and had become friends with some of the tellers over the years. He had watched Wesley rise from a clerk in the bank to Mr. Miller's right-hand assistant.

Wesley was the second child in a family of six children. His parents lived in a small, four-room house on the east side of Pittsburgh. His father worked in the steel mill, and his mother was a seamstress. As Wesley got older, he helped his parents out by delivering ice when his brothers and sisters were in school. Wesley enrolled in night school, and he was at the top of his class and earned a high school diploma. Some of the teachers were so impressed with Wesley, they gave him college books to continue his studies. His math teacher, Eunice Jeffs, saw his potential and got Wesley a job at Pittsburgh Federal Savings as an apprentice clerk. Wesley quickly learned the banking system and understood the bank better than anyone.

After a couple of years, Larry Stevens, the teller supervisor, approached Wesley about working as a full-time teller. Wesley was overjoyed and threw himself into the work. Larry kept an eye on Wesley as he soaked up the workings of the bank, and because of his suggestions, Wesley was promoted and given more responsibilities. In the seven years that Wesley worked at the bank, his drive and thirst for knowledge and responsibility was unsurpassed by anyone.

Mr. Miller realized that the bank was growing and started looking for an assistant. In a discussion with all the tellers as to who would be the best assistant, it was suggested that Mr. Miller promote Wesley. Larry wanted to suggest himself but instead asked one of the other tellers to nominate him. Larry was not much older than Wesley but had started at the bank years before, following in his father's footsteps. He was a competent man but was not as imaginative or proactive as Wesley.

Mr. Miller chose Wesley, and again, Wesley jumped at the chance and soon became indispensable to Mr. Miller. Mr. Miller and Wesley worked side by side for many years. Mr. Miller enrolled Wesley in night school and watched as he got his degree. A party was thrown for Wesley at Mr. Miller's house, and many of his friends and customers were invited. It was there that Wesley met Eloise, Mr. Miller's daughter.

After two years of courting, two years of Wesley proving himself to Mr. Miller and saving every penny he had to give Eloise a good life, Wesley asked Mr. Miller for Eloise's hand. He knew he was not of the same class as the Millers but hoped that Mr. Miller would honor him and say yes. Mr. Miller took a week to answer Wesley, and when he did, it was a resounding yes.

Wesley and Eloise were married, and for a wedding gift, Mr. Miller moved them into the large carriage house on his property. The couple stayed in the carriage house for many years and were very happy.

At the bank, Wesley assisted Mr. Miller in every task, started to sit in on the board meetings, and advised Mr. Miller on policy changes and what the customers thought about the changes in the bank. As Mr. Miller got older, he relinquished many tasks to Wesley and began spending more and more time away from the office, knowing that the bank was in the best care.

When old Mr. Miller was ready to retire, Wesley was approved unanimously by the board and was inducted in a lavish banquet honoring Mr. Miller as the outgoing president and Wesley as the new president. Larry Stevens, though outwardly happy for Wesley, was deeply resentful at being passed over for the promotion. It became common knowledge around town that Larry thought he should have had the job.

In the nine years that Wesley Danvers had been president of the bank, they had to expand the bank vault twice and tripled the amount of staff that worked at Pittsburgh Federal Savings. "That is some story. I always thought that hard work would pay off, but I never saw it happen to this extent," Walter said. "I have seen him around town, and I would never have believed he didn't come from money."

"Mrs. Danvers, Eloise, is just as down to earth," Walter's mother said. "I have run into her in Mrs. Hill's shop with her daughter. I believe her name is Sheila. Cute little girl, and so well behaved. She never has a maid tagging along like some of the other high-society ladies. She carries her own bags, doesn't expect special treatment. I have seen her wait up to twenty minutes to be waited on and will allow others to go before her if she is undecided about a purchase."

"Talk around the market is that Wesley is getting pressure from the other society gentlemen about not having a maid, butler, and other help around the house," Sarah said.

Walter's father threw his head back and let out a loud laugh. Shirley looked up from her book and started giggling with her grandfather. "Wesley doing something that everyone does? Pressure from the other men? Not Wesley! There is no way he would do something because it is considered correct. Wesley is his own man. If he is hiring help for his wife, then it is because he feels she needs help. She is just as headstrong as he is, so I am sure it took some convincing to change her mind."

"I have heard the same thing," Walter's mother said. "Mrs. Danvers probably heard someone talking about needing a job, or the poor working conditions somewhere, and decided to help out by hiring someone in her household."

"That sounds like Eloise more than needing help. I think it would be a good idea if Sarah went over to the interview and applied. I know I am a bit biased"—Walter's father winked at Sarah—"but I think that you and Mrs. Danvers would work well together. You are smart, talented, a hard worker, and anyway, what will it hurt?"

"Walter? What do you think? I just don't know." Sarah looked around the small house. "It would be a nice change of pace from Mrs. Hill."

Walter knelt in front of Sarah's chair. "Darling, you can do anything you put your mind to. I think you should go."

"Then it is settled," Walter's father said as he slapped his hand on the table. "Sarah will apply at the Danvers and we will go from there. Now, where is that fine cake you made?"

At the mention of cake, Shirley squealed and jumped from her chair, book forgotten.

Smiling, Sarah got up and brought the cake to the table. As she set it down, Walter looked up at his wife and saw the worry still on her face.

Chapter Two

Walter and Sarah talked about the interview over the next few days. Every time Sarah started to back out of going to the interview, Walter reminded Sarah how Mrs. Hill talked to her, the rude and sharp tone in her voice. He reminded her that every time Sarah asked to be hired as a full-time employee, Mrs. Hill said she did not know the business well enough to work with the customers, as a full-time employee would, that her position was to stay in the back and sew. Walter also speculated that the pay and the working conditions would be much nicer at an estate, than in the cramped back room of Mrs. Hill's dress shop. Sarah thought about the amount of money that Mrs. Hill paid her. Sarah averaged about $3.50 a week, and it was only that high because she was fast with the needle. After being reminded about all of this, and hearing what Walter's parents had told her about the Danvers, Sarah decided that she had nothing to lose by going and talking to Mrs. Danvers. She liked what she had heard and wanted to meet them. If she did not get the position, then she was no worse off than she was now.

It was a hot day in August, but Sarah dressed carefully in her best dark blue skirt and white blouse and freshly polished worn shoes. She arrived at the Danverses' mansion and was not surprised at the line of applicants that were milling around the ornate fountain in the middle of the driveway. Sarah gave her name to the butler at the door and waited patiently for her turn. As she was waiting, she strolled around the driveway and marveled at the estate's grounds.

The Danverses' house was located at the top of High Street. High Street boasted houses that were set back from the road, with long, sweeping driveways and rolling, manicured lawns. When approaching the house, perfectly manicured trees, shrubs, and colorful flower gardens could be seen. The driveway curved to the front of the house under the large porch so guests and family members did not get wet when entering or leaving the house to get into a carriage if the weather was bad. The driveway then continued around a large fountain, which was said to have the largest cherub in the city. There was a "Y" in the driveway. The left fork wound its way back out the main gate, and the right fork continued toward the carriage house. Next to the carriage house was the stable, which was connected by a covered walkway. It was told that the stable was manned by six stable hands and was among the cleanest in the county.

Knowing it would be some time before her turn, Sarah walked toward the stable. She remembered when her father used to bring her to the horse auctions. She loved the earthy smell of the stable and the welcoming whinny of the horses. She supposed that was partly why she had married Walter. He, like her father, loved horses and worked in the stables. When he came home at the end of a long day and folded her into his strong arms, she'd take a deep breath and be reminded of family, past and present.

She cautiously stepped inside the stable, not wanting to appear nosy, and looked around. It had a unique design. In the center of the building was a large archway leading inside. There were two large doors that swung wide to admit horses or the family carriage. It opened to a short, spacious hallway that intersected the main isle.

When coming to the main aisle, looking to the left, Sarah saw the aisle housed eight stalls on either side. A stable hand was feeding one of the horses, and he turned and saw her. Sarah was quite embarrassed to be caught wandering and turned quickly to leave.

"Good morning! How are you on this hot day?" the stable hand said as he walked toward Sarah.

"I'm f-fine. I'm sorry for intruding! I was waiting for my turn and I was curious and, oh my, I'm so embarrassed," Sarah stammered.

He laughed. "Please, do not be embarrassed. I am Ryan. I work here. May I ask your name?"

"I'm Sarah Green. I'm here to talk to the Danverses about the position of maid."

"Sarah. Very nice to meet you. Would you like me to give you a tour while you wait? It is much cooler in the barn than out on the driveway."

"Oh, thank you, no, I don't want to take you from your duties. I'll go wait outside with the others."

Sarah turned to leave when Ryan called to her.

"It's no problem. I would very much like to show you the barn. We, the other stable hands and myself, are very proud of our jobs and feel very blessed to be working here. The Danverses are such wonderful people. You're in for a surprise when you meet them."

Sarah hesitated only a moment before curiosity won out. She was very interested to learn more—both about the stables and about the Danverses.

The Danverses had two teams of carriage horses. One set of four horses were snow white, with matching black stars on their foreheads. The other set of four horses were coal black, with white socks on all four feet. There were also two Morgan horses, one sleek black and one charcoal gray; these were Mr. and Mrs. Danvers' horses. The Danverses could often be seen riding together on a Sunday afternoon. The grooms kept the stalls in pristine condition. At the end of the aisle, the doorway led to a large paddock for grazing.

Ryan pointed out to Sarah the pictures and ribbons on the walls of the stable.

"All the stable hands or grooms, whichever you like, are encouraged to enter local competitions for riding, showmanship, or anything else they are interested in. The Danverses insist that the awards and photographs be displayed. They attend every meet and are very proud of us."

As Sarah finished looking at all the ribbons and awards, she turned and saw the large indoor riding ring, including jumps. The ceiling was at least thirty feet high, and it gave the appearance of being outdoors. Sarah stepped into the ring and noticed the floor was covered with sawdust. When walking it felt like a cushion was underfoot. Sarah stood a few feet inside the ring and looked around and up at the high ceiling.

"Pretty nice, wouldn't you say?"

"It's amazing."

She walked back to the aisle and saw that to the right of the main entrance were multiple storage rooms. There was a large tack room and a room that housed the family carriage, a smaller carriage, and a buckboard. As Ryan and Sarah slowly walked down the aisle toward the storage rooms, she could see that the room also held many of the ribbons and trophies the grooms had won.

"This is where the rest of the awards are located. The ones on the wall outside are the most current. When one of us wins a new award, it gets hung on the wall and the award it replaces gets put in this room."

The Danverses were very proud of the grooms and wanted them to be proud of themselves and their accomplishments. No other employer allowed their grooms to participate in the competitions.

Across from the large tack room was the storage room, which was divided into two areas. One was for the grain sacks. The other side held medicines that might be needed to keep the horses healthy along with a stall in which a sick horse could be kept away from the other horses while recuperating. There was still a lot of storage room left over, and everything was kept in an orderly fashion.

"This stable is incredible," Sarah said as she looked around.

"Yes, it is. Are you familiar with stables?"

Sarah nodded. "My father, Scott Atworth, was a consultant, hired to evaluate horses for purchase. I accompanied him to many farms, auctions, and stables."

"Scott Atworth? He was your father? He is a legend among stable hands. I wish I had been able to meet him. But if you are his daughter, it is just as good." Ryan smiled at Sara.

Sarah grinned. "My parents could not afford to have a large stable, but we spent so much time at auctions and other people's stables that it didn't matter we didn't have our own. It would have been nice to have a stable like this. I think my father would have thought he died and went to heaven." Sarah's eyes traveled from the sturdy stalls to the equally stout rafters. The magnitude of the place took her breath away.

Ryan touched her arm. "Come let me show you more of the stable."

Smiling, Sarah composed herself and followed Ryan. As they walked back toward the main entrance, she saw a doorway that was partially opened. She peered inside and noticed the staircase that led to the upstairs floor of the stable. Sarah had heard from people in town that the stable hands lived above the barn, and the quarters were quite nice.

"That's where the stable hands live. We mostly have single men working here, and the upstairs has apartments. The Danverses had the servants' quarters built the same time they had the barn built, just in case there was a need for larger apartments. When someone gets married, they are moved into the larger quarters. The Danverses are considerate that way. The apartments in the servants' quarters are larger, for families. I live there with my wife, Megan, and our son, Timothy."

Sarah thanked Ryan for his tour of the stable and went back to the front of the house to wait with the other ladies from town. Sarah saw many friends and made more as they talked and waited for their turn. As she chatted with the other applicants, she told them what she had learned from Ryan. The other ladies were interested to know about the accommodations in the barn. Sarah knew they were treated far better than at other households and, because of that, they were very loyal to the Danverses.

To the right of the stable, closer to the house, was a smaller building that was built for the families that Ryan told her about. She could see the covered walkway from the back door of the staff house to the kitchen door of the main house. From what Ryan had told her, the apartments were quite large. Sarah could not imagine living in a large apartment that did not smell like bleach. She tried to imagine Shirley having her own room and there being room for a sofa to relax on after the day was over.

Mrs. Danvers had enlisted the help of the stable hands to pass out lemonade to the waiting applicants. All the women were very surprised, and of course, that brought on a new speculation about what the Danverses were really like. By the time it was Sarah's turn, she was tired and a bit wilted from the sun beating down on her straw bonnet.

A young woman opened the door and called out Sarah's name. Sarah came forward brushing the imaginary lint from her skirt and slowly entered the house. A cool breeze washed over her face as she removed her bonnet. As she walked into the foyer of the Danverses' mansion, she was surprised at the vastness of the entranceway. There was a large, crystal chandelier hanging in the main hall. An oval carpet of deep blue covered the entrance hall floor. In the center was an ornately carved cherry table with a marble top. In the center of the table was a large oriental vase with brightly colored flowers. A curved staircase rose from the right corner of the hallway around to a small landing. The railing was made of cherry wood and was smooth and polished to a high shine. The stairs were carpeted with a deep blue oriental runner up the center of the stairs. On the wall along the staircase were many pictures of relatives, past and present.

Under the stairs was an archway that opened into a large, comfortable kitchen. Sarah could see a center island with pots and pans hanging overhead. She could make out the edge of what looked like a new icebox.

Mrs. Danvers entered the foyer and watched Sarah look around the entranceway.

"Isn't it lovely? All the pictures are of our relatives, many of whom are not with us any longer. The carpet was brought all the way from the Orient, and the chandelier is from England. I'm Mrs. Danvers, and you are?"

Startled that she was being watched, Sarah turned around quickly. "Sarah Green, ma'am." She curtsied to Mrs. Danvers.

"Sarah, what a lovely name. May I call you Sarah?"

"Of course, Mrs. Danvers."

"Come this way, Sarah. I would like you to meet my husband. He's waiting in the library."

Mrs. Danvers led Sarah through a large oak doorway into the library. Sarah let her eyes wander around the room. The difference was amazing. This room looked lived in, warm and cozy. To the left of the entrance there were two large windows that were as high as a person was tall. At the end of the room was a large oak desk, with ornate carving on the front. The wall behind the desk was lined from floor to ceiling with shelves that contained books and art objects. In front of the desk were two leather chairs with a small table in between. To the right was a large fireplace that looked like it was carved into the wall and outlined with white marble. On the mantle were ivory carvings of elephants and lions. Above the mantle was a stunning oil portrait of Mr. and Mrs. Danvers. In front of the fireplace were two very comfortable-looking couches with a table in front. On the table was a silver tea service with china cups that were ornately painted with small, purple flowers.

Finally, Sarah let her eyes rest on the other person in the room. Standing next to the fireplace was Mr. Danvers. As he turned to greet her, a large, welcoming smile spread across his face, and he walked over to shake Sarah's hand.

Wesley Danvers was a handsome man. He had dark hair, a thick moustache, and clear green eyes that sparkled when he smiled. Eloise moved to stand next to her husband. Mr. Danvers put his arm around his wife and gave her a small hug while he kissed the top of her head. Mrs. Danvers blushed, and a small smile crept across her face. They made a striking couple. Her golden blonde hair was coiled into a bun. Her blue eyes were framed by long, brown lashes. She had rosy cheeks and ruby red lips. Sarah suppressed a sigh. She was the picture of femininity, and he, the picture of masculinity.

"Wesley, this is Sarah Green. Sarah, my husband, Wesley Danvers."

"Pleased to meet you, sir."

"Please sit down. Would you like some tea?" asked Mr. Danvers.

Sarah turned to ice inside. Since hearing Mrs. Danvers say they would be meeting Mr. Danvers, she had become increasingly nervous, for it was normally the mistress of the house, not the master, who conducted interviews for the hired help. This was a new situation that gave way to speculation that he was a hard taskmaster and did not think his wife would be able to find, much less handle, the household staff. Sarah feared that it would be worse than working for Mrs. Hill.

"No thank you. I had some lemonade outside."

"Oh, yes," Mr. Danvers said. "Eloise insisted that the stable hands bring the lemonade to the waiting applicants. It's such a dreadfully hot day, and we wanted to make you more comfortable."

"Thank you, sir, ma'am. That was most kind."

Sarah was very confused. This was not going the way she had thought, and she was unsure as to how to act. She was expecting the litany of harsh questions, not to be treated like a guest. No wonder the wait was as long as it was.

"So, Sarah, please tell us a little about yourself and your family. Are you originally from Pittsburgh?" Mrs. Danvers asked as she poured two cups of tea. She handed one to her husband. Mr. Danvers sat back on the sofa, drinking his tea as he watched his wife.

"Yes, I am originally from Pittsburgh. My father was Scott Atworth, and we lived near the large stable in town. My husband, Walter, works there now."

"Yes, I knew your father a little. Wonderful judge of horses. It was such a tragedy when he died," Mr. Danvers said.

The compliment and resulting memories eased Sarah's tension somewhat—enough to where she could make a complete answer. "Thank you. I learned what I know about horses from him, and my mother taught me to sew quite well. I currently work with Mrs. Hill, the seamstress in town. I love to sew and it gives me time to be with my daughter, Shirley. Mrs. Hill allows me to bring her into her shop and let her play in the workroom."

"I know of Mrs. Hill," Mrs. Danvers said. "I have purchased some of her fine dresses. I take it that you are the genius behind the craftsmanship? They're just lovely. Although, Mrs. Hill herself can be somewhat difficult to deal with, from what I have heard."

"She is a nice woman." Sarah rushed to Mrs. Hill's defense, in fear of speaking harsh words and Mrs. Hill hearing about them.

"I understand, Sarah," Mrs. Danvers said. "There is some talk about how she treats people. Even the people on High Street hear what goes on in town." Mrs. Danvers smiled at Sarah and gave her a small wink. Mr. Danvers continued to sit back and let his wife ask the questions. The look on his face as he gazed at his wife was one of complete tenderness and love. Sarah recognized the look, as she often saw her husband looking at her with the same expression.

Sarah relaxed and realized that nothing would get back to Mrs. Hill, that her reputation had preceded her. Her opinion of the Danverses shifted the more time she spent with them. Sarah realized that Mr. Danvers was totally smitten with his wife and would do anything for her. She could see the love as they looked at each other. Her first impression of Wesley Danvers was all wrong. He was a brilliant businessman, but at home, he was a man hopelessly in love with his wife. The rest of the interview supported her observation.

"Well," Mrs. Danvers concluded, "the position that's open, as you know, is for a maid in our house. It is a rather large house, and even though I have no problem keeping up with the cleaning and the cooking, we find that we are in need of help, now that we have started our family. The job will require cleaning and polishing the house, cooking the meals, which you and your family may share, running errands, for which a stable hand will take you in one of our carriages, and serving at the occasional party we host. There will also be laundry and some mending. This position is not a traditional maid's position. The hours will be set by me, on an as-needed basis. There will be some days that we would need you early, and some days that you'll be here late such as when we have a party. There would occasionally be weekend work, but for the most part, you will have weekends off."

"How does that sound, Sarah?" Mrs. Danvers asked.

"It sounds like a great deal of work, but I know I can handle it. I hope you can give me a chance to prove it," Sarah replied.

Mrs. Danvers smiled. "You are a very honest and lovely girl. Would you like a tour of the house before you go?"

"That would be wonderful. I'm most curious about this beautiful house."

"I'll leave you in the capable hands of my wife. It was a pleasure to have met you, Sarah," Mr. Danvers said as he held out his hand.

Sarah shook his hand and thanked him.

"This way." Mrs. Danvers led the way out of the library, and they re-entered the foyer. As they walked throughout the house, Mrs. Danvers gave a running monologue of the improvements and quirks that were built into the house.

"This is the foyer, which you have already seen. Under the stairway is the door to the kitchen. We have a fully modern kitchen, including a new icebox, large wood-burning stove, and here is the woodbin. It is loaded from the outside, and if you lift this hatch, you can take out what you need and never have to go outside. The island here is where we take our meals. Although we do have a dining room, we seldom use it, unless we are having guests over. It's just Wesley, myself, and our young daughter, Sheila. The back door, here, leads to the covered walkway that connects with the servants' quarters."

"How old is Sheila?" Sarah asked.

"She will be six shortly and will be starting school soon. She is very excited, but she doesn't like to be away from Wesley or myself, so we will see how that goes."

"I have a daughter, Shirley, who just turned six. School is right around the corner. I hope she will enjoy it as much as I did when I was her age."

Sarah looked around the kitchen and felt a pang of jealousy. She had never been in such a large kitchen. Her entire house would fit in this large room, twice. But she quickly pushed the thought from her head; she was blessed with what she had, with Walter and Shirley.

"How wonderful! Children are such a blessing. In through this doorway is the formal dining room. This arch leads to the formal living room or parlor, as we like to call it. Do you play the piano?"

"No, I have wanted to learn, but we don't own a piano, and lessons cost too much. It would be great fun to be able to sit down and play beautiful music. To be able to entertain family and friends. Our daughter Shirley loves to dance, and it would be nice to see her dance around the room." Sarah walked over to the piano and ran her fingers along the edge. "I love to listen to the piano player in the saloon next to the laundry where we live. Walter and I sit on the front porch, after Shirley is in bed, and listen to the music. Sometimes, when they play a slow ballad, we get up and dance." Sarah blushed and quickly said, "It would be wonderful to be able to play."

"Wesley bought this piano, and it looks lovely in this room, but neither of us are very good. I fear I am all thumbs when it comes to playing. We are hoping that Sheila will want to learn. When we have parties, we hire the local music teacher at the school to come entertain our guests. He is a wonderful man, and he is so talented. He enjoys our fine piano as much as we enjoy listening.

"And here we are in the foyer again. Now upstairs," she said as she turned to climb the stairs, "we have a few bedrooms and indoor water closets. That was Wesley's idea. He hated the fact that we had to put in an outhouse, so the minute he heard it could be done, he had it installed and tore the old outhouse down. It is a wonderful invention and makes life so much easier."

"I have never seen one, nor used one. It must be wonderful not having to go outside in the cold Pittsburgh winters."

"Indeed it is. We loved it so much, we installed them in the stable apartments and also in the servants' quarters."

Sarah thought about the rundown outhouse that was behind her small home, about how cold it was, and began feeling very uncomfortable in such a fine house. She tried to wipe the worried look off her face as Mrs. Danvers turned to smile at her.

They reached the top of the stairs and Mrs. Danvers turned to the right. "This is the master bedroom, water closet, and sitting room. The next room is Sheila's."

As they looked inside, they could see toys everywhere and a child sitting in front of the largest dollhouse Sarah had ever seen. At the table in the corner sat a young girl, and she immediately sprang to her feet when Mrs. Danvers entered the room.

"This is Michelle. She is the niece of one of our stable hands and has been helping me with Sheila while we are doing these interviews and occasionally cares for Sheila when Mr. Danvers and I go out to dinner or attend a function at the bank. This position would also take care of Sheila when we go out. Michelle, this is Sarah Green. She has come about the maid's position."

"Nice to meet you, ma'am," Michelle said as she curtsied.

"Nice to meet you too, Michelle."

When she heard her mother's voice, Sheila turned and let out a squeal of delight. She dropped the doll she was holding and ran toward her mother. Mrs. Danvers bent down and lifted up the smiling child. "This cutie is our daughter, Sheila. Sheila, say hi to Sarah."

Sheila held out her hand to Sarah, and when Sarah reached for the outstretched hand, Sheila quickly pulled it back and hid her head in her mother's shoulder.

"She can be outgoing and sometimes very shy. We never know which. Come, I'll show you the rest of the bedrooms and our water closets. Michelle, I'll take Sheila with us for now. Thank you, for watching her. You have been a godsend!"

Smiling and blushing slightly, Michelle hurried out of Sheila's room and disappeared down the hall.

Mrs. Danvers put Sheila down and, holding Sheila's hand, showed Sarah the rest of the house, which included a large nursery at the end of the hall. This room was also cluttered with toys and books, enough to keep an army of children happy. Sarah thought about Shirley and how few toys she had. She wondered what her reaction would be if she were allowed to play in this room. A feeling of sorrow came over her, knowing she would never be able to give Shirley a fraction of the toys she saw on the shelves. But Shirley was happy and content. When they had finished touring the upstairs, they descended to the foyer. As they reached the bottom of the stairs, Mr. Danvers came out of the library. The moment Sheila saw her father, she jumped from the bottom stair into her father's outstretched arms. Mr. Danvers caught Sheila and proceeded to tickle her.

Mrs. Danvers turned to Sarah and held out her hand. "It was very nice to have met you, Sarah. We'll be deciding in a week or so and will let you know. Thank you for coming."

"Thank you, Mr. and Mrs. Danvers. It was a pleasure meeting you and your daughter. I look forward to hearing from you."

Sarah walked out into the sunshine, replaced her bonnet, and started down the driveway. Sarah replayed the entire interview and felt pangs of jealously at all the Danverses had been blessed with and how little she and Walter had. As Walter's father had told them, she knew that Mr. Danvers worked hard for all the lovely things he had, but she also knew that Walter worked very hard. Why didn't they have a nice house? Why did they have to live in a tiny shack smelling of bleach? Anger welled up quickly and just as quickly it was gone. She immediately felt guilty for being jealous, she was raised to appreciate everything she had, to work hard and not be spiteful or jealous. She lifted her head to the sunshine and counted her blessings as she walked home.

Chapter Three

A week went by and Sarah went on about her life. She assumed another person got the job at the Danverses' estate, although she had not heard any gossip in town about who was hired. She wasn't sure what to make of that, but she knew that eventually the lucky person's name would filter down. She was a little sad and wished it had been her, but she had a job and a wonderful husband and family—she felt very blessed.

It was a Wednesday, and she had just gotten home from Mrs. Hills's store and was preparing the evening meal when there was a knock on the door. Sarah opened the door and was shocked to see Mrs. Danvers standing there. Her shock quickly turned to embarrassment, and her hand went to the stray strands of hair that had broken free from her bun and were hanging damply around her face. She wiped her hands on her apron and quickly untied it when she looked down and saw the collage of stains. Taking the apron off and putting it on the back of the chair, Sarah smoothed her wrinkled skirt and finally found her voice.

"Mrs. Danvers. What an unexpected surprise. Please come in. Please excuse the way I'm dressed. I just returned home from work and was starting our evening meal. Please sit down. Oh, let me move that for you." Sarah moved the bundle of clothing from the chair and motioned for Mrs. Danvers to sit down.

"It's nice to see you again, Sarah."

As Mrs. Danvers entered the house, Sarah felt more self-conscious than she ever had before. Here was a fine lady, used to the best things in life, standing in her kitchen, with the smell of bleach from the laundry hanging in the air. As Mrs. Danvers entered the house and walked to the chair, Shirley looked up from her picture book and said hi in a very loud voice. Mrs. Danvers walked over to the chair where Shirley was sitting.

"What a lovely child. What's your name?"

"Shirley, ma'am."

"Shirley. What a beautiful name. And how old are you, Miss Shirley?"

Giggling Shirley replied, "I am six. Do you want to see the book I got for my birthday from my grandparents?"

Shirley held the book out for Mrs. Danvers to see. Mrs. Danvers leafed through it and smiled.

"I know this book. It is one of my favorites. I love to read this to my daughter before bed."

"You have a daughter? What is her name? How old is she?"

"Her name is Sheila, and she is six also." Mrs. Danvers handed the book back to Shirley and turned to Sarah. "She's just beautiful. She reminds me of Sheila. She's the same way."

Laughing, Sarah said, "I know what you mean."

Sarah offered Mrs. Danvers lemonade, and she accepted. What a picture they made, Sarah and Mrs. Danvers drinking from chipped cups in her ramshackle house.

"Sarah, I would like to offer you the position of maid in my home. There would be a few conditions we would have to agree on first."

Unable to trust her voice, Sarah just nodded as she sank into the chair across from Mrs. Danvers and waited for her to continue.

"First off, you'll need to move into the servants' quarters next to the house. It will not be a traditional job but on an as-needed basis, and I need you close. Second, your salary will be ten dollars a week, room and board will be included in your salary, so the ten dollars will be yours, free and clear. And you'll have the option of having your daughter go to the same school as Sheila. If you would prefer her to go to another school, I will have one of the stable hands take her to and from school, so you will be free to do your duties. Can we agree on these terms?"

Sarah was still trying to grasp the idea and started nodding. Finally she found her voice.

"Yes, that's more than fair. Thank you. When would you like for us to move in?"

Summer of Gold and Water

"How's this weekend? I will send one of the stable hands with a wagon to help you pack and move you to the servants' quarters. You can get settled and start on Monday morning."

"This weekend would be fine, ma'am."

Mrs. Danvers stood and hugged Sarah. "Welcome to the family. It will be wonderful! See you on Saturday."

Mrs. Danvers turned and walked out to the waiting carriage. Sarah closed the door and returned to the table and sat heavily in the chair. As Sarah waited for Walter to come home, she thought about everything that had happened and still could not believe it.

When Walter arrived home an hour later, he found Sarah singing as she cooked the stew with Shirley dancing around the room. He stood in the doorway and watched his family. They were extremely happy, and although his was a happy household, this was unnatural. He approached her slowly. "Sarah, honey, what's the matter? Are you all right?"

"I'm wonderful!" she shouted and grabbed Walter and danced a jig with him. Walter danced with her with a confused look on his face. When she finally stopped, she said, "We are moving…to the Danverses' estate!" She started dancing around again.

"What? Moving? When? Where? Why?"

"Oh honey, we've been so blessed. Mrs. Danvers was here this afternoon. Right here in this house! She sat at our old table and drank lemonade from our chipped cups like it was the most natural thing in the world. She offered me the job as their maid, but said we must move into the servants' quarters on her estate. She is sending one of her grooms to help us move on Saturday! It looks like eighteen seventy-five will be our year!"

"Saturday? Really? Did she say what the pay would be for your job?"

"Ten dollars a week! Plus we don't have to pay for our rooms or food. We can eat with them, or eat in our own apartment, after I fix it of course, and our children will be educated alongside her own, if we want. She has a daughter, Sheila, who is just turning six." As Sarah continued to dance around the small room, Walter, who was stunned at the news, sat down heavily in the chair Sarah was dancing around.

Sarah picked up Shirley, went over and grabbed Walter's hand, and pulled him from the chair. There was barely enough room for the three of them to move, let alone dance, but dance they did until they were all exhausted. They sat down at the table that rocked unevenly and ate the stew that Sarah had made and chatted about the day and all the things that needed to be done before they moved to the Danverses' estate. Luckily they had a few days to plan and for Sarah to quit her job, and as they talked, they realized they would be very busy for the next few days.

Chapter Four

Saturday morning, there was a knock on their door. When Walter opened it, he was amazed to find a stable hand, dressed in a crisp uniform. Behind the man was a large wagon hitched to an impressive team of black horses with shiny silver harnesses.

"My name is Ryan. I'm here to help you with your things."

"Hello, Ryan. I am Walter, and this is my wife, Sarah. And that blonde ball of energy is our daughter, Shirley. We are ready. There is not much to load."

"Hello again, Sarah. Walter. I remember you from the livery stable. I'm glad you will be working at the Danverses' estate. I enjoyed the tour I gave you. Now you'll be able to really explore all the estate has to offer."

As Walter started to take the table out to the wagon, Ryan stopped him.

"You won't need to take any furniture. Your apartment is furnished. There is a kitchen that's stocked with pots and pans and dishes, so you may leave them behind. I told you that we were well taken care of. Just take your personal belongings and clothes, and we will be off."

Walter looked at Sarah, shrugged, and set the table back in the small kitchen.

"Yes, it's nice to see you too, Ryan. I look forward to meeting your family you told me about." Sarah looked at Walter. "Ryan was kind enough to give me a tour of the stable while I was waiting for my interview. He and his wife live in the servants' quarters next to the barn I told you about."

"Nice to meet you, Ryan. Now let's get these things loaded and be off!"

They grabbed their suitcases and a few boxes and piled them into the back of the wagon. The wagon had two rows of seats, and

Walter lifted Shirley onto the seat and then reached for Sarah. As he was lifting Sarah into the wagon, he saw Shirley trying to climb over the seat to sit with Ryan. As Ryan looked back to see if the Greens were aboard, he noticed Shirley, and with a huge grin on his face, reached to help the small child over the seat. By that time Sarah and Walter were settled on the back seat. Ryan turned to urge the team on. As he was picking up the reins, Shirley walked in front of him and proceeded to climb into his lap.

"Shirley, you should sit next to the nice man, not in his lap. He needs to guide the horses," Walter said.

"It is all right, Walter. She is welcome to sit on my lap. I have a son a little younger, and he does the same thing. She's welcome to help me guide the horses."

With a triumphant grin, Shirley settled in Ryan's lap and her small hands grabbed the bottom of the reins. Ryan showed Shirley how to hold the reins, and as soon as her small hands were in the proper position, Ryan flicked his wrist and the horses started toward their new home. Walter and Sarah smiled as they heard Shirley and Ryan laughing.

"This was our first home. It's bittersweet leaving, but we are heading to something wonderful," Sarah said.

"As long as we are together, as a family, everything is perfect."

The ride to the estate was not a long one. When they reached their destination, Walter could not believe his eyes. It was exactly as Sarah described it when she came home from the interview. They were even more surprised when Mr. and Mrs. Danvers came out and greeted them as they climbed down from the wagon. Behind Mrs. Danvers's skirt, a small head of dark curls framing a cherub face peaked out.

"Welcome to our home! Now your home also," Mr. Danvers said as he reached out to shake Walter's hand. "I have been looking forward to meeting you and your daughter. Your wife is a wonderful person. Let me introduce you to my family. My wife, Eloise, and our daughter, Sheila, who is almost six."

When Walter regained his composure, he said, "It's nice to finally meet you. Sarah has told me great things about you and your wife. This is my family. Sarah, whom you already know, and our daughter, Shirley, who is six and a half. I want to thank you for the wagon and the help with our things. It was most kind."

"You are most welcome," Eloise said. "Now let us show you your new home. I hope you like it. If there are things you need or want to change, let me know and we can discuss it. We want you to stay and be part of our family, and for that to happen, you need to be happy. The apartment is this way."

Walter and Sarah went to grab their bags from the wagon, and Ryan told them that he would bring their belongings to their apartment, they did not need to carry them. Walter had never had anyone carry his bags or treat him with the respect that Ryan was showing. With a shocked look on his face, Walter took Sarah's arm and followed the Danverses toward a building that was connected to the main house by a covered walkway. A usually outgoing and inquisitive Shirley stayed close to Sarah's skirt, unsure of the new place and the other little girl who was walking with them.

As they reached the building, the front door opened into a large vestibule. There were two doors on either side, and in the center was a staircase.

"Your apartment is upstairs. These down here are for some of our stable hands, the ones with families. There are two apartments upstairs, yours and one that is vacant. It is just in case we hire more help, or one of our families needs more room."

As they reached the top of the stairs, Eloise walked down the hall to a door on the right side of the hallway. She beckoned the family in after her. As the Green family walked into the apartment, they were speechless. They looked around the large room and saw it was furnished with couches, chairs, tables, and oil lamps on the tables. To the right of the doorway was a small kitchen. It had a small stove and a table with four chairs. There was also a sink with indoor plumbing—no more walking outside to get water. A large vase of brightly colored flowers sat in the middle of the table. There was also an icebox in the kitchen.

To the left of the doorway was a comfortable living room. It had a long couch and two chairs. There were a couple of tables with oil lamps, and there were some oil lamps attached to the wall. There was a large picture window that overlooked the gardens in the back of the house. An explosion of color was visible. They walked past the living room and down the hall, where they found three bedrooms. Two smaller bedrooms were to the right, and one larger one to the left. The first bedroom on the right was painted in light blue. It held a sturdy bed, a dresser, and a sturdy wardrobe. There was an open box in the corner that was piled high with toys for a young boy.

The next bedroom on the right was painted pale yellow. It had a bed with a canopy of pale yellow lace above it, dresser, and wardrobe. The covers on the bed were yellow with sunflowers on them, and the curtains matched the covers on the bed. Inside the door was a small vanity with a mirror, and on top were brushes and ribbons, everything a young girl needed to coif her hair in the latest fashions.

On the left was a larger bedroom. It held an enormous bed, two wardrobes, and a double chest of drawers. A vanity stood next to the wall, with an ornate mirror and an array of colored bottles and brushes on the top.

At the end of the hallway there was a door. Sarah thought this was the linen closet, and when she opened it up, she was shocked to find indoor plumbing. It was a water closet.

As the family drifted back into the main room, Eloise saw the shock and disbelief on their faces.

"Is this adequate? Do you like your new home?"

"Are you sure this is all for us? All of it?"

Eloise smiled. "Yes, this whole apartment is yours. I want you to be happy."

"Thank you. This is magnificent."

"We'll let you get settled. Sarah, I need you to come to the house at three p.m. today. We have to talk about the hours and the routine. I see that Sheila has found a friend. I hear the girls in Shirley's room. Is it all right if she stays? If you would like to get settled, I can bring her back another time."

"No, it is fine. It will help ease the change for Shirley. I will bring her with me when I come at three, if that is all right with you."

"That is fine. Nice to have met you, Walter. I look forward to all of us working together."

"Okay then, we will see you later," Mr. Danvers said as he led his wife out and closed the door.

Eloise and Wesley stood outside the door, while inside the apartment, Walter grabbed Sarah and swung her around, laughing until they were both dizzy. They whooped and hollered and danced around the living area. On the landing, Eloise and Wesley looked at each other and smiled and then turned and went downstairs.

Three o'clock came, and Sarah walked down the path toward the main house with the girls racing in front of her. The pathway ended at a door that opened to the kitchen. As soon as they entered, Sheila grabbed Shirley's hand and raced to her room upstairs. Sarah waited for Mrs. Danvers. She shifted nervously while looking around the large kitchen. As she was inspecting the stove, Mrs. Danvers came in.

"Sarah, I'm so glad you are here. Let's sit and talk about the job and our routine."

As Sarah sat at the large kitchen table, Eloise asked, "Would you like some tea?"

"I can get it," Sarah replied as she started to get up.

"No, please sit, your employment does not start until Monday, so today we are just friends."

Sarah was floored. *Friends?* Thankfully, Mrs. Danvers's back was turned and her attention focused on the tea. Sarah clenched her hands in her lap and schooled her features into a pleasant smile. She could be friendly with this beautiful creature…right?

As she waited for the kettle to heat up, she asked, "How do you like your apartment?"

"It's wonderful. It's so spacious. We are not used to all that room. I was not expecting anything so lavish. Are you sure you want us in such a large apartment? We would be happy in one of the smaller ones."

"A smaller one? No, my dear, a family needs room, and you are right where you need to be. To get and keep good employees and keep them loyal so we don't have to change and retrain over and over, employees must be happy. One way is to make the family comfortable and make it so they do not worry about housing and expenses, so they can do their jobs. Too often we have found, through our friends, that if their help was unhappy, or in poor living conditions, they kept looking for a better job and were not loyal and did not stay. That meant getting new help, retraining them, and hoping they did not also leave. So when Wesley and I moved in here, we decided to do things a bit different. So far, we have not had any employees leave or become unhappy. And it's not because this is not a hard job, it is. We work people pretty hard around here, but they like their jobs, and their families are happy and safe, and that makes them want to do a better job and work harder. So in the long run, everyone wins."

The kettle started to boil, and Eloise fixed two cups of tea. She brought them over and set one in front of Sarah. She then brought the milk and sugar to the table and sat down.

"Thank you." Sarah paused before putting milk and sugar in her tea to make sure her hands stopped shaking. All this talk about being happy, content, and friends, she was not sure how much was real or how much would fade away in the coming days. Eloise was thankfully focused on the pad of paper before her, so she did not see the frown that creased Sarah's brow. Sarah quickly put a smile on her face; she did not want Eloise to think she was unhappy or worried. Eloise was so excited and happy, and Sarah tried to mirror her mood.

"Now, our schedules. We have breakfast every morning at seven a.m. You and your family are welcome to join us. Wesley leaves for the bank at seven thirty. Dinner will be at seven. As for Wesley's schedule, as I said, he leaves for the bank at seven thirty a.m. and will return at six thirty p.m. every night. Very rarely will he work on the weekends. The weekends are very relaxed around here. We ride in the park or have parties or just relax. If there are any parties that we host or attend, I will let you know ahead of time so you can plan accordingly. As for me, I have various charities and luncheons that I will attend. I will let you know what is going on, since it changes so often.

"As for your job, meals will be on the schedule I just gave you. Lunch will be just you, me, and the girls. On the weekends we will play it by ear. The house needs to be kept clean and the laundry done. You can set your own schedule for these chores. The children will be in your care. There is a nursery upstairs, and Sheila is quite content to play in her room. Shirley is welcome to play there too. The rest, we will make up as we go along. How does that sound?"

Sarah waited a few moments before responding, to make sure all of what Eloise had said sunk in. She wanted to make sure she asked all the questions she had now, just in case the mood changed between them. All this was just too good to be true, and Sarah did not want to become too familiar or comfortable with Eloise for fear of being disappointed later.

"Fine. Do you want me to do the shopping also?"

"Oh yes, I will give you money each week to get the things we need. One of the stable hands will take you to the store. If, at any time, you find we need something else, let me know. Sarah, I want you to be comfortable here. I want us to become friends."

Sarah picked at the napkin in her lap, trying to make sense of all that had happened. "Yes, ma'am."

"Sarah, please call me Eloise. This is an informal household. Do you have any more questions?"

"Only one, ma'am, ah, Eloise." Sarah looked down, unable to meet Eloise's gaze. She twisted her napkin in her lap and tried to get her hands to stop shaking. "I'm uncomfortable asking, and feel that I'm imposing, but my husband, Walter, he works in town, and we don't have a horse for him to go back and forth to work. When we lived in town, he would walk to work. Would it be acceptable for him to borrow one of your horses, until we can afford our own?"

"Yes, that is most acceptable. I will ask Ryan to show you which horse Walter can use, and in the case of bad weather, Ryan can to take him in the buggy. That will be Walter's choice."

She could not believe her ears. "Thank you, ma'am. I know I have not really started to work yet, and I'm uncomfortable asking for this huge favor, and I want to say thank you very much. It's not something that Walter and I discussed when I applied for the position, for I never thought I would be hired. But it is a concern, and I want to thank you for your generosity."

"I want you to feel you can ask me anything, Sarah. Any more questions?"

"No, ma'am." Sarah hurriedly tried to straighten out the twisted napkin so Eloise would not see. She folded it and placed it next to her teacup.

"Now that the formalities are over, let's really talk. I want to get to know you and you get to know me."

Eloise sat back, her aristocratic posture softening. The effect on Sarah was the same as if she'd let her hair down. The knots in Sarah's shoulders and stomach loosened, and for the first time she allowed herself to meet and hold Eloise's gaze.

"So Sarah. Tell me about your family."

"Well, my father worked at the livery stable that Walter works at. He also would help people purchase horses. He taught me to ride. My mother taught me to cook and sew. We would sit after supper and mend the clothes at the laundry that my mother worked at. Now and again when the garment couldn't be repaired, the customer would leave it with my mother for her to throw out. She would use the material and make the best of it. She taught me to use what you have. Sadly, they both died when their wagon crashed into a tree."

"Oh, I am so sorry. It must have been such a hard time for you. How old were you when this happened?"

"I was sixteen when they died. Walter's parents took me in after it happened. My grandparents were elderly and could not raise me. I was supposed to go live with distant cousins in New York City when Walter asked his parents if I could stay with them. They agreed, and when I became of age, Walter and I got married. I was twenty at the time."

"First love. How wonderful."

"What about your grandparents? Are they still living? Do they live in Pittsburgh?"

"Yes, they live in town. They live down the street from Walter's parents. Walter and I get over to see them as often as we can."

"It is nice to have family around. Wesley's parents live down the road, as do mine. They both are very busy and come to see us on holidays and special occasions. We sometimes see them at the charity events and dinners that we go to. It seems we are both blessed with still having our parents. I don't know what I will do when that day comes." Eloise shuddered and waved her hand. "Enough sad talk. Everyone is healthy, and we must be thankful for that."

"Shirley just loves her grandparents. They try to spoil her rotten, always bringing her things, but I think she loves the attention more."

Eloise laughed. "Sheila is that way also. She will be polite and open the present and become engrossed in it for a while, but then she will put it down and climb on the nearest empty lap and settle in. It doesn't matter what we are talking about, she just wants to be on someone's lap, getting hugs and kisses. It warms my heart to watch her."

Sarah had become more comfortable sitting and chatting about family and other things, but when the conversation lulled, she snapped back to the present and sat up a little straighter. She twisted her wedding ring. She was not sure how to act. What should she do now? Clear the table? Or should she wait for Eloise—Mrs. Danvers to tell her what to do?

"Well, Sarah. We have talked the afternoon away. Why don't we start Monday morning? I'll give you the weekend to get settled. Please feel free to explore the estate. There are many trails and beautiful flowers to see."

They stood and, as Sarah turned to leave, Eloise hugged her. "I'm so glad you're here."

Surprised and not knowing what she should do, Sarah slowly put her arms around Eloise and returned the hug. "Thank you, ma'am. I'll see you on Monday."

"I'll bring Shirley over later, when she and Sheila are done exploring. That will give you some time to get settled in your apartment. If you should need anything, please feel free to ask."

~~~

As Sarah walked back to the apartment, she committed the schedule to memory and smiled at their good fortune. When she entered the apartment, Walter came out of the bedroom.

"Everything all right? You were gone a long time. Where is Shirley?"

"She's playing with Sheila at the Danverses'. Everything is fine. The schedule is simple enough, and as she said, I believe it will be a lot of work, but they are nice, and I'm not a stranger to hard work. I believe we will be happy here."

"I suppose on Monday I will have to get up pretty early to make it to work on time."

With a Cheshire catlike smile, Sarah said, "I asked Mrs. Danvers about letting you borrow a horse, until we could afford one. She graciously agreed and said you need to check with Ryan as to which horse will be available to you. Also, in bad weather, Ryan will take you to work in the buggy, so you don't get your pretty head wet." She ruffled Walter's hair.

"Really? Are you certain? I think we will *definitely* be happy here. I can't believe it! She really said that?"

"Yes, she really did. Our prayers have certainly been answered." Sarah stopped and faced her husband. "Walter, this is not at all what I expected. I feel like it is all a dream and we are going to wake up in the small apartment smelling of bleach. I don't know how to act around Mrs. Danvers. She asked me to call her Eloise. Eloise said she wants us to be friends, I wasn't expecting that. It is very uncomfortable for me. I was raised to call the upper class Mr. and Mrs., not by their first names. I get so nervous, I am afraid I will mess up and she will fire me. Then what will we do? Where would we go?"

"Darling, come sit on the couch." He took her hands in his and said, "Sarah, honey, you are worrying about nothing. You heard what my father said. They are as honest and down to earth as you and I are. You will do fine, and you will see that they are just what they seem to be. Now, put a smile on that beautiful face and come help me unpack, and then we can take a walk and explore the trails that Mrs. Danvers told you about. It's such a lovely day."

Sarah smiled at Walter. "With pleasure, my darling."

Together they unpacked, first their own clothes and then Shirley's. When they were done, Walter went to the toy box and opened it up. Inside was a huge pile of blocks, dolls, doll clothes, and a tea set.

"Shirley will be overwhelmed. I'll make her a small table and chairs for her to set the tea set on. She'll feel like a princess."

"I think that would be lovely. I cannot believe how generous the Danverses are, and what a great apartment this is! Sure beats the smell of bleach and the heat from the fires boiling the water."

"Come, darling, let's go and explore the grounds." Walter put his arms around Sarah as they headed toward their adventure.

At the bottom of the stairs, one of the apartment doors opened. Out popped a small redheaded boy about four or so, and ran directly into Walter's legs and bounced back and fell on his behind.

"Whoa there, tiger, where're you going in such a hurry?"

As Walter picked the boy up and set him on his feet, his father walked out of the apartment.

"Hello again, Ryan. I take it this bundle of energy is your son?"

"Walter, Sarah, hello. Yes, this is Timothy. We were on our way to feed the horses. Timothy is my big helper, and he's in quite a hurry today."

Walter went down on one knee, held out his hand, and said, "Hello, Timothy. I am Walter, and this is Sarah. Nice to meet you. We have a little girl; her name is Shirley."

Timothy got an attack of the shy bug and raced back to hide behind Ryan's legs.

"Oh, don't be so shy, son. They are nice people, and they'll be living upstairs from us. Please say hello."

"Hello," he said in a very low voice.

"Hello, Timothy." Walter got up and faced Ryan. "Sarah and I were just about to explore the grounds. Do you think you and your dad would have time to give us a tour of the barn and these lovely horses?"

Timothy looked up at his dad and cried, "Do you think we can, Dad? Can we? I want to show you my favorite horse!" Timothy's shyness vanished into thin air. With that he grabbed Walter's hand and started to pull him out the door toward the barn. Laughing, Walter followed the young boy.

As Sarah and Ryan started across the lawn, they saw Timothy still pulling Walter. He was taking baby steps and trying not run Timothy over. Sarah and Ryan could hear Timothy talking a mile a minute about the barn and his favorite horses.

"How old is your son?"

"He'll be four next month. We moved here before he was born, so this is all he knows. The Danverses have been very good to us. My wife, Megan, and I used to live above the stable, and when Megan became pregnant, we were moved to this building. We have been very comfortable here, and we love watching Timothy grow up in such a nice place."

"I'm glad. The Danverses have been very generous to us already. They are letting Walter borrow a horse to get to and from work in town, until we can purchase one for ourselves. And in the bad weather, I hear you have been nominated to drive him. I hope that it's not too big an inconvenience."

"Nonsense. It will give us a chance to become better acquainted. I would do anything the Danverses asked. They are good people."

"I agree. I think I hear Timothy down this way," Sarah said as she turned to the right and started down the row of stalls.

"I knew he would be here. Blaze is his favorite horse. Timothy was there when Blaze was born, so he's very partial to him. Blaze has taken quite a liking to Timothy also."

Sarah and Ryan approached the stall that held a beautiful black horse with a white face. Walter was holding Timothy up so he could peer into the stall. Ryan reached into his pocket and pulled out a carrot. Timothy eagerly took the carrot and held it out to Blaze. The colt came over and very slowly and carefully took the carrot from Timothy, and when it was gone, Blaze bobbed his head up and down a few times to say thank you.

"See? He likes carrots. He's saying thank you," Timothy cried.

Laughing, Walter said, "I see that. You have quite a beautiful friend, Timothy."

Walter set Timothy down, and Timothy raced off toward the loft. "Want to come see the kittens? They were born about a month ago. Their mother is Tabby. She helps keep the mice away from the barn."

"We would love to."

The group followed the smiling youngster up the stairs to the loft. Back in the corner, a mewing could be heard. Slowly they approached the corner and saw a straw bed with an orange cat stretched out, and nestled next to her were six kittens of various colors. Tabby sat up a bit straighter at the group approaching until Timothy called out to her.

"Tabby, it's me. These people are okay. We won't hurt you."

To Sarah, it looked as though Tabby was listening intently to Timothy and visibly relaxed when he came into view. They all sat on the floor to watch Tabby feed her babies and then give each of them a bath. Timothy reached over and picked up one of the kittens, after its bath, and held it ever so gently. After showing everyone the kitten, Timothy put the baby back near Tabby, and the attentive momma promptly gave the baby another bath and pushed it toward the others for their nap.

When all the babies were nestled next to their mother sleeping, Tabby proceeded to give herself a bath and then settle down for a rest.

"Aren't they great?" Timothy whispered. "I don't want to wake the babies, so we need to talk really quiet."

"They are very special," Sarah said. "And I see that you are taking very good care of them. You are a special young man, Timothy."

Timothy sat up straighter and beamed at the compliment. Walter helped Sarah from the floor, and the group tiptoed back the way they had come.

As they reached the bottom of the stairs, Ryan said, "Timothy, we need to finish our chores. Walter and Sarah are going to take a walk. I'm sure we will see them around, now that they live upstairs from us."

"Yes, Father. Bye!" With that he dashed off to the supply room to get ready to feed the horses.

"Nice seeing you, folks. If you need anything, please ask. And welcome to the Danverses' home!"

"Thank you. You have a wonderful son."

"Thank you. We think he is special too. See you around." Ryan started off in the direction that Timothy had taken.

"They are lovely people," Walter said as he turned to his wife. He held his hand out to her. "Let's go explore the grounds."

"Yes, let's."

Sarah and Walter walked out of the barn and started down the path that led toward the gardens.

Chapter Five

As time went on, the families fell into a comfortable routine. Sarah found herself looking forward to the days, even though, as Eloise had said, it was hard work. She enjoyed the job, and because the Danverses were so generous to her family, she found herself going out of her way to make them happy. Eloise and Sarah spent a great many hours together. Over time, Sarah found herself letting go of her anxiety and relaxing around Eloise. She would go home at night and not feel like she had been working, but spending time with a good friend. Sometimes Eloise would be doing needlepoint and Sarah would be working, or other times they would sit and enjoy a cup of tea together. Shirley and Sheila were inseparable. They played well together and kept each other amused while Sarah was working.

Four years passed in a blink of an eye.

One night after dinner, Wesley stood up and said, "Walter, can I see you in the study?"

Although Walter and Wesley had become friends, Walter thought Wesley's tone was off and found this request to be a bit strange.

"Of course, Wesley. Ladies, would you excuse us?"

Walter followed Wesley into the study, and Wesley turned and shut the door. Walter grew increasingly nervous at Wesley's actions and slowly turned to face his friend. Flashbacks of the conversations that he and Sarah had had when they first moved in crossed his mind, and his stomach started to churn.

"Please sit down. Would you like a drink?"

"Thank you. Whatever you are having would be fine."

Wesley poured the drinks and sat down behind his desk. Whenever they were in the study, they sat in the chairs in front of the desk, now Wesley was behind the desk. Walter got a sick feeling in the pit of his stomach as he watched Wesley swirl his drink and did not meet Walter's eyes for a long time. Walter's nervousness increased the longer Wesley waited.

"Walter, I have a business proposition. I'm sure you know my head groom, William."

"Yes, we're good friends. Is something wrong?"

"Well, William came to me last week. He will be leaving us at the end of the month to return to Philadelphia to care for his sick mother. This is very sad news, as William is well liked and a hard worker. None of the other stable hands are qualified to fill his position, and that is the problem. I was wondering if I could hire you away from your position to work here and fill William's shoes."

Walter was stunned. He was not expecting a job offer, and he sat in silence and waited for Wesley to continue.

"When I was in town yesterday, I spoke to your boss, Mr. Arnold, about you. I asked him what he thought of your work ethic and your knowledge of horses. He told me that he thinks very highly of you. He is amazed at your knowledge of horses and has marveled at the way you handle them. He has seen you calm the most nervous of animals and train horses that most would have just shot. He told me about the time you talked one of his most stubborn horses into getting into the harness and pulling the iceman's cart when his horse was ill." Wesley paused, studying Walter. "I hope you are not upset that I spoke to him, without coming to you first, but I wanted to find out what kind of work ethic you have. I know what kind of friend and husband you are, but the worker side, I needed to understand."

"No, I'm not upset," Walter said, still puzzling about the whole offer.

"And as Mr. Arnold said, he is very pleased with your work and wishes he had more men like you. As I have known him for years, I trust his judgment, and when William came to me and told me he was leaving, I knew that you would be a good addition to our staff. I understand if you need time to think about it, and talk to Sarah, but if you could let me know by the end of the week, I would appreciate it."

"What? No, no, it is not that." Walter ran a hand through his hair and laughed at how shaky it was. He shook his head and met Wesley's concerned gaze. "I am honored and a bit shocked. This was not what I expected to hear. I accept your position. I know Sarah will be thrilled and will be very angry if I turned you down."

Wesley stood up. "Wonderful! I am so glad. Eloise told me you would accept. Will you be able to start on Monday?"

"Yes. That would be great. I can work with William over the next two weeks, to get caught up on things, and be ready to take over when William leaves."

"Great, I know that Eloise and Sarah are in the parlor, and if I know Eloise, she told Sarah and they are both waiting for the good news. Let's not keep the ladies waiting!"

Wesley put his arm around Walter, and they went to find their families. As they entered the parlor, Shirley and Sheila, who were playing on the floor, each screamed with delight as their fathers walked into the room. Walter picked up Shirley and tossed her in the air. Feeling left out, Sheila got up and ran to her father, crying, "Me too, Papa!" Wesley picked the smiling girl up and tossed her into the air. Sarah interrupted the play.

"Well? What did you decide?"

"It was a really hard decision. I'll have to think about it," Walter said as a huge smile broke across his face.

"You bum!" cried Sarah as she got up to embrace her husband. "Why do you do that to me?"

"Because I can. I need to work with William the next two weeks or so until he leaves, to learn what is going on and how things are run, and then it will be just me!"

"That is wonderful. Now I won't have to worry when you go to work in the snow and ice. This is just wonderful."

Wesley walked over and sat next to Eloise. Sheila came over and sat on his lap. He put his arm around Eloise, and she laid her head on his shoulder. They watched Walter and Sarah embrace and gently glide around the room to an unheard melody. When the dancing stopped, Walter and Sarah sat on the couch, with Shirley bouncing on Walter's knee. It was a comfortable feeling, and they all sat in silence and watched the flames flicker in the fireplace.

The silence was broken by a loud hoot owl perched in the tree outside the window. Brought back to the present, Eloise realized there was something else that she needed to talk to Walter and Sarah about.

"Now that you are working for us, I don't feel torn in asking you this. If Walter had said no, then I would not have been able to ask, although I would have wanted to badly. It looks like eighteen seventy-nine will be an exciting year. We have been asked to join a new, exclusive club. The club will not be open for members for another month, as they are putting the finishing touches on the clubhouse and some cottages, but they are getting the members lined up and excited about it, so when they do open, it will be a grand event. The club is going to be located on a large parcel of property outside of Johnstown. The resort will be called the South Fork Fishing and Hunting Club. Our family is one of the first to join, and so far there are sixteen families that are members. There will be a large clubhouse that will house all the members, initially. If a family would like more privacy and more room, the club owns a great deal of property and members will be allowed to build their own cottages. The clubhouse will serve all our meals, and will have a ballroom, billiards room, boat rental, swimming, hunting, fishing, and plenty of fresh air and lively fun.

"They are working on the transportation, but as it stands now, we will take the train to Johnstown, where we will be met by carriages to take us to the lake. I'm told it is supposed to be very relaxing, and the children will be together to swim and go sailing. We would like you to come with us. I will purchase a membership for your family along with ours as a bonus. I did not want to tear you away from Walter if he had turned down the job, but since he has accepted, we can all go. There will not be as much work, and the atmosphere is so relaxing. Food is provided, cooked at the clubhouse, the laundry is done, and anything else we need, we have only to ask. It will be a vacation for you and your family also. So what do you say? Would you like to come?"

Walter looked at Sarah, who was already nodding her head yes. "We would love to come!"

Wesley got up and poured four glasses of sherry and filled in some of the holes in Eloise's explanation.

"There is an encampment of immigrant workers who live near the dam. They help with odd jobs, maintenance, and other tasks that need to be done at the club. The members are encouraged to bring their servants, and if they choose not to, the townspeople are willing to help out. The servants will stay in the annex of the clubhouse. It's not as lavish as the main clubhouse, but it's comfortable. But since you will be members, you will stay in the main clubhouse, in your own rooms. The roster at the club will show that you are members, and will be treated as such."

Walter hesitated and looked over at Sarah. He saw the same worried look on her face that he was feeling. Walter squeezed Sarah's hand to reassure her he knew what she was feeling. "If you are sure that is how you want it, we are most happy to stay in the annex with the other servants. We do not expect you to purchase a membership for us and to be treated like the members," Walter said.

"Nonsense. This is our decision. Eloise and I have talked at length about this, and we feel that you both have earned this bonus, and we want to share it with you. In the past few years, you and Sarah have become family. Shirley is as close to us as Sheila. We have thought about this and discussed it, and if you are comfortable with it, then we are too."

"If that is what you wish, Wesley. We agree."

"Excellent!"

About an hour later, Walter and Sarah bid good night to the Danverses, picked Shirley up from where she had fallen asleep on the floor, and went back to their apartment. Walter tucked Shirley into bed and came back to the living room, where he saw Sarah pacing. Walter sat on the couch and watched as her steps got more and more agitated.

"Walter, I am not so sure about this. Going as members? I just don't know about this."

"I feel the same way, honey. Please sit down and we can discuss this."

Sarah sat next to Walter, but she continued to wring the handkerchief she had in her hands. "We shouldn't be going as members. We should be staying in the annex. You know there are people who will be there that know we work for the Danverses."

"I know, but this is what they want. I will make you a deal, if this year is too uncomfortable for you and Shirley, then next year we will stay in the annex. Let us put our faith in the Danverses that they know what they are doing."

"Well, I guess so. They were very excited about us going with them, weren't they?"

"Yes, they were. Now wipe the worry off your beautiful face, and let's get some sleep."

Chapter Six

The next month passed quickly, and soon it was time to go to the club for the first time, and the families were very excited about going. As they got off the train in Johnstown in the early morning light, they were met by two carriages, one for each family, and a large wagon to bring the clothes and other items that they had brought with them. As they climbed into their carriage, Sarah sat by the window, with Shirley on her lap, and marveled at the scenery. Sarah's fears about the club were replaced with excitement as they traveled to the lake.

The carriages wound their way up the slope to the top of Prospect Hill, and as they were riding along the ridge, they could look down on the bustling city of Johnstown. They could see the train depot they had just left, and the big stone church in the center of town. They watched as the people moved through their morning rituals and made their way to work. They heard the wheels of the wagons on the cobblestone pavement and the jingle of the harnesses on the horses.

As Johnstown slid out of sight, the scene around the road changed. They passed through a wooded area, and they could see trees, taller than they imagined, covered with lush, green leaves, some with white flowers on them. Farther along, the towering trees gradually gave way to meadows that stretched as far as the eye could see, and Sarah caught a glimpse of a herd of deer in the distance. There were patches of flowers that erupted in a riot of colors that provided quite a contrast to the green rolling hills.

They passed many small towns where they saw the same scene as in Johnstown. People getting started with their workdays, young children running to and fro, older children going to school or on their way to the fields to help with the family chores. The driver of the carriages told them the names of the towns as they passed. To

Sarah, the names were musical—Woodvale, Mineral Point, Valley of the Little Conemaugh. They all marveled at the stone viaduct that they passed under.

Occasionally they would pass a farm or two, or a cluster of houses, outside of the towns. The workers in the fields would wave, and the children would run along side the carriage for a short while. The fields of wheat and corn waved in the breeze as they went by, bidding them welcome. Some of the local people had been hired to help out at the club during the summer, so they would meet them soon. The coachmen explained that they were approaching the club and would be there in a few minutes.

The road ran alongside a lovely stream, and now and then they would get close enough to see pools of swirling water and rushing rapids. Near the pools of water, Sarah could see some children fishing. They waved as the carriage went by and resumed their concentration on catching a big one. It looked like a wonderful way to spend the morning.

The ride took about two hours but passed quickly as the wondrous sights floated past the carriage window.

"Look at this scenery! Shirley, have you ever seen so many trees? I can't believe that we are so close to Johnstown. You can't see any of the larger buildings, and it looks like we stepped into a different world. Who knew this beauty was only a few hours away!"

"Look at the cows and horses, Mother! Look, look! That one is running!" Shirley cried.

"The club is talking about putting in a train depot near the club," the coachman explained, "to make the ride more pleasant and shorter for the guests, but the town council is putting up objections, and they are still working on it. So for now, the carriages take the guest to the club. It is a pleasant ride and the scenery is just lovely."

As the carriages approached a dirt bridge, the drivers stopped and said to the families, "To your left, across the dam, is the spillway. This drains the overflow water from the lake. It is a very popular place for cooling off, playing in the water, or a romantic picnic. I will take you across the dam so you can see. If you look to your right and up ahead of us, you can see the clubhouse. Next to the clubhouse are two of the cottages that are owned by some members."

The drivers started up the teams and crossed the dam. When they reached the middle of the dam, they stopped so the families could see the entire lake. The view was breathtaking. Sarah was in awe at the vast expansiveness of it. On either side, gentle mountain slopes rose up with green carpeting. There were so many trees. As the group sat taking in the sight, a large flock of geese rose from the lake, calling to each other. Sarah switched places with Walter and looked over the dam. She could see the gorge where the water from the spillway ran down the valley. The water tumbled over the rocks in a gentle waterfall to the valley below and hurried around the bend. There were many trees lining the river, and Sarah thought she caught a glimpse of a raccoon digging in the rocks. The families marveled at the scene before them and were startled when the drivers started the carriages. They continued across the dam, and the driver stopped at the spillway.

"If you look to your left, you will see the opening to the spillway. In front of the spillway, under the surface of the water, is a net. The net holds the fish in the lake, so they don't all drain into the river. The lake is stocked with a minimum of one thousand black bass for the members to catch. We don't want our investment running downstream." He chuckled. "If you take that trail to your left, you can walk beside the spillway. It is a very beautiful spot and very romantic."

The drivers sat a minute and then turned the teams around and headed across the dam to the clubhouse. "There is a boardwalk that is in front of the clubhouse. It continues past the two cottages and up the hill to Brown's General Store, which is past that cluster of trees. The Browns have the only store here, as the club provides everything you can possibly want and more. The Browns also have a store in Johnstown and have agreed to have a smaller version here, for the members, during the summer. Just past the Browns' store, up that road, is a stable. It is a very large stable with a two or three dozen fine riding horses and carriages. There are many trails around the club, and you are welcome to rent the horses for a ride through the hills. There are wagons that are also housed there, for the freight that you will occasionally see being brought up from Johnstown. Many of the people who work at the club live nearby, and the club has agreed to let the people use the stable, year round, to house their wagons, plows, and horses in exchange for them hauling freight to the club during the summer. On the opposite side of the lake, you will see a house. That belongs to Mr. Timmons, the owner of the club and our host for the summer. His house is like a sentry, silently watching from afar."

The drivers pulled up next to the clubhouse and jumped down to open the carriage doors. Everyone disembarked and thanked the drivers for the ride and the tour. They tipped their hats, climbed back on the carriages, and urged their teams back toward the depot.

As the drivers pulled away, Sarah stood and marveled at the lake that was no more than a few yards from the boardwalk and ran in front of the clubhouse. A small beach was in front of the cottages, and the lake sparkled as if diamonds were scattered on top. There were many sailboats tied up to the docks that were to the west of the clubhouse beach.

Sarah turned and saw that the clubhouse was large and very neat. It had a porch that wrapped around the front and side. The building was three stories high and had large windows. The curtains fluttered as the light breeze from the lake entered the house. As she looked across the shimmering lake, she could see Mr. Timmons's house on the opposite side. It seemed smaller, like a dollhouse nestled in the side of the hill. It was a quaint house with a large porch. She could see a man standing on the porch looking across the lake and taking in all the details. He then turned and went into the house.

Sarah resumed her assessment of the clubhouse, grounds, and the lake, and looked toward the dam. From where she stood, she could see the carriage road they had just come across and the bridge that went over the river that lead to the spillway.

"Sarah? Are you coming?"

Snapped out of her daydreaming, Sarah turned to see Eloise calling her and the rest of the families staring at her.

"Coming."

Together they all walked toward the clubhouse and mounted the stairs. As they walked across the large porch, they could see that it wrapped around the building and was lined with chairs, with a clear view of the lake. As they reached for the door, a man came out and welcomed them inside.

"Welcome, I am Seth Daniels. I am the manager here at the club. Anything you need, you have but to ask. Your rooms are ready, Mr. Danvers, Mr. Green. If you will come this way, I will show you around."

They entered and walked into a large room. As the families stood and took in the room, Mr. Daniels started his tour.

"This is the main room of the clubhouse. This is the room that all the meals are served in, as well as when the club has dances, which are held every Saturday night and on special occasions. And here at the club, every day is a special occasion." He laughed.

"To the left, through that door, is the pool room. There are two billiards tables that can be rented by the hour or by the game. Behind the billiard room is a library. The library is well stocked with all the latest books for our members to read while they are here. There are many comfortable couches in the library, and it is very quiet. Behind the library and billiard rooms are the kitchens. All meals are prepared there and served to the guests in the main hall. On the nights that we have a dance or other special event, the tables are moved to accommodate the dance floor and the band we bring in to entertain everyone. At night the fireplace is lit, which adds warmth and light to the main room. Up the stairs are the guest rooms. The servants' quarters in the annex are accessed by the stairs that are next to the kitchen. If you will follow me, I will show you to your rooms."

Mr. Daniels climbed the stairs with Wesley, Eloise, Walter, and Sarah close behind. Shirley and Sheila had wandered into the billiards room and stood watching the men play pool. When they realized their parents weren't behind them, they turned and dashed out the door and up the stairs.

Mr. Daniels climbed to the second floor of the clubhouse. He stopped at room twenty, opened the door, and said, "This is your room, Mr. and Mrs. Danvers. I hope you will be comfortable. Mr. and Mrs. Green, your room is next door, room twenty-two. Right this way."

Mr. Daniels went to the next room and opened the door for Walter and Sarah. "Your bags have been brought up and have been put in your rooms. If you should need anything, please feel free to ask. I will let you get settled." With that, Mr. Daniels retreated down the hall and disappeared down the stairs.

Walter and Sarah walked into their room. In the corner was a large bed, with very fluffy pillows and comforters on the top. On the opposite side of the room was a smaller bed, just right for Shirley. There was a bureau with five drawers and a large mirror on top against the wall. Shirley immediately jumped on the bed, squealing with delight. Walter and Sarah went over and sat on their bed, still in shock at the lavishness of the room. Through the open window they could see the lake, and they felt a warm summer breeze. Sarah broke out of her trance first, and seeing that their trunks had been delivered prior to them being shown their room, she proceeded to unpack.

When they were done, they went next door to see if they needed help unpacking and found that Eloise was done with her clothes. Sheila and Shirley were tugging at their fathers' hands.

"Let's go exploring, before I lose my arm," Wesley pleaded with Walter.

Wesley let Sheila lead him down the stairs and out the door, with Walter and Shirley close behind.

Chapter Seven

They walked down to the edge of the small beach area, marveling at the clean, white sand at the edge of the lake. The club had purchased a half-dozen or so sailboats for the members to use, and they were lined up at the docks like racehorses ready for the big race.

"Wouldn't it be nice to be able to sail one of these?" Walter commented as he looked at the sailboats.

"I'll be the best sailor at the club," Shirley stated.

"I'm sure you will become a fine sailor, when you get a bit older. You are only eleven, my dear. I don't know if they will allow you to learn until you are older. We will have to see what the age limits are."

"Sheila and Mr. Danvers must learn also, then we can have races, and you will see that Sheila and I will be the best and no one will be able to beat us. Not even you, unless we let you, of course." Shirley giggled.

"We shall see, my dear."

They walked to the edge of the beach to test the water to see if it was warm enough to swim. The water held a slight chill but would be quite refreshing on a hot day. They then proceeded to walk out onto the pier to see the boats. As the families neared the boats, Walter looked back and noticed that Sarah had not joined them on the pier, but waited nervously near the boardwalk.

Walter turned and walked back to where Sarah was pacing, and when he put his arm around her, he could feel her entire body shaking. "Is something wrong, Sarah? You're trembling."

"I am terrified of water, Walter. I always have been. When I was younger, I slipped and fell into the pond at one of the farms I visited with my father. We were walking out on the pier to the small rowboat to take a short ride on the pond, and as I tried to get into the boat, I slipped and fell in. My father jumped in right after me, but since I couldn't swim, I went under. Ever since then..." Sarah shook her head, staring out at the expanse of water, willing her limbs to stop trembling.

"This summer I will show you that the water is fun. By the end of the summer, you will be splashing about with the rest of us."

Sarah frowned at him. "So you say. We shall see, Walter. I don't mind if it is shallow, like a brook, or like the spillway that we saw on our way here. I cannot walk out on the pier. I am afraid I will fall in. Come, let's not talk of this further. Here come the others, please do not say anything to them. I do not want to ruin their good time."

"Your secret is safe with me, as always, my love. Come, let's finish our exploration of the club."

Walter and Sarah caught up with the others as they strolled down the boardwalk. They passed the two cottages that had been built by other members, marveled at the view they had, and wondered which cottage belonged to whom. Farther up, there were open areas where more cottages could be built. As they rounded the bend of trees at the end of the boardwalk, they came upon Brown's General Store. It was discreetly hidden behind a copse of trees so that the members would not feel like their sanctuary was being invaded by commerce.

They all entered the store and were immediately enveloped with the smell of fresh-baked bread. It filled the store with heavenly goodness. As their eyes adjusted to the dim light inside the store, they began to make out neat rows of shelves and racks with hats, clothing, and other assorted items. Near the counter was a row of glass jars all filled with brightly colored candies of different sizes, shapes, and flavors.

"Welcome to our store!"

The families looked toward the bonnets, and coming from between the rows of hats was a kindly woman. She had gray hair pulled into a bun. Her face was round and her blue eyes sparkled, as if she held a secret.

"Welcome, I am Frances Brown. My husband, Richard, and I own this store. If there is anything you need or cannot find, please feel free to ask."

"Thank you. I am Wesley Danvers. This is my wife, Eloise, and our daughter, Sheila. This is Walter and Sarah Green and their daughter, Shirley. Pleased to meet you."

"Very nice to meet you all. Is there anything in particular you are looking for?"

"No, we have just arrived and are exploring the club grounds. You have many beautiful things here, and the bread smells heavenly."

"Please join us. Richard and I were about to have a slice with some fresh honey. We would be honored if you would join us. We want to get to know the people who will be our neighbors for the summer."

"Thank you, but we don't want to intrude."

"Nonsense! I insist. We can sit on the porch and enjoy the nice breeze. Come."

"If you insist, we would be delighted."

They all went on the porch and sat at the tables that were scattered around. Frances came out holding a tray with the bread and honey, and right behind her a man wearing coveralls emerged carrying a tray with a large pitcher of lemonade and glasses. He wore wire-rimmed glasses, and his face looked as if he never stopped smiling.

"This is my husband, Richard. He is a train conductor in Johnstown, where we live most of the year. He comes up here when he's not working to help me out. Our son, Justin, and his cousins help out from time to time in the summer. We also have a store in Johnstown, and my sister-in-law, Margaret, looks after that store during the summer while we are up here."

Richard poured generous glasses of lemonade and passed them out, while Frances cut the warm bread and dipped honey onto the slices. She passed them around and as each person took a bite of the warm bread, many sounds of delight could be heard.

Sarah's eyelids fluttered with pleasure. "This is wonderful! Would you please give me your recipe for this bread? It is much softer and more flavorful than the bread I make."

"I would be delighted. My mother gave me this recipe, and it has a few family secrets which I will share. I'm so glad you are enjoying it."

Richard took a seat next to Wesley.

"I'm looking forward to hunting and fishing," Wesley ventured. "Pittsburgh is not exactly the fishing and hunting capital of the world." Wesley laughed.

"You will find the hunting and fishing is unparallel. I have heard that the club has hired the best guides in the area," Richard said. "There will also be hunting and shooting competitions. I don't know if they will have fishing competitions, but you never know. This lake has been stocked with black bass, and they are fun to catch."

"Great. I look forward to it. Will you join the competitions, Richard?"

"No, I am far too busy with this store, the store we have in town, and running my routes on the train to be able to hunt and fish. I may try and make some time to spend with you, if you do not mind?"

Wesley laughed. "Of course, you are always welcome to hunt or fish with us. And when you are not here, we will make sure that Frances does not work too hard."

"Thank you, that sounds like good fun. Now, I must get back to the crates in the back room. We want to have all our new merchandise out when the rest of the guests arrive. It was very nice to have met you, and I look forward to a pleasant summer." Richard got up and took his plate into the store.

Frances watched him leave, a worried crease in her brow. Sarah leaned forward and placed a hand on the older woman's arm. "Your husband's a very nice man," Sarah said.

"Yes, he is great. He works so hard. I hope he will relax some this summer."

"We promise to do our utmost to lure him away for a few hours of recreation. Well, we must continue our exploration, or I fear that Shirley and Sheila will run off without us. It was so nice to have met you, Frances," Wesley said as he rose from his chair.

"Here, let me help you with those dishes," Sarah said as she started to gather the plates.

"Nonsense, you run along, I will take care of these," Frances said as she gathered the plates and glasses on the tray and started for the door. "Take care and enjoy your summer. I look forward to seeing you. Sarah, I will have the recipe for you, so make sure you stop by."

"Bye, we will see you later. Thank you for the fine bread and honey," Eloise said as she walked down the stairs to join her family.

Shirley and Sheila had already decided the direction the family would take as they raced off toward the barn. They could see the horses in the corral and wanted to get a closer look. Walter raced after them as Wesley waited for the ladies. By the time Sarah reached the corral, Walter had the girls on the fence, and they were petting some of the horses that came over to see them. Walter was showing the girls how to pet them nicely, so they didn't spook the horses. The horses at the house knew them, and Walter reminded the girls that these horses didn't know them and were a bit wary. As Sarah approached, Shirley climbed down from the fence and grabbed her mother's hand and started to drag her toward the barn.

"Mom, I saw a pretty cat go in the barn. Let's go find it."

"I'm coming."

As they entered the barn, they paused to let their eyes adjust to the dimness. They looked around the interior of the barn and saw that it was quite large. There were twenty stalls, which appeared to be empty. On either side of the aisle and on top of the stalls were two lofts, each filled with straw and hay. In the center was a large pulley with rope attached to lift the bales to the loft. The stalls were neat and clean, and the center aisle was free of clutter and swept clear. They spotted the cat as it crawled up the ladder and disappeared over the edge of the loft. Shirley dropped Sarah's hand and scrambled up the ladder. Sarah, seeing where she was going, scrambled right behind her so she would not fall. Walter entered the barn just in time to see his wife climb into the loft. He could hear Shirley calling to the cats, and Sarah rustling around in the hay to find where Shirley had disappeared.

Sarah found her daughter sitting with the cat along with six baby kittens all snuggled around the mother. Shirley was holding two of the babies and laughing as they tried to suckle on her fingers. Sarah crawled over to where Shirley was and was handed a baby kitten. It was so small and soft.

"Aren't these the cutest kittens, Mom? They are so small and soft. Just like the ones at home, the ones Timothy takes care of."

"Yes, they're adorable."

They turned when they heard a noise and saw Sheila crawling toward them and reaching for a kitten. Right behind her was Wesley, trying desperately to catch her, but she was just too fast for him.

When Wesley reached the group, they all sat and watched the cats in silence. Every few minutes, Shirley would pick up a different kitten. Not wanting to be left out, Sheila did the same. After fifteen minutes or so, Walter called up to the group, "Are you coming down or do we need to come up there? There's so much more to explore."

"We're coming. Girls, put the kittens with their mother and let's get going."

Amid groans, the girls did as they were told and crawled to the ladder. Wesley had gotten there first and helped each of them down the ladder. Walter was waiting at the bottom, and when they saw him, each one leapt into his arms when they reached midway. Sarah could hear their squeals of delight and smiled as she crawled to the ladder. Wesley helped Sarah negotiate the ladder and then climbed down after her. The next few minutes were spent pulling hay and straw out of their hair and off their clothes. When they felt they were presentable, they continued through the barn.

On the other side of the barn was a smaller shed. Upon inspection they could see it was filled with carriages and wagons and all the tack for the horses. Behind the shed they could see a barn and larger paddock filled with mules and workhorses. Unsure why they were there, they decided to venture closer to the paddock. As they approached, they surprised a stableman who was cleaning the stalls.

"Hello! I don't mean to startle you. How are you?" Walter said.

The man turned and pushed his hat out of his eyes. "Well, now that my heart's slowing down, I'm doing better." The man held out a dirty hand, saw the dirt, quickly wiped it on a rag on his waist, and then thrust it toward Walter once more. "Hello, my name is Steven Stamper. How are you folks today?"

"We are fine. We're out exploring the grounds and came upon the barn and wondered why there were so many mules and workhorses here."

"In exchange for helping out at the club, the local people are able to stable their wagons and work animals here. The club provides grain, straw, and hay. We feed and water our animals, but the club maintains the barn and paddock for us. It is a workable deal that many of us are taking advantage of. My father, Joseph, is the main caretaker at the club. He does all the maintenance and helps Mr. Timmons out during the off-season. My brother, Michael, and I help out when we can. We run our farm and help with the chores at the club."

"That sounds like a win-win for all. My name is Walter Green, and this is my family, Sarah and Shirley. This is Wesley Danvers and his wife, Eloise, and their daughter, Sheila. We got caught up looking at the horses and then Shirley spotted a cat. You have a fine family of cats in the loft. I am sure they will be great mousers."

"Yes, that is Patches. She produces the best mousers. We often sell or give away her kittens for those who need mouse control." Steven laughed. "She is well known in this area, and her kittens are in high demand."

"She is so cute, and the babies tried to suck on my fingers when I held them," Shirley said.

"Yes, she had that litter a few weeks ago. They are growing by leaps and bounds and will be running all over soon."

"Well, we will let you get back to what you were doing. It was nice meeting you, Steven."

"Likewise, Mr. Green." Steven shook Walter's hand again as the family called good-byes and drifted back toward the club.

Steven watched the two families walk away. He was surprised that they had been so polite and friendly. Some of the families, he had heard, were not that receptive to the nonmembers. He smiled as he went back to work on the stalls.

They strolled back toward the clubhouse and took in the sights as the children raced here and there, checking out all the buildings and the lake. When they had finished walking up and down the boardwalk and were relaxing on the porch, Mr. Daniels suggested they might want to walk down to the spillway. It was built as a relaxation place and was very romantic. The families started off down the road that the carriage had come across when they arrived at the club. They stopped on the dam and marveled at the view toward the lake. The lake looked larger and more beautiful from the dam. As they continued walking, they found a path that led to the spillway. As they rounded the corner, they stopped at the breathtaking sight.

The spillway was made of massive flat rocks that were arranged in a stair formation that let the water flow naturally down the side of the hill to the river below. There were some flat and depressed parts of the top of the spillway, where the water pooled and created a deeper swimming hole. Along the banks of the spillway were larger rocks that were low enough for people to sit on. As they rounded the corner and approached the area, they could see a few people sitting on the rocks with their feet dangling in the water to cool off. The water going over the spillway was not a fast-flowing stream, and they could see some children playing in the water as it ambled its way down the embankment.

Shirley and Sheila quickly sat down and pulled off their shoes and stockings and went over to the other children, where they were quickly accepted. Soon they were all splashing water on each other and squealing with delight. Walter and Sarah walked over to the place where another couple was sitting and introduced themselves. Wesley and Eloise came over, and the three couples sat and watched the children play in the water.

After a time watching the children, Wesley and Walter took off their shoes and socks, rolled up their pant legs, and went over to where the girls were playing. Sneaking up behind them, they each scooped their daughters high in the air and pretended to throw them over the cliff. When the screaming stopped, they set them down and the girls proceeded to splash Walter and Wesley until all parties were soaked. A water fight ensued, the children against the adults. Everyone won in the tussle, all were soaked and exhausted.

Tired from the water fight, Walter and Wesley sat on the rocks next to the ladies and warmed themselves in the sun. The girls proceeded to find shiny rocks and pebbles in the water and would occasionally run over to show their parents. They left the prettiest ones with their mothers and raced back to find more. Soon they were tired and the men were dry, so everyone put on their shoes and stockings and the families walked back to the clubhouse.

When they got to the clubhouse, they realized it was lunchtime. They were seated at a table where four of the chairs were already taken. As they approached, a tall gentleman stood up and said, "Welcome. I am Robert Powell, and this is my wife, Dorothy, and our children, Darryl and Susan."

Wesley was closer to Robert and stretched out his hand. "Thank you, we would enjoy that. This is my wife, Eloise, and our daughter, Sheila. This is Walter Green, his wife, Sarah, and their daughter, Shirley."

As they all went to their chairs to sit down, Darryl jumped up out of his chair and pulled the chair out for Sheila. Blushing, Sheila sat down and murmured, "Thank you." Robert looked at his wife and smiled.

The waiter came over to the table. "Welcome to the club. I am Edward, and I will be your waiter for this afternoon. Lunches here at the club are family style. We have one menu for lunch and we will bring out the food, and you may take whatever you would like, as much as you would like. I will bring out a couple pitchers of milk and beer in a minute. If you would like more of something, please let me know. Enjoy your lunch!"

In no time at all, Edward was bringing out steaming bowls of potatoes, vegetables, and stew.

Walter picked up the bowl of potatoes, put some on his plate, and then passed the bowl to Sarah. "Are you from Pittsburgh, Mr. Powell?"

"Please, call me Robert. Yes, we are. I am a lawyer at Marcus, Smith, and Powell. Do you live in Pittsburgh also?"

Walter was unsure how to answer Robert. He glanced at Sarah and saw his worry mirrored in her eyes. If he said yes, then the next obvious question was where did he work, he didn't want to say he worked for Wesley, but hesitated long enough for Wesley to see his quandary and answer, "Yes, we live in Pittsburgh. I am the president of Pittsburg Federal Savings. The Greens are our good friends who joined with us."

"I thought you looked familiar. I bank there and have seen you often. I just couldn't place you."

Wesley nodded his head. "When we arrived, we took a stroll around the grounds, I was amazed at the spaciousness of the club. Shirley noticed the sailboats and that they would be giving sailing lessons. That of course piqued Sheila's interest, so we will be investigating when the classes are and if there is an age restriction."

Walter was grateful to his friend for changing the topic of conversation. As he relaxed he said, "I am anxious to learn to sail a boat also, so I think we can all take lessons together. What do you think, girls?"

He was rewarded with a strangling hug from his exuberant daughter.

Walter pried Shirley's arms from around his neck, chuckling as he did so. "I do insist, and I am sure, Wesley, you will insist also, that the girls take swimming lessons. Accidents happen in boats, and we want to make sure you know how to swim. It will be fun. We can all take lessons together."

"Absolutely. I know how to swim a little. It will be good to get instruction and learn to be a stronger swimmer. What do you say, dear?" Wesley looked at Eloise.

"Good idea." Eloise looked at Sarah and saw that she was looking at her hands and that they were busy twisting the napkin that was in her lap. "Sarah, don't you think it would be a good idea for the girls to learn how to swim?"

Sarah looked up quickly, masking the worry on her face. "Yes, I think it is a great idea."

"Then it is settled. Robert, Dorothy, will you be joining us for swimming lessons?" Wesley said, looking from his wife across the table to where Robert sat.

"Well, we really haven't talked about it. Darryl, do you think you would like to learn how to swim?"

"Yes, I would love to learn."

"I guess it is settled. Looks like we are in for a bit of competition on the water this summer. What a grand time it will be."

~~~

The swimming classes were for two weeks and were held every morning at ten. The sailing classes started the second week and were held in the afternoon. The club wanted to be sure that all who were taking the sailing classes had a basic understanding of how to swim, perchance the sailboat turned over, they would be safe.

After lunch, the children ran off, and the adults went onto the porch to talk and discuss the things they would do during the summer. The rest of the day was spent strolling the boardwalk or visiting with the other guests. The men talked about all the hunting and fishing they would do, and the ladies came up with the idea that they could learn a popular play and they could rehearse and perform the play at the end of the summer for the rest of the guests. They found out that a large number of the other guests liked to perform, so it next came the job of deciding which play to perform. They spent the rest of the afternoon picking out a play and then setting up auditions.

By the end of the day, Shirley and Sheila were exhausted. They could barely keep their eyes open at dinner, and soon after they were sound asleep.

Chapter Eight

The next week came much too quickly for Sarah. She was not looking forward to taking swimming classes, but she put on a smile and got into her bathing outfit. As they walked down toward the beach, Sarah looked at what the other women were wearing, and then looked down at her bathing outfit. When Eloise told them of the club, Sarah used some leftover material she had and fashioned her family bathing outfits. They were all handmade, and Sarah was afraid it was not in the latest fashion and that her family would not be as well dressed as the rest of the guests. As she looked around, all the other outfits were ones that Sarah had seen in the shops, new and professionally made. Although Sarah was adept with a needle, she was still apprehensive about the clothes she wore. No one seemed to care what they were wearing, and Sarah's fears turned from the clothes to the water.

Everyone who was taking the class met at the beach where the instructors were waiting. They were broken up into smaller groups, each with a qualified instructor. The first day was spent on the beach, learning about the things in the lake that can help them stay afloat and the correct way to move your arms and feet when swimming. It was easier to show them how to do this while they were lying on their towels. Once they got the hang of the strokes and were comfortable with the movement of their arms and legs, they would try it in the water. Sarah got a kick out of lying on her towel pretending to swim. Thinking it might not be so bad after all, she relaxed and listened to the instructor's voice.

Day two was spent standing waist high in the water, practicing the arm motions and taking a breath while swimming. They learned a few different strokes while standing in the water. The instructors then got the group used to the feel and the resistance of the water. Sarah grew increasingly more comfortable as the classes progressed. Shirley and Sheila were having a great time and were anxious to get off their feet and swimming around.

For the next few days, they alternated with the arm strokes and learning to kick in the shallow water. The instructors made sure their legs stayed straight, helping build up strength. The first week was pleasant, and Sarah grew more relaxed in the water. Walter was glad to see Sarah smiling and enjoying herself. It was nice that the whole family, plus the Danverses, were learning, so when they made mistakes, they helped each other. The weekend came, and the classes were halted. They would resume on Monday morning. During the weekend, they practiced in the water by the beach, went to the spillway, and visited Frances and Richard Brown at their store.

When Monday morning came around, as they met for their swimming classes, they learned that they would be working with a partner. Each person would have someone to help hold them up as they attempted to float for the first time. Sarah felt her apprehension grow, and when the instructor called her name, she found she was paired with Walter.

"Sarah, relax. I will never let anything happen to you. Do you trust me?"

"Yes, I do trust you, but I am still scared."

"I know, I can feel your hand trembling. Remember, I am here. I will not let you go."

Sarah took a deep breath, squeezed Walter's hand, and walked with him into the water. Walter held his arms out for Sarah to lie across. Sarah's mind was racing with flashbacks of the fateful fall off the pier. She hesitated as she looked at Walter's arms stretched out before her. She looked around and saw that everyone else was lying in the water, being held up, and no one was drowning. Slowly, she lay down on Walter's arms. She felt his strength and looked up at his face, smiling down at her, giving her strength to do this. As she lay in Walter's arms and felt the water around her, she started to relax a bit.

The instructor called out, "Now that everyone has gotten comfortable with the water around their bodies, and what it feels like, I want everyone to move their hands slowly side to side, this will help you stay afloat. Take a deep breath, and now I want the holders to slowly lower their arms so your partner is floating. Those of you who are lying in the water, start moving your arms slowly, take a deep breath, and float."

Okay, Sarah girl. Just take a deep breath and float. You can do this—

Walter looked down at Sarah. "Ready, love? Remember, I am right here."

"I...guess....so."

Sarah moved her arms as the instructor had said, took a deep breath, and then nodded that she was ready. Walter inched his arms away from her, and Sarah started to float. With a grin of relief and pride, Walter moved his arms from beneath her completely, and Sarah started to sink. Water flooded Sarah's mouth. Sarah thought Walter had let go too soon, and now she was drowning! In a blind panic, Sarah thrashed her arms and legs. She could feel the water pulling at her. Flailing, she fought off the assailant surrounding her and connected with a body.

Walter grabbed a hold of Sarah's swimming outfit and pulled her up. Sarah gasped and wrapped her arms around Walter's neck.

"Put your feet down, Sarah. You can stand. it is not that deep."

As his voice penetrated her fear, she did as she was told and found she was not drowning. She opened her eyes and saw Walter standing there, holding her. The next moment, she was racing toward the beach. She reached her towel and sat down, shaking.

As Walter approached, he heard Sarah talking to herself.

"No more. Never. I am not going back in. No way."

"Sarah? Honey, are you all right?" Walter asked as he knelt beside her.

"No more. Never. I am not going back in. No way. Can't make me," she repeated through chattering teeth.

"Sarah, it's Walter. Are you okay, honey?"

Sarah's gaze snapped to his face. "Walter, I am fine. I just don't want to do that again. I can't float or swim, never could. I sink like a stone. You go learn. I will stay here, where it is safe."

"I will let you rest, but I would like you to try again. Maybe tomorrow?"

"We will see. No promises. I will watch you and Shirley from here."

"Are you sure? We can go back to the clubhouse."

"No, you and Shirley swim. I will be here when you are done."

Walter walked back to where the class was waiting. When Walter assured them she was fine, they went back to taking turns learning to float. There were a couple of people that could not float. They started to sink, just as Sarah had done, but none of them had the reaction that Sarah had. Each stood up and tried again. By the time the class was over, each person, with the exception of Sarah, had floated, some for long periods and others for a few seconds. They had all started to get the hang of it as the class ended.

The group exited the water, talking excitedly. Sarah got up and joined her family. Having recovered, she was happy to be leaving the beach. They went back to their rooms and readied themselves for lunch.

After lunch, Walter asked Mr. Daniels about the sailing lessons.

"Any member who is twelve or older is allowed to rent the sail boats. Each person must complete six hours of training with our instructor before they are allowed to take the boats out by themselves. We want to make sure that everyone knows how to safely operate the boat and all the safety features. If you and your lovely daughters would like to learn, the classes start next Monday afternoon by the boats."

"Thank you, Mr. Daniels. The girls are too young right now, but will they be allowed to learn alongside of Wesley and myself? This way they can learn, and when they are older will be able to take the boats out themselves."

"Yes, they are welcome to attend the classes along with you and Mr. Danvers. I believe they will enjoy it, and as they get older, they will be very knowledgeable and capable sailors."

Walter explained to the family what the rules were. Shirley and Sheila were disappointed they wouldn't be able to take the boats out themselves until next year but were very happy they could learn.

Shirley and Sheila soaked up every word the sailing instructor said and memorized the boat parts and the rules for safe sailing. When they all went out sailing, Walter and Wesley let the girls steer and run the boats completely. Even though they were not allowed to take the boats out by themselves, when they were on the lake, they were the captains. It was enjoyable to ride along and let the girls man the boat. Walter and Wesley often sat in the back of the boat and just enjoyed the view.

Toward the end of the summer, Walter and Wesley each rented a boat, and when they got to the end of the lake, let the girls take over and race back to the club. Each girl was quick, and the races were very close. Sometimes it was Shirley and Walter who crossed the imaginary finish line first, and sometimes it was Sheila and Wesley. Their races were the talk of the club, and as the boats sped toward the finish line, most of the members would be on the banks cheering. Sarah got scraps of material from the Browns' store and made a blue ribbon for the winner of the most races of the summer. The first year, Sheila won the blue ribbon, but by a very narrow margin.

As the first summer at the club came to a close, the club organized a hunting competition for the men. This was the first annual contest, and the winner would get a trophy and bragging rights until next year. Walter and Wesley entered the contest, each having become an avid hunter over the summer. There were two dozen other men who joined, and the competition was going to be fierce.

Mr. Daniels walked up to the front of the group. He held his hands in the air for quiet. "Thank you. The club is pleased to announce the first annual hunting competition. The rules are very simple. Each man will have four hours to hunt the woods around the club. The competition will start at ten a.m., and each man must be back at the club at two p.m. If you are not back at two, you will be eliminated from the competition. The one who accumulates the most points will win. Each bird is given a point value. We will be hunting game birds: quail, pheasant, turkey, and grouse. Turkeys carry the most points at five for each bird, a pheasant is four points, quail are three points, and grouse are two points. These birds will be given to the cook, and we will have a feast of game birds tonight for dinner. Are there any questions?"

All the men were standing around shaking their heads, so Mr. Daniels said, "All right men, go and get your rifles and prepare for the competition. You have one hour, and we will meet here to all leave for the woods together. For those of you who do not have your own guns, there are guns for rent at the clubhouse. If you will follow me, we will get everyone what they need, and get this competition off to a good start. Good luck to all of you, and may the sharpest shooter win."

Walter and Wesley followed Mr. Daniels to the clubhouse with a number of their friends. Each man was given a muzzleloader gun, a bag of powder, a bag of shot, and a large burlap sack to bring home their spoils. Each bag contained over two hundred shots, and Mr. Daniels thought that it would be enough for each man. They were to bring back the unused shot when the competition was over. As the guns were handed out, each member checked them out, made sure they were in working order, and then went to the porch to wait for the competition to begin. They all discussed where they could go, and although some of the men shared their secret places, some of the men were curiously silent about the best places to hunt. Wesley and Walter were two such silent men. They had hunted extensively during the summer and had their spot they wanted to try.

Ten o'clock came around, and Mr. Daniels fired a small handgun to announce the beginning of the tournament. Each man walked quickly into the woods, and soon they were all swallowed up by the trees. The women and children cheered them on as they walked away, and when the men were out of sight, they sat and talked or walked away. The children ran to the beach or to the other play areas and quickly forgot their fathers.

As the day wore on, Sarah could hear shots in the forest. She prayed that Walter would be safe and that he would enjoy himself. She hoped that he would get some birds, so he wouldn't have a bad showing. Sarah and Eloise had tea on the porch, and then Eloise drifted off to talk to some of the other guests. Sarah had brought her needlepoint down and was working on making a pillowcase for Shirley's room. Sarah was lost in her work, when she heard someone say, "Excuse me, can I sit with you?"

Startled, Sarah looked up and saw a woman of about thirty-five, trussed in the latest fashion. "By all means, I would enjoy the company."

The woman sat down stiffly. "I am Dora Stevens, Larry Stevens's wife. You are Sarah Green, correct?"

Sarah forced her smile to stay in the place. The woman was peering at her like she was a cockroach she'd found in the kitchen. "Yes. Nice to meet you, Dora."

"You may call me Mrs. Stevens. I know who you are. My husband told me that you work for the Danverses! It is an insult to all of us that you are allowed to stay in the main part of the clubhouse and not in the annex with the servants, where you belong."

Speechless, Sarah could only stare at Dora's face. Her cheeks had changed from their usual pallid color to an angry flush, and her mouth was contorted in an ugly sneer.

Mrs. Stevens continued her rant. "I have half a mind to go to Mr. Timmons or Mr. Daniels and tell them that they are being fooled by you. That they should throw you out and throw the Danverses out also, for making fools out of all of us with this charade."

Sarah could not think of anything to say. She had thought the same thing since Eloise told her about their offer to make them members but wasn't able to hurt her friend's feelings by saying what was on her mind.

"Dora! Really, how can you sit there and be such a snob? You will do no such thing. You know that you are only a member of this club because of the money your parents left you when they both passed away. If not for that, then you wouldn't be a member, nor have a big house or the fancy clothes."

Eloise walked up to where Sarah was sitting and stood behind her chair. Placing her hand on Sarah's shoulder, she silently challenged Dora to continue with her tirade.

Seeing that she had hurt Sarah, that was enough for Dora. With a satisfied smirk, she thrust her chin out, got up quickly, picked up her skirt, and turned and walked into the clubhouse. The other ladies saw her march into the clubhouse and, after she had passed by, looked over to where Eloise and Sarah were. Sarah had her head down, and Eloise had a smile on her face as she watched her go. The ladies on the porch smiled at Eloise and Sarah and went back to what they were doing.

Eloise pulled a chair next to Sarah, took her friend's hands in hers, and forced her to look up. She saw that Sarah was crying, and it broke her heart.

"Sarah. Please do not let what Dora said upset you. You have a great many friends here, and what you do for a living doesn't matter to them."

"That is what you say. But you know that Dora is right. We don't belong here, staying with you in the clubhouse, when we should be in the annex. I knew that this would happen, and I don't want you or Wesley to think we have ruined your time here and your friendships. I have been worried all summer that someone would find out and that they would kick you out of the club."

Eloise smiled. "Please do not worry. That old biddy Dora and any of her friends can just shimmy up a pole. I believe your secret is safe, and I do not think Dora will say anything to anyone. Please do not worry or cry."

Sarah sniffed into the hankie Eloise handed to her. "I hope you are right. I would feel just awful if you and Wesley got kicked out over us. I know you love it here, and it would just break my heart if I did anything to jeopardize it."

"Okay, enough of this. Dry your eyes and let's go and have a nice lunch. You will see—everything is just fine."

Sarah put her needlepoint aside and followed Eloise into the dining room. They found a table with two empty chairs and sat down with some of the other ladies whose husbands were hunting. Sarah looked around and saw Dora sitting with some of her friends, watching her with undisguised hatred on her face. Feeling a chill, Sarah turned her attention back to the women she was sitting with. Shortly thereafter, Shirley and Sheila came barreling into the dining room looking for their mothers. They stopped short inside the doorway, and when their eyes adjusted to the light, they spotted them and ran over.

"Hi, girls! Where have you been?" Sarah asked.

"We built a nifty sand castle on the beach, and we want you to come see it before someone tears it down," Shirley said as she grabbed her mother's hand and started pulling her toward the door.

"You too, Mom," Sheila said.

Sarah and Eloise found themselves being dragged out of the dining room to the surprise of the waiter who was just bringing their food. "We shall be right back, Edward," Eloise called as she went out the door.

Smiling, Edward put the plates on the table and went to get the pitcher to refill any glasses.

"What unkempt ruffians those two are. They need a good whipping to bring them into line," Dora said to anyone who would listen.

"Those two ruffians," Dorothy said, "as you called them, are the sweetest, prettiest girls at the club. So you just keep your mouth shut, Dora Stevens. I do not think Mr. Danvers would appreciate the wife of one of his employees saying such nasty things about his daughter. I would hope your husband is good at his job, so he can find another quickly, if word of this got out!"

Dora closed her mouth and bit off the retort she was thinking because she did not want to be the one to cause Larry to lose his job. Dora was quiet the rest of the meal and quickly left as soon as she was done.

Sarah and Eloise came back a short time after Dora's comeuppance and resumed their places at the table.

"So how are the sand castles?" Dorothy asked.

"Just lovely. It was a group effort, and I think all the children pitched in. It was quite a huge castle. Then after a while, they counted to three and they all jumped on it, and it was demolished. All the children were laughing and squealing."

Dorothy smiled. "Sounds like they had a great time."

"Which is what this place is all about!"

The ladies all finished lunch, and no one breathed a word to Eloise or Sarah about the tirade that Dora put on. They all felt that they did not need to be upset by the hateful words.

∿

An hour later, Eloise and Sarah waited impatiently for the men to come back from hunting. The men had started to come in, a few at a time, and Walter and Wesley were nowhere to be found. It was getting near two, and Eloise feared they would not make it back in time to be among the contestants. Sarah's fears went deeper. She was afraid that something had happened to them, a hunting accident, a bear, or something else. All she wanted was to see Walter's face, and the nerves cramping her stomach would stop.

She spent the next ten minutes wringing her hands and pacing around the boardwalk, all the while looking in the direction that the men had gone. As she turned to pace some more, she noticed two men walking across the dam and realized it was Walter and Wesley. She picked up her skirt and ran to where they were. Not caring if he was sweaty or dirty, she launched herself into his arms. Walter saw her coming and put the bag of birds down along with the gun just in time for him to catch Sarah. Walter was nearly knocked down but somehow managed to stay on his feet.

He kissed Sarah, and when he pulled back, he saw the worried look on her face. Setting her down and picking up the bag and gun, he maneuvered his wife toward the clubhouse.

"What is wrong, Sarah? Why do you look so worried?"

"When you were later than the others, I started to think all sorts of things that could have gone wrong."

"Then why are you still upset? We are back, safe and sound, and hopefully the winners of this competition."

Sarah looked around and saw that Wesley had continued on and was almost at the clubhouse. Because he was out of earshot, Sarah told Walter what had happened while he was gone. "Dora Stevens said some things to me this afternoon. Awful things, and it is not that they were untrue, but just the amount of hate in her voice and on her face made me shudder."

Walter stopped and turned to face Sarah. "What did she say?"

"That she knew we worked for the Danverses and that we were not supposed to be members of the club, that we should stay in the annex. And she threatened to tell Mr. Timmons and Mr. Daniels and have us and the Danverses thrown out of the club."

"Then what happened?"

"Eloise heard her and put her in her place, but not before everyone heard her. I was so humiliated, and I think that was her intent. Walter, you and I have talked about this. You know as well as I do that we should be here as servants, not guests. She hit a raw nerve, and I am afraid that the Danverses will suffer more than us."

"So what did Eloise say after this happened? Was she concerned or upset?"

"No, you know Eloise. She was more concerned that I was upset than any effect this will have on them. Oh Walter, I just don't want to hurt them, they have been so good to us. Will you talk to Wesley about this, and next year we can stay in the annex?"

"If it will make you smile, my dear, I will speak to Wesley about it. I am sure that Eloise will fill him in, so when we talk, he will know about the incident and we will work out a plan. Now smile for me, and let's go see if I won this competition."

Walter put his arm around Sarah, and as she smiled, he kissed her and they joined the rest of the people at the clubhouse.

All the men brought their bags up to the edge of the porch. The ladies all waited on the porch looking down at the bags that were placed side by side. One by one, Mr. Daniels dumped the bags onto the ground. Mr. Daniels counted the birds and tallied the shooter's points and kept them on a scorecard. He announced the total for each person when he was done.

"Mr. Powell. You have two turkeys and four pheasants. Your total is twenty-six points. Mr. Stevens. You have four grouse and two quail. Your total is fourteen points." And on down the line he went until he reached Wesley and Walter, who were the last two to have their bags tallied.

"Mr. Danvers. You have two turkeys, four pheasants, and six quail. Your total is forty-nine points. Well done!" He turned to Walter. "Mr. Green, you have six turkeys, three pheasants, and four quail. Your total is fifty-four points. We have a winner! The club champion for this year, eighteen eighty-one, and the winner of the trophy is Walter Green! Congratulations, Walter!" Mr. Daniels handed Walter the trophy and shook his hand. "Looks like we will have quite a feast tonight!"

A loud cheer went up. Shirley launched herself at Walter, and he caught her and twirled her around. Sarah approached and gave Walter a kiss. "My hero!" Sarah said.

"Congratulations, my friend," Wesley said as he approached the group. "I'll get you next year."

"Maybe, or maybe I will continue to reign as champion!"

"We will see, we will see! Come, I am hungry. Let's go to the clubhouse and get something to eat. We also need to start packing. The carriages will be here in the morning."

"But we already ate lunch, Daddy," Shirley said as she rode into the clubhouse in Walter's arms.

"Well, Mr. Danvers and I have not eaten, so you can sit and watch us eat," he said while tickling her. Her laughter could be heard above all the talk in the dining room.

The staff waited patiently until the guests were in the clubhouse before they came with large tubs to collect all the birds and begin the task of preparing them for the party that evening. There was a celebration luncheon going on for the men who were hunting and didn't get to eat, and everyone was there. Mr. Daniels reminded everyone that there was a final dance that evening for all the club members and the wonderful birds that had been shot at the competition would be served for dinner, to round out the summer.

The dance was a lively affair in the clubhouse, and the decorations that had been put up gave a very festive atmosphere. By the end of the dance, everyone was exhausted, and they all slept soundly.

In the morning, there was a line of carriages waiting to take the guests to the train depot in Johnstown. As Sarah came out the front door, she could see all the people she had come to know milling around saying good-bye to everyone. There were a few tears for those who would not see their friends until next summer, as some of the guests did not live in Pittsburgh. Sarah said good-bye and found the carriage that was loaded with their trunks. As she looked back to the clubhouse, she saw Mr. and Mrs. Stevens coming out the door. Dora looked at Sarah, lifted her chin in the air, and continued to walk toward their carriage. Sarah felt a twinge of sadness, not for herself—she was used to being treated like that—but for Eloise and Wesley. They had been so good to her family, and their friendship meant the world to Sarah. She didn't want any adverse affects because of Eloise's generosity. She hoped that when they returned to Pittsburgh, Dora didn't cause any problems for Eloise. She believed her friend when she said things were fine, but deep down, the old fears resurfaced. After all, she hadn't said anything about Sarah that was untrue.

The family climbed aboard and settled in for the journey to Johnstown and eventually Pittsburgh. There was very little talk as everyone was still tired from the night before. Everyone seemed a bit sad that they would be leaving this paradise to go back to the real world.

Sarah had missed cooking and cleaning and was not used to being waited on, being from the working class. She wanted to get home, where things made sense, and she didn't have to worry about being a fraud with all the rich people.

Mrs. Danvers's social schedule would be heating up once again, and there would be parties to get ready for, and the holidays were approaching also. The Danverses liked the holidays and always had many parties, and the decorations that they put up took quite a bit of time. Walter usually had the younger stable hands help with the decorations, and the place looked like a snow palace when they were done. And as was the case in Pittsburgh, the snow was plentiful, and it added to the glitter and shine of the house.

Sarah also missed seeing Walter's parents. Sarah had made it a point to stop by when she was in town shopping for the Danverses and have tea with them. They were getting on in years, and Sarah dreaded the day that they would lose them. She enjoyed sitting and having tea, hearing about their friends and what trouble their children had gotten into or what triumphs they had. Walter's parents wanted to hear all about Shirley, and occasionally Sarah would bring her along when she did the shopping, knowing they would be thrilled to see her, as she was to see them.

Before she realized it, the carriage was pulling to a stop near the train station and everyone was getting out. As they moved to the train, Sarah took in the hustle and bustle of the station and was surprised to see Richard Brown coming their way. Sarah reached for Walter's arm and pointed to where Richard was.

Walter turned and, taking Sarah by the arm, walked over to greet his friend. "Richard! I don't know why I am surprised to see you here. You did tell us that you ran the train."

"Walter, Sarah, so nice to see you," Richard exclaimed as he shook Walter's hand. "Did you enjoy your vacation at the lake?"

"Yes, we did, thank you."

"I enjoyed hunting with you and Mr. Danvers. I hear you won the trophy this year for hunting, Walter. Good job!"

"Thank you. It was fun. Now I know I have to sharpen my skills next year. There are a lot of fine shots at the club. I think this time was a fluke, but we shall see when next summer comes around."

The train whistle split the air, and some of the smaller children covered their ears. Almost everyone noticeably jumped when the whistle sounded.

When the whistle stopped, Richard said, "I think you should get aboard. I don't want to fall behind schedule. It was nice seeing you. I hope to see you soon." With that, Richard turned and walked back to the engine.

"He is such a nice man. I am glad we became friends. Maybe sometime during the holidays we can come to Johnstown and see Frances and Richard. What do you think, Walter?"

"We shall see what the weather decides to do this winter. They have been pretty snowy lately, but we will try very hard to get back here to see them," Walter said as he took Sarah's arm and led her back to where the Danvers were waiting.

Summer of Gold and Water

When they arrived in Pittsburgh, they found Ryan waiting with the carriage to take them home.

"Welcome home! Let me get those bags for you."

"I can get them, Ryan, thank you. I am not one of the upper class, although we have been treated like that. I need to get back to working for a living and not being one of the pampered. I won't say it wasn't fun, but you and I know the reality of life," Walter said as he picked up his and Sarah's luggage.

"I understand. I guess I am just used to doing it all. Welcome back. We have missed you. Timmy keeps asking about Shirley, and Megan is dying to catch up with Sarah. Good to have you home," Ryan said as he shook Walter's hand.

It took Ryan and Walter several trips to get all the luggage loaded in the carriage. Ryan climbed up and was not surprised to see Shirley sitting next to him. She giggled and took the reins from him to drive the horses home. It was a welcome sight to pull up into the driveway. Walter helped Ryan carry the Danverses' luggage into the house and then came back to help Sarah with their own. It was nice to be home, and after they got the clothes put away, Sarah and Walter sat in the quiet of their living room and just relaxed.

"It has been a long day. I am bushed. How about you, my love?"

"I am tired too. I am glad we are home, and now things will get back to normal. I like being at the lake, but it is a weird feeling when everyone thinks we are the same class as them and that we have money. I would have preferred to stay in the servants' quarters and be with our own kind. Did you get a chance to talk to Wesley about what Mrs. Stevens said?"

"Yes, I did. Eloise had told him what was said and how angry it made her. Wesley said that we should not worry about it, that the fallout will be minimal, and that we were not to worry about them. I told him of your fears, and he wanted me to assure you that nothing will come of this. He indicated he might have a word with Mr. Stevens about what his wife said. She may not have told him, but I am sure she heard it first from her husband and was just vocalizing it. Wesley is going to make sure that Mr. Stevens knows the lay of the land and will advise him strongly to keep his opinions to himself and to make sure his wife does the same."

"Remember, it was Wesley's decision to make us members. I know he thought he was doing us a favor and he was, but I don't think he realizes just how different we are and how much some people would resent it. Wesley does not treat us like servants, and never will, but I think he got a taste of how different he and Eloise are with Mrs. Stevens's comments. I don't think they regret the decision, and I don't think they will change anything about the way they act toward us or anyone. They aren't snobs, and they have no tolerance for snobs."

Sarah shook her head. "I know, but it isn't really for us that I am worried. One day Shirley will be old enough to be interested in boys, and I don't want her to think, or the boys to think, that she is of that class, because she will get her heart broken if she falls for a boy in the upper class."

"We will just have to make sure that she knows where she comes from and what the rules of society are. I think that she is a levelheaded girl and will understand."

"I hope so. Would you put out the light? I am very tired," Sarah said as she climbed into bed.

Walter put out the light, and she could feel his weight shift on the bed. Soon she was lying with her head on his shoulder and his arm around her. She felt safe and secure and soon drifted off to sleep.

Chapter Nine

The weather turned colder as fall turned into winter. As was the custom at the Danverses' estate, Mr. Danvers ordered a turkey for each of his employees for their Thanksgiving dinner. He invited all of his employees to his house for Thanksgiving dinner, and normally they all attended. He held his dinner on the Saturday after Thanksgiving so the families could spend Thanksgiving Day with their families. Then on Saturday, they all gathered at the Danverses' home to celebrate and give thanks for the year that just passed and pray for the year to come.

Eloise hosted two dinners every year. One for both Wesley's family and her family and then one for the workers and their families. Sarah was instrumental in helping pull these massive dinners off without a hitch. Sarah started at the beginning of the week, making sure the supplies were bought and stacked. She made sure the baking of all the pies, cakes, fudge, and cookies, which were a tradition in the Danvers home, was completed early, giving her time for the turkey and the side dishes. The house smelled heavenly all week. In addition to making sure that the food was prepared correctly, Sarah also did an extra thorough cleaning of the house, polished the silver, and made sure the crystal was sparkling.

Thanksgiving, along with Christmas, was the busiest time for Sarah. It kept her going from sun up to sun down, but she was pleased with what she was doing and always felt self-satisfaction. During the Thanksgiving break from school, Shirley helped her mother out with all that needed to be done.

Because Sarah was so busy cooking on Thanksgiving, she enlisted the help of Walter and Shirley to help serve and clear dishes. Dinner on Thanksgiving Day was a sit-down affair, unlike the Saturday dinner, which, due to the number of workers, was a buffet style, so everyone could help themselves. The Saturday dinner was much easier on Sarah, since the wives of the stable hands and gardeners would help her with the serving and cleaning. They were all used to working, and this was a treat they enjoyed. It was also a time for catching up and visiting with the families of the people they worked with. It was not often that they were all free at the same time, and it gave everyone a chance to relax and enjoy the holiday.

As soon as Thanksgiving was over, the flurry started about Christmas and New Years. All during the month of December, the Danverses either hosted parties or were invited to them. When they were invited, Sarah helped Eloise get the clothes ready and helped her with her hair, and after they left, she watched the children. When Eloise hosted the party, well, that was a different story. The entire household was turned upside down for a week before the party. The gardeners and grooms made sure that the driveway and walkways were clear of ice and snow, Sarah was busy baking and cleaning the house, Walter and Ryan put up decorations and set up tables and chairs, and the kids tried to stay out of the way. Usually when the party happenings were going on, all of the children went to Sarah's apartment to play. They didn't want to be dragged into helping, and they stayed out of the way of the busy adults.

When Eloise announced the Christmas party following their first year at the club, Sarah was immediately filled with a sense of dread. Dora Stevens's words came back full force, and although usually excited about the parties, she grew very quiet and subdued. Eloise was so excited, and was talking a mile a minute, that she didn't notice that Sarah was unusually quiet. When she was done, Eloise went upstairs to check on some decorations. Sarah turned and went into the kitchen. She sat at the counter with a pad and pencil to start planning the meal that she would present to Eloise for final approval.

About a half hour later, Walter came in looking for Sarah. He saw her sitting at the counter, frozen like a statue. He walked up behind her and put his hands on her shoulders and was about to kiss her cheek when she jumped. Walter jumped backward, also startled.

Summer of Gold and Water

Sarah turned around to see Walter standing there. "Walter, you scared me. Please don't sneak up on me. You gave me such a fright!"

"I made as much noise as I could, barring singing, when I came in, and you didn't move. You looked so far away. I think that's why you didn't hear me," Walter said as he took the stool next to her. "What are you writing?"

Sarah looked down at the paper. "I am making a menu for the party Eloise is planning next weekend. Guess I didn't get too far," she said, showing Walter her empty pad.

"Is there something wrong? It isn't like you to daydream while planning a party. You love doing that. What's wrong, sweetheart?"

"When Eloise was telling me about the party and who was to be invited, I flashed back to the lake when Dora said those horrible things. I know you talked to Wesley about this, but this will be the first time we have seen these people."

Laughing, Walter said, "We have seen these people many times here at the house for parties, dances, and dinner. I don't know why this party is making you so nervous."

"Because, Walter, this will be the first time we have seen them after spending the summer at the lake. You remember the lake? Where we were treated as equals, talked to instead of ordered around? Yes, I know that we have seen them here many times before, but before, they didn't notice us, we were just the help. Now when they come, they will see us not as equals but as the servants that we are, and they'll notice us this time because we spent so much time with them. Do you understand?"

The light went on, and Walter nodded. "Yes, I understand your fears. But they are all nice people, and I don't think they will be rude or talk like Dora did. I am sure that they know that Wesley will not have any of that. They know he is a good and kind man, and if he treats someone a certain way, then there is no one who will go against him."

"I am not worried about at the party, but after the party. It will be the talk of the town, what frauds we are and how gullible the Danverses are to let us be treated as equals. I just don't want a scandal that involves the Danverses. They are such wonderful people. I am not worried about us, I can handle us, but it is the Danverses' reputation I am worried about. Do you understand?"

"I understand, dear. Would you like me to talk to Wesley about it?"

"Oh no! Please don't. Let it just be our secret fear. I pray I am wrong."

"Things will be fine. Just wait and see," Walter said as he put his arm around Sarah and gave her a hug. Sarah put her head on his shoulder and let herself be comforted by his touch. Then she went back to planning the party.

To shake off the feeling of dread, Sarah threw herself into cleaning the house, the crystal, and silverware and making sure that the rugs were beaten clean and the drapes were taken down and washed. She had Ryan take her to the store to get all the supplies for the menu that she and Eloise had finalized. Every day she worked until sundown, cleaning and baking. She would fall into bed bone tired, asleep when her head hit the pillows. Her plan for keeping the worry at bay at night was working. But during the day, she would be caught unawares during the middle of some mundane task with the premonition that a storm was about to hit her dear family. The day before the party, there was a knock on the door. When she opened it, she was surprised when she saw Dora Stevens on the other side.

"I see you do know your place after all!"

"Mrs. Stevens, nice to see you again. How can I help you?"

"Give this to Eloise," Dora said as she thrust an envelope at Sarah.

"I will. Thank you."

"See you tomorrow, maid!" Dora turned and strutted to her waiting carriage, waiving impatiently to the groom to open the door.

Sarah watched Dora ride away, and as she turned to close the door, she heard Eloise come out of the kitchen.

"Who was at the door?"

"Mrs. Stevens. She asked me to give this to you." Sarah held out the envelope for Eloise.

Sarah looked toward the ground and started off toward the kitchen.

"Sarah, is something troubling you?"

Sarah stopped but did not turn around. She wiped the tears from her eyes and slowly turned to face her friend. "No, ma'am. Nothing is wrong."

"Ma'am? Sarah, come in the library and tell me what is the matter."

Eloise didn't wait for Sarah but turned and walked into the library. Sarah had no choice but to follow. As she entered the library, she looked up and saw Eloise standing in front of the sofa.

"Come, sit down, please."

Sarah walked over and sat next to her friend.

"Is it Dora?"

Sarah could not look Eloise in the eye and looked toward the fireplace. "Not really. She just reminded me of my place. I am very afraid that tomorrow night will begin trouble for you and Wesley. This is the first time we have seen the people from the lake, they will know that we are not equals but your servants. My fears will be realized tomorrow and you and Wesley will pay the price for our friendship."

"Pish posh! I know my friends. They will not say anything against you or the fact that you are members of the club. You will see. Please, dry your eyes, and try not to worry. Nothing will change how Wesley and I feel about you and your family, and nothing, I repeat, nothing, will happen to our reputation."

Sarah dried her eyes and looked at Eloise. Love and confidence glowed like a hundred candles from her face. "I trust you. I will try to put aside my fears."

"Good. Now let us finish the preparations."

They got up, and Eloise gathered Sarah in her arms and gave her a long hug. Sarah felt the love flow into her and started to relax. As Eloise stepped back, she smiled one more time at Sarah, took her by the arm, and they walked back into the foyer to finish the preparations for the party.

∾

The night of the party arrived, and Sarah was standing in front of the mirror, putting her hair in a bun, when she heard her husband enter. She turned to face him as she put the last pin in place. "Well, what do you think?"

"Beautiful as always!" he said as he planted a kiss on her cheek.

"Walter, I am just so nervous. I know I have done this many times, but tonight, well, I just don't know if I can do this. I keep picturing Dora's face as she walked away from the house yesterday. What if she started talking or does something at the party to embarrass me or, more importantly, Eloise and Wesley? I don't know how I will be able to handle it," Sarah said as she sat on the bed.

"We have to trust Eloise. Just do the best you can and let the chips fall where they may. Wesley and Eloise are on our side, and I know that nothing will happen. Do you trust me?"

Smiling, Sarah said, "Of course I trust you. Thank you. Now, let's get going, I have to make sure everything is perfect." Sarah got up and left the room. Walter sat there a minute longer, thinking about what she said. He hoped he was right, that the people they spent the summer with would not care that Sarah was serving the food and not eating it with them. He wondered if Sarah would mind not sitting down with people she saw as her friends this past summer. Slowly, he got up and followed Sarah to the Danverses' kitchen.

When Walter arrived in the kitchen, it was a flurry of activity. Eloise had hired extra help to make sure that Sarah wasn't run ragged and that the party was a success. The same people from town came to help as in past years, so everyone knew what was expected, where things were, and what they needed to do. Sarah was there to supervise the cooks and waitresses along with checking to make sure everything stayed on schedule. Huge platters of food waited to be brought out to the guests, and the smells from the oven were heavenly.

On the other side of the kitchen door, Walter could hear guests arriving and the four-piece orchestra that was playing on the balcony. Walter walked to the front hall to give Ryan a hand at opening the door, helping people down from their carriages, and taking their coats from them. He saw many of the people that he had spent the summer with arrive, and as he took their coats, they asked how he was and said they were looking forward to the weather being warmer. They told him it was nice to see him and then entered the house. There were no snide remarks or surprises as he took their coats. Walter started to relax when he saw Mr. Stevens and his wife arrive in the next carriage.

"Ryan, I will help the Stevenses," he said and walked into the driveway to help Mrs. Stevens from the carriage. She thrust her chin in the air, took her husband's arm, and walked into the house. No words were spoken, and Walter was not sure that she even knew who he was or had even looked in his direction. She just expected the hand to be there to help her out of her carriage, and it was. It didn't matter whose hand it was. Walter saw them enter the house and watched as Ryan took their coats to hang them up. She did not cast him a second glance; she just turned her back, expecting him to take her coat. That was her world. Walter marveled at the difference between the Danverses and the Stevenses.

Walter and Ryan continued to help people from their carriages and take their coats, each taking turns being outside, as it was getting dark and with the lack of sunlight, getting colder. When all the guests had arrived, Walter and Ryan went back inside to make sure there was nothing left to do, and then retreated to the kitchen. As they walked through the kitchen door, Sarah spotted them and asked them each to take one of the heavy platters into the dining room. They grabbed the platters and proceeded to make their rounds among the guests with the goodies Sarah had prepared. The tray that Walter had was loaded with stuffed mushrooms, scallops, small meatballs, and tiny quiche. Ryan's tray had a variety of cheeses with crackers and an array of fruit, such as melon balls, grapes, cantaloupe slices, apple slices, and tangerine slices. When each of the men had made their rounds, they went back to the kitchen to refill the trays and then placed them on the side boards strategically positioned around the living room and the dining room.

At eight o'clock, Sarah appeared in the doorway of the living room, rang a bell, and announced that dinner was being served in the dining room. All of the guests funneled their way into the dining room and took their respective seats. When they were all settled, Wesley stood up at the head of the table and said, "Welcome, all my friends and coworkers, to this happy holiday party. Eloise and I are overjoyed that you have all decided to share this holiday season with us. After dinner, we will have dancing in the living room, and I hope you will all stay and dance the night away. Please enjoy your dinner."

At each plate was a cup with shrimp cocktail and cocktail sauce. Everyone started to eat, and as each finished, Sarah, who was standing by the door, whisked in and took the empty plate away. When all were done, the next course was brought out by Walter. He carried the heavy tray out of the kitchen for Sarah and placed it on a table near the door. Sarah then took the creamy tomato soup and served it to each of the guests. When the soup was done, she took the plates away and out came the main course. Sarah had prepared Cornish game hens for each of the guests, with baby carrots, red potatoes, and rhubarb on the side.

As people finished their dinner, Sarah once again took the plates away. When all the plates were cleared, Sarah asked who would like dessert. The desserts had been placed on the sideboard, and all the guests had a chance to see them before dinner. A few jokes were made about eating dessert first and the meal later.

When dinner and dessert were finished, Wesley got up and said, "That was a magnificent meal." And with that he raised his half-empty glass of wine in Sarah's direction and toasted her. "Thank you, Sarah. You have outdone yourself!"

Blushing, Sarah could only nod. The rest of the guests raised their glasses also and said "Here, here!" As Sarah looked around the room, she saw nothing but smiling faces, until she got to where the Stevenses were sitting. They had not raised their glasses and were in fact looking down at their empty place settings. Before anyone noticed the Stevenses' reaction, Dorothy, who was sitting next to, Larry, leaned over and spoke to the couple in hushed tones.

"If you don't act as a polite human would do, and toast Sarah, I will make it my personal quest to ruin your reputation and cause your husband to lose his job. You won't be welcome in polite Pittsburgh society again. I guarantee it!"

Immediately, both Mr. and Mrs. Stevens faces got beat red, and they picked up their glasses to toast Sarah. Dorothy looked at Sarah and winked. Sarah smiled back, very grateful that things were not like she envisioned.

"Now, let us go work off some of these calories that Sarah has inflicted on us all!" Wesley said as he went to help Eloise out of her chair and led everyone to the living room. As they walked through the foyer, they could see that the small orchestra had moved their place to the living room and struck up a waltz when they entered the room. Sarah could hear the music and the rustle of the skirts. She relaxed and looked at the table. Walter came out of the kitchen, and together they cleared the table. When they finished, Sarah went to the living room to see if there was anything else that needed to be done. As she looked around, she saw Wesley guiding Eloise around the floor. While she was waiting, Dorothy approached her.

"Sarah, what a wonderful meal. You are such a talented person. I have missed our needlepoint sessions. I learned so much from you this past summer."

"I have missed those sessions also."

"Why don't you and Walter come and join us for the dancing? I know you and he are accomplished dancers."

"This is not my party, Mrs. Powell. It wouldn't be right. We will save our dancing for the summer."

"Dorothy, please. Nonsense!" Just as she said that, Wesley and Eloise were gliding by. Dorothy grabbed Wesley and pulled them off the floor. "I was just telling Sarah that she should go get her dancing shoes on and snag her husband to do some dancing with us. Don't you agree?"

"Of course, by all means. We have asked them before, but they don't feel it is their place, but you can't turn down a request from one of our guests, can you, Sarah?" Wesley said as he smiled and winked at Sarah.

"Maybe next time. Walter and I are tired, and we are going to retire. I just wanted to make sure everything was all right and that we were no longer needed."

"I believe we are fine. But I wish you would come join us," Eloise said.

"I will discuss it with Walter."

By then the music had stopped and the band started a lively jig. Everyone started to dance, and Sarah left the room still shaking her head. She and Walter loved to dance, and to be asked to the party was something she never expected. Walter could see the confused look on her face as he waited in the kitchen for her.

"We have been invited to dance. Eloise said to put on our dancing shoes and come back."

"Would you like to? If Eloise asked, maybe we should. It would be fun."

"Eloise didn't ask. Dorothy did. Eloise just agreed to it. Why not? It is the holidays, and we deserve some fun."

Walter and Sarah went back to their apartment and changed clothes, cleaned up a bit, and came back to the dancing. They had a wonderful time, and Sarah was relieved that her fears were unfounded. It was well after midnight that Walter had gotten the last coat and bid the guests good-bye.

"Good night, Eloise, Wesley. It was a wonderful party. Thank you for allowing us to join your friends," Walter said.

"They are your friends too. I am glad you decided to join us. We will see you in the morning. Good night, Walter, Sarah."

Walter and Sarah walked back to their apartment and, shortly after checking on Shirley, were fast asleep themselves.

Chapter Ten

In the early spring of 1882, Sarah began to feel poorly. Unsure of what was wrong with her friend, Eloise called the doctor.

"Doctor, is Sarah going to be all right?" Eloise asked as the doctor came out of Sarah's bedroom.

"Sarah will be just fine. What she has will be gone around Thanksgiving. Do not fear."

"Thanksgiving? Why so long?"

"Sarah is with child, and the baby will be born after Thanksgiving. Sarah is healthy, and there should be no complications. She will be over this bout of morning sickness in a couple weeks."

"Oh, what a relief," Eloise said as she collapsed into a chair. "I was just so worried. She is always so healthy. She really gave me a scare."

"She will be just fine. Are you feeling all right, Mrs. Danvers? You look a bit pale yourself."

"I am fine, just a bit nauseous. Must be something I ate."

"Let us go back to your house. I want to give you a physical while I am here. Just to make sure."

Sarah heard them leave and was lying in bed smiling. She could not wait to tell Walter the great news. He was just a short distance away, but she wanted to tell both Walter and Shirley together. Mrs. Danvers had given her the afternoon off, so she got up and walked slowly around the apartment. She stopped in the bedroom, decorated in blue, and started to imagine what it would look like with a crib and a rocking chair. Her hand absently rubbed her belly, where her child was growing.

She went to the window and saw the doctor leaving. He seemed to be smiling. Sarah remembered him telling Eloise that he wanted to make sure she was okay, so Sarah walked to the house to check on her friend. She found Eloise sitting in the living room, humming and doing needlepoint. She looked up when Sarah walked in and put the needlepoint down.

"Are you all right, Eloise? I heard the doctor say he wanted to examine you."

Eloise only smiled and patted the seat next to her. "Please sit down with me. It seems we will both be having additions to our families about the same time. I am pregnant also."

"That is terrific. Congratulations!"

"Congratulations to you also. This will be a year to remember!"

"Have you told Wesley?"

"No. I swore Dr. Baker to secrecy. I want to be the one to tell him."

"As did I. I was waiting for just the right moment to tell Walter. I have an idea. Why don't we tell them tonight at dinner?"

"I think that is a great idea."

Both ladies lapsed into a comfortable silence and thought about the babies they were carrying and how happy everyone would be that night.

Dinner came, and when everyone was assembled, Eloise said, "I would like to say grace tonight, Wesley, if that would be acceptable to you."

Startled, Wesley replied, "That is fine with me, dear."

"Dear Lord, bless this food and our families. Grant us peace and tranquility in the coming days and years. Bless the new additions to our families, and let their entries into the world be smooth and uneventful. In your name we pray, amen."

When she had finished, Eloise started to eat her dinner. The rest of the family sat stock still, in shock at Eloise's words.

"Eloise? Is there something going on?" Wesley asked.

"I was just giving thanks for our families and the new arrivals," Eloise said.

"New arrivals?"

"Yes, Dr. Baker was here, and he informed us of our maladies. Both Sarah and I are pregnant! We are both due sometime around Thanksgiving. It will be a blessed time for us this year."

All of a sudden everyone started talking at once. Walter sprang from his chair and went to hug Sarah. Wesley leaned over and gave Eloise a kiss. When everyone calmed down, they resumed their seats and started suggesting names for both boys and girls. Dinner was forgotten until it was cold, but no one noticed.

~~~

Eloise's and Sarah's bellies continued to grow over the summer at the lake and into the fall. As Thanksgiving approached, so did everyone's apprehension. Walter was glad he was not far from the house, and Wesley was reluctant to go to work, for fear his child would arrive in the world without him. Sarah and Eloise thought this was very cute and a bit funny. The stable hands had a pool as to who would deliver first. But whoever delivered first, both children would be welcomed into the world with open arms. The two women had decorated their nurseries and all was in preparation for the arrival of the babies.

Sheila and Shirley were anxious about a new brother or sister and were looking forward to helping take care of them. The girls had pitched in to help with the chores around the house so Sarah could be off her feet as much as possible. Shirley was becoming a good cook, and she was teaching Sheila. Both girls were naturals, although some of the meals were a mystery to all. The family ate whatever was prepared, so as not to hurt their feelings. After the meal was done, Sarah would talk to the girls as they did the dishes and give them hints as to what to do better next time.

Thanksgiving was a festive affair. Walter invited his parents, Ryan volunteered to bring Sarah's grandparents to the house, and with the addition of Eloise and Wesley's parents, there was quite a crowd at the Danvers house. All the stable hands and their families were invited, but they all had families in town and chose to go have their dinner with them. Mr. Danvers gave each one a large turkey as a Thanksgiving bonus and also gave them a few days off to enjoy their families. Dinner was delicious, and every time Sarah or Eloise winced or rubbed her belly, the room got quiet until they were sure that it was not time to deliver the babies.

As dinner wound down, Shirley and Sheila helped Sarah clear the table, and the families moved into the living room to rest and have an after-dinner drink. Everyone was talking quietly when a dish shattering and a scream of pain broke the pleasant spell. Walter leapt to his feet, looking around frantically and, after realizing Sarah was not in the room, ran toward the scream. As he neared the kitchen, he heard more cries of pain. He burst through the door and saw Sarah doubled over. A dish that had held the last of the potatoes lay broken on the floor. Shirley was helping her mother to a chair, and Sheila was putting her coat on. Sheila ran out the back door before anyone could stop her.

Walter knelt down next to Sarah. "Is it time?"

"I think so. Please get me to my bed."

Walter picked Sarah up as if she weighed nothing and walked out the back door. The rest of the family followed behind them. Shirley ran ahead of Walter and opened the doors for him. As he was carrying Sarah down the walkway toward their apartment, he saw Sheila race out of the stable on her horse.

"I am going for the doctor!" she yelled as she galloped down the driveway.

Walter made it to their room, and everyone went into action. Walter's father pumped the water into the pots and set them on the stove. Walter's mother lit the stove and started boiling water while Walter placed Sarah on the bed. He tried to make her comfortable with pillows and sat next to her. Shirley hovered next to her great grandmother by the door until Sarah called her over.

"Come sit on the bed next to me. Hold my hand and just be here. Having a baby is a wonderful thing, although it is a bit painful. I am glad you are here to share in the joy of your new brother or sister."

The labor pains came and went, and everyone in the living room started pacing or just stared out the window, waiting for the doctor. Walter's mother had helped deliver Shirley, so she stayed with Sarah in case the doctor did not arrive in time. Shirley took some time to arrive, and Walter's mother feared the second child would take some time also. Sarah was comforted by the thought of her mother-in-law and grandmother being there to help. She had long ago felt that she was as close to her mother-in-law as she would have been with her mother, had she been alive.

Summer of Gold and Water

Wesley was staring out the window when suddenly he raced out the door and down the stairs, running for the stable. Sheila was back, and as soon as she got her horse in the stable, the doctor's carriage came up the drive. Wesley hugged his daughter.

"That was quick thinking, my dear! Dr. Baker, it's Sarah. She's in labor. The pains started a couple hours ago."

"Let's go take a look. If I remember correctly, Shirley took her time coming into this world, so this baby may take a while to come, but we will see."

The three of them walked into the apartment, and the doctor went back to Sarah's room.

"Well, I see this little one doesn't want me to have a proper Thanksgiving dinner!"

"Sorry about this, Doctor. I waited as long as I could. I was hoping the pains would not get closer together until tomorrow."

"How long have you been having pains, Sarah?"

"Since last night. They came about once an hour starting around midnight. They woke me up. But after dinner they started to come every fifteen minutes, and now it seems like it is long and steady, although I know there is some break in between."

"Walter, would you please bring in some water, and then leave us? Have your mother and Sarah's grandmother come in if you would."

"May I stay and help, Doctor?" Shirley asked.

"If that is all right with your mother, you may stay. It will be very educational for you."

"Yes, Shirley, you may stay and help the doctor and your grandmothers. Why don't you ask Sheila also?"

Shirley went to the living room and got Sheila. Together they entered the room. Walter brought in a basin of hot water and left, closing the door quietly behind him. He joined his father, Sarah's grandfather, and the Danverses in the living room. Together they all waited and paced, occasionally bumping into each other.

After a few hours, there was a long, high-pitched scream from the bedroom. Then there was absolute silence. Faintly, they could hear a baby cry. It got louder and louder, and there was laughing and cheering in the living room. The doctor came out of the bedroom, wiping his hands on a towel.

"Congratulations, Walter, you have a fine, healthy son. Sarah and the baby are just fine."

"A son? Really, a son? That's great."

Walter felt the pats on the back and heard the words of congratulations, but all he could think about was getting to Sarah's side and seeing his son. He stumbled down the hall, and as he stood in the doorway, he looked at Sarah. She was drenched with sweat, but in her arms was a small, red-faced bundle. Shirley was standing to the side, wiping off her mother's face.

Walter walked slowly over to the bedside. He looked down at the tiny face, and just as the baby looked up at Walter, a loud wail erupted. They all laughed as Sarah calmed the baby down.

"Why don't we call him Tyler? What do you think?"

"Tyler, that is a good, strong name. I think it suits him perfectly. Are you well enough to see the rest of the family? They are anxiously waiting outside."

"Yes, they can all come in. I would like to introduce Tyler to them."

Walter walked to the door and called to his family and friends. "Come meet Tyler Green, the newest member of our household."

Everyone walked in softly and gathered around the bed. They marveled at the tiny hands, and just to show them his lung capacity, he let out a loud wail and then proceeded to suck his thumb.

After about an hour, when the doctor had declared that the baby was healthy and Sarah was fine, he was escorted to the driveway by the Danverses. Just as he was getting into his carriage, Eloise cried out. She doubled over, and Wesley caught his wife before she crumpled to the driveway. Wesley picked her up and carried her into the house, with the doctor trailing close behind. Just as they were disappearing into the house, Sheila came out of the Greens' apartment. She raced back inside and told everyone that her mom was having her baby also. Wesley's and Eloise's parents quickly went to the house. Walter's parents stayed but promised they would come to see how Eloise was doing before they left.

About three hours later, Sheila came bursting into the apartment.

"Mom had her baby! It is a boy too! They are going to name him Thomas! He is so cute! I have to get back, wanted you all to know. Mom is doing great!"

"This is just wonderful. I am glad she is all right and the baby is doing well. When you are feeling better, Sarah, we will go and see her."

"Sounds good to me."

For the remainder of the evening, Shirley and Sheila spent their time alternating between the two newborns and their mothers. They made sure that their mothers wanted for nothing. They fetched drinks and made sure they were comfortable. Both girls were fascinated with their baby brothers and loved to just sit and watch them sleep.

Chapter Eleven

Shirley and Sheila were entering the ninth grade and were very excited to be going to an exclusive, coed, private high school that the elite of Pittsburgh attended. It was more of a social club than a school, although the girls were taught all the subjects. The school had an extracurricular program where anyone could take cooking or sewing classes. A few of the girls took these classes, but the majority of the girls did not take them because they knew no other life than having servants to wait on them, so they felt the classes were a waste of time. Shirley and Sheila knew a different side of life, and both attended all the classes that were offered. They enjoyed learning and would often persuade Sarah to let them cook what they had learned in school for dinner. These meals were received by their families with some trepidation. Some of the meals were superb and some were very questionable. Even Shirley and Sheila would cringe when the meal did not turn out right, but luckily they had Sarah to help them and guide them as to what would make it better and what would make it edible.

They found they enjoyed cooking, but it was during one of the sewing classes that the girls got their inspiration. Both liked to draw, and when it came time for the final project, the class was to design and create their own outfit, dress, skirt, blouse, or bonnet. The only rule was that it had to be an original creation. They had to show the teacher the original drawing, any patterns they made for the garment, and, of course, the final product. The girls were so excited, it seemed that it was all they talked about. They could often be seen with their sketchpads out, sketching away, stopping frequently to examine the other's drawings, and talking nonstop the entire time.

One afternoon in early March, the girls were walking home from school, talking about their projects, when they passed the park that was short distance from their home. They could see a snowball fight going on. It looked very spirited, and as they passed, they noticed a boy crouched down on one of the benches. They both said hi, and as he raised his head to say hello, a snowball caught him unawares and knocked his cap off, showering his face with snow. From the other side of the park, gales of laughter could be heard as the boy turned slowly to face his attacker.

As he wiped the snow from his face, Darryl yelled, "Hang on a minute!" and turned to face Shirley and Sheila. As he gazed at the two lovely visions in front of him, he was assaulted with a final snowball to the center of his back. This one he ignored as he stared intently at Sheila. The girls giggled in the silence, and the boy seemed to snap out of his trance. As he slowly bent to retrieve his fallen cap, he said hello.

"Hello," Sheila replied. "I am sorry we distracted you and you got hit with a snowball. It must be cold."

"Not so much. It is not the first snowball that has hit me. My friends and I often have snowball fights, and everyone wins because everyone gets hit. My name is Darryl Powell."

"I am Sheila Danvers, and this is my friend Shirley Green. I remember you from the lake."

Sheila watched as Darryl knocked the snow off his cap and replaced it on his head. She noticed he had thick dark hair and clear blue eyes. She noticed that his mouth had a scar on the side, and it made a curious *S* shape when he smiled.

"Yes, I remember. Do you live around here? Are you from around here? I live on the other side of the park, on Pine Crest Drive. My father is a lawyer with Marcus, Smith, and Powell."

"Yes, we live on High Street. My father is Wesley Danvers, president of the bank."

"I am pleased to see you again, Sheila Danvers, and you as well, Shirley Green. I must be off. I hope to see you again very soon." With that parting comment, Darryl tipped his snowy cap and dashed off to find his friends.

Sheila watched him rejoin the snowball fight. She kept looking to see if he would look back at her. Shirley had to shake her to snap her out of her daydream.

"Sheila, Sheila! Hey!"

"What? Oh, yeah. Isn't he dreamy! Did you see those big blue eyes?"

"Yeah, he was cute. Come on, we will be late for dinner." Shirley tugged at Sheila's coat until her friend was pointed in the right direction and walking toward home. All the way home, Sheila was quiet, not paying attention to anything. Twice Shirley had to grab her friend so she would not walk into a tree. As they were walking along, they rounded the corner to go up High Street when out of nowhere a horse and sled came barreling down. Shirley could see that they were not going to make the turn. They were going too fast. She looked for a place to run, but with the recent snows, the sides of the streets were piled high with snow banks and there was no place to go.

Sheila was still walking dreamily next to Shirley and at the last second heard the jingle of the harnesses as Shirley screamed and jumped out of the way, dragging Sheila with her. The girls dropped their sketchpads and books and tumbled into the snowdrift on the side of the road. As they rolled down the other side, Shirley was stopped abruptly by a large rock that was partially hidden from the snow. She banged her head and fell unconscious in a heap.

The driver of the carriage managed to get the horse slowed down right before making the turn. When the horse had stopped, he tied it to a tree and came over to see if the girls were all right. The door to the carriage opened and out stepped a well-dressed man. Sheila was shaking the snow from her coat when she looked around and didn't see Shirley. She expected her to be standing next to her, shaking the snow from her coat also. When she saw Shirley lying in the snow, she fell to her knees next to her friend and started to shake her.

"Shirley! Shirley! Wake up! Please wake up!" Sheila cried. She kept shaking her as the man came up to them.

Sheila grabbed his sleeve. "Mister, my friend won't wake up. Can you help?"

"I'm not a doctor, but let me see what I can do." The well-dressed gentleman rolled Shirley over so she was lying on her back and gently shook her and slapped her face. Just as Shirley was opening her eyes, Darryl and his friends came running over.

"Is she all right? We heard the carriage and then heard you both scream. Sheila, are you hurt?"

Sheila was sprawled in the snow next to her friend, her clothes out of sorts, snow in her hair, and shaking with worry. "No, I am fine. Shirley wouldn't open her eyes for a while, but it looks like she is doing better."

They looked at Shirley and saw that she was sitting up, rubbing the back of her head. The stranger was helping her up, and soon Shirley was on her feet.

"Ouch! What happened? Sheila, are you hurt?"

"No, you pulled me out of the way just in time. Guess you hit your head on a rock or tree under the snow," Sheila said as she went over and hugged her friend, glad she was not seriously hurt.

Shirley walked to the road and quickly became embarrassed when she saw that Darryl and his friends were there and people had stopped along the road to make sure she was not seriously injured.

"I can give you a ride the rest of the way to your destination, if you like. Where are you headed? Your coat and shoes are quite wet. It will be warmer in the carriage," the well-dressed stranger said to Sheila.

"Thank you. We would like that. We were headed home from school," Sheila replied. "Do I know you? You look very familiar to me."

"I do not believe we have met. My name is Mr. Stevens. I work at the bank in town."

"I remember you. You work for my father, Wesley Danvers. I have seen you many times when I have come into the bank with my mother," Sheila said as she placed a steadying arm around Shirley.

"Now I remember you. Sheila and Shirley, right? You are Walter Green's daughter, the stable hand of Mr. Danvers," Mr. Stevens said as he looked at Shirley.

"Yes."

"All right, girls, hop in the carriage. I will have my driver take you home," Mr. Stevens snapped.

Shirley and Sheila looked at each other, wondering why Mr. Stevens's tone was so clipped and abrupt all of a sudden. He had been very concerned about them, and upon finding out who they were, he was very cold.

"Good-bye, Darryl. Thank you for coming to our rescue," Sheila said as she and Shirley climbed in Mr. Stevens's carriage.

"I am glad neither of you are seriously hurt. I hope to see you again soon," Darryl said as he turned to join his friends.

Mr. Stevens climbed up in the carriage after the girls, slammed the door, and yelled to his driver. The ride to their house was short and very quiet. Both girls wondered at the change in Mr. Stevens, and it seemed to them that he was suddenly in a hurry to be away from them. They pulled up in front of the house, and the girls got out.

"Thank you for the ride, Mr. Stevens. It was very kind of you to give us a lift," Shirley called.

"You are welcome. Next time, do not walk in the middle of the road." With that, he slammed the door, and the horses took off down the slippery driveway.

"How do you like that? He causes us to almost get killed by running his poor horse down the hill like that, and he gets mad at us?" Sheila said. "I think I will ask my father about him. He doesn't seem to like us much. Let's get you inside and dry before you go see your mother. Otherwise, she will be very upset."

"Good idea."

Just as Sheila reached for the door, it opened, and there stood her mother.

"Hello, girls. Did I just hear a carriage pull up?" Eloise said as she took one step outside and looked around.

"Yes, Mr. Stevens brought us home."

"Mr. Stevens? Why in the world would he bring you home? It is very cold. Come in before you get a chill." She put her arm around the two girls and guided them into the house. As she did she said, "My goodness, Shirley, you are soaked to the bone, and, Sheila, you are wet also. What have you two been doing?"

"It wasn't our fault." Sheila fairly radiated anger as she retold the tale. "We were walking home from school, and we had just passed the park and were turning onto High Street, when a carriage came barreling down the road—the poor horse was frantic. He was going way too fast for that hill with the snow on it, but the guy on top kept flicking the reins and making him go faster. The horse was trying to slow down, but the road was very slippery. Finally he got the horse slowed down enough to make the turn, but the carriage slipped on the snow and we jumped into a snow bank to avoid being run over. We got a bit wet, and Shirley banged her head on a rock or something and didn't wake up for a few minutes. The guy in the carriage finally came over to help us and offered us a ride home. He was really nice and sorry about it until he found out who we were, and then he got mean and told us we shouldn't be walking in the middle of the road. It was his fault!"

Shirley sat by the fire, rubbing her head. "We were on our way to change clothes before you saw us. I don't want my mother to see me like this. She will be frantic with worry. I will tell her later, when she can see I am all right."

"Come here. Let me take a look at your head."

Shirley walked over and turned around. She pointed to where her head hurt, and Eloise parted her hair to take a closer look. "That doesn't look so bad. Just a small bump. It will hurt for a while, but you will live." She smiled at Shirley. "Now, go and change, your mother needs you in the kitchen."

"Thank you, Mrs. Danvers." Shirley went out the front door and over to her apartment to change her clothes. She then went to the kitchen to help her mother prepare the evening meal. As she entered the kitchen, she took the apron off the hook by the door and was tying it on when Sarah noticed that Sheila was not with her.

"Wash up, and come help me set the table."

"Coming, Mother."

"Where is Sheila? Is she feeling all right?" Sarah asked.

"She is fine. She met a boy and has been daydreaming about him. She did that all the way home, and I had to keep her from running into a tree! And I got hurt on the way home."

Sarah turned suddenly and looked at Shirley, checking to see if she was bleeding anywhere.

"I am all right. I just got a bump on the head. Sheila and I got very wet, so I had to change before I came in to help so you wouldn't see me and worry. Mrs. Danvers caught us before we had a chance to change and looked at my head. She said it is just a small bump, and I will have a sore head for a few days."

Sarah walked to Shirley and gave her a huge hug and then looked at the bump on Shirley's head. "I am glad that you are all right and didn't get hurt too seriously. So why did you have to keep Sheila from running into a tree, wasn't she paying attention?"

"No, I told you, she was daydreaming about Darryl ever since she met him. We had just seen him in the park, and she was thinking about him and not paying attention. She is probably upstairs right now, writing his name on everything. I don't think she will be down to help us. She was wet too."

After the table was set, Sarah called everyone to the table. Sarah watched as Sheila walked slowly to the table. Sarah could see ink stains on her hands. She smiled, knowing what Shirley had said was true.

At dinner that night, Sheila told the family about running into Darryl at the park. "Remember, Father, he was at the lake this past summer with his parents."

"Yes, I remember him. He is a fine young man. His parents are very nice also. Robert told me that Darryl is studying to be a lawyer and works in the law firm part time, to get the feel of the place. Maybe we should invite the Powells to dinner sometime, then we can all get to know Darryl better. What do you think, Sheila?"

When Sheila didn't immediately respond, Mrs. Danvers answered for her. "I think it would be great. Shirley, are you feeling all right after your run-in with the runaway carriage?"

"Yes, thank you. My head is a bit sore and I think I ripped my favorite skirt, but that is all."

"Father, it was Mr. Stevens who was the driver of the carriage. He stopped to help and was very concerned, but after he offered us a ride home and he found out who we were, he got very cold and mean. Why is he like that?" Sheila asked.

"Mr. Stevens works for me at the bank. He has been there longer than I have, and I think he feels that the promotion that Mr. Miller gave me should have been his. He is a good, hard worker, but he lacks imagination and will not rise above the position he currently has at the bank. He is resentful toward me because of that. I am sorry he took out his frustration with me on you both."

Everyone lapsed into a comfortable silence and finished the meal. The children went upstairs, and Wesley and Eloise went into the den. Walter and Sarah cleared the dishes, she said, "Walter, I can't believe that Mr. Stevens could be so mean to the girls. After all, they did nothing to him."

"He is everything that Wesley is not, and he is jealous of everything that Wesley has and does. So therefore, he will lash out at anything that is connected to Wesley. Unfortunately, the girls happened to be in his path today. I don't think the girls will think twice about this after tonight. Now, let's get these dishes cleaned up and enjoy the rest of the evening."

Sarah smiled at Walter and started to wash the dishes.

Chapter Twelve

March moved into April, and soon it was the beginning of May and the school year was coming to a close. Each day Sheila looked for Darryl in the park when they passed by. And each day she was disappointed. Shirley tried to brighten her friend's mood with talks of their project and of the summer at the lake, but nothing seemed to work. Their projects for the sewing class were due, and as Shirley and Sheila worked on the finishing touches, Sheila started to talk about Darryl.

"I guess it was silly of me to think he would remember me. I am just a child compared to him. He is an adult. Why would he be interested in me?"

Shirley thought about what her friend was saying and knew how badly Sheila wanted to see Darryl again. She thought about what she should say to comfort her friend, but no words came. As Shirley finished up the last stitches of the skirt she made for her project, she held it up for Sheila to see.

"What do you think? Do you think the teacher will like it? Do you think my mom will like it, since I made it for her?" Shirley said.

"Yes, it is lovely. I think your mom will be thrilled. I know that my mom has been asking over and over to see what we are working on, but I wouldn't show her. Do you think my mom will like my dress?" She held it up for Shirley to see.

"It is great. Do you think if we wanted to continue making clothes that your dad would get us material and stuff?"

"I am sure. He wants us to be creative, and it is cheaper than buying new clothes. Maybe next time we can make stuff for Thomas and Tyler," Sheila said.

"They would be quite a challenge, getting them to hold still to get measurements." Both girls started thinking about measuring their little brothers, who were not known for holding still for very long, and started to giggle. Shirley felt better when she saw her friend laughing.

The next day on the way to school, as the girls were passing the park, Shirley noticed a well-dressed man sitting on the bench where they saw Darryl the first time. He was wearing a top coat and a top hat with his head bent down reading the paper. As they passed, Darryl picked up his head and startled the girls.

"Good morning, Sheila and Shirley. I have come to this park every day to see if I could catch a glimpse of you, and each day I seem to come at the wrong times. So I decided, since school was ending, I would need to camp out here on this bench, all day if necessary, so I could talk to you."

Startled, Sheila said, "Darryl, what a nice surprise. I have thought about you often since our first meeting and was hoping to see you again before school let out. Soon we are leaving to go to Lake Conemaugh for the summer, and I would not have seen you again until September."

Shirley was amazed at the calm in Sheila's voice. She knew how excited she was about seeing him but was able to keep that from showing. She noticed that Sheila was acting somewhat shy, which was not like her, and was also batting her eyes and blushing.

"The club? Usually in the summer I just study or clerk in my father's law firm. He and my mother go to the lake all the time. Maybe I will have to consent to go again this year. I must be off to work, and you must be off to school. I believe it will be a wonderful summer after all! Farewell, lovely ladies. We shall meet again soon!"

With that he tipped his hat and strolled into the park. Shirley could hear him whistling as he walked away. Sheila stood there watching him. Stunned that he had remembered her and also that she would be seeing him that summer at the lake. When Darryl was out of sight, Sheila let out a loud "*Whoopeee!*" Shirley and Sheila laughed and continued their way to school.

All day, any time Shirley saw Sheila, she was smiling. Now was the final class; they walked into the sewing room and found that

Summer of Gold and Water

instead of the usual chatter, it was very quiet. Everyone had brought their final project to be graded and displayed in front of the class. They all knew that if their project was not up to standards, the class and especially their teacher would not hesitate to tell them. It was different when you showed your best friend or family, but here was the real world and it was time for judgment day.

Shirley was called on first to present her project. Nervously, she got up from her desk and walked to the front of the class. She laid out the drawings she made and attached the pattern across the blackboard, she then pulled the finished skirt out of a bag.

Shirley held the skirt up for all to see. "As you can see, I chose to make a skirt. I chose to layer the skirt to give it a dressier feel. The waistband is blue velvet, and there are blue velvet cloth buttons down the front. The bottom layer is dark blue, hangs to the floor, and has white lace around the bottom. For the next layer I chose a medium gray blue and hung it three-quarters of the way down the length of the skirt. If you looked closely, the material has pale blue flowers embroidered around the skirt. For the top layer I chose a pale blue that hangs halfway down the skirt." As she ended her description, Shirley looked toward the teacher.

When Shirley was done, Sheila stood up and started clapping. The rest of her classmates joined, and Shirley blushed profusely. When the clapping subsided, the teacher said, "That was wonderfully done, Shirley. The skirt looks a little big for you. Who did you make this for? Part of the assignment was that the garment was made for someone specific."

"I made if for my mother. Her favorite color is blue, and she has been talking about getting a nice skirt to wear when we go to the lake in the summer. I wanted to surprise her with this gift."

"And just how did you get the correct measurements for your project?"

"I borrowed one of the skirts she wears all the time and took the measurements from that. She never knew it was missing from her closet for a day."

"Wonderful. Your grade is an A. You pass this course."

"Thank you," Shirley said as she gathered her drawings and went back to her seat. She was grinning ear to ear as she passed Sheila's desk. Sheila gave her a big grin and mouthed, *I knew you could do it!*

The teacher called a few other students who all showed their garments off. There were a multitude of skirts and shirts, but none had taken on the challenge of an entire dress. Sheila was up next, and she carried her drawings and bag to the front of the room. Slowly she set up the drawings of the garment and then the pattern that she used to make this garment. Everyone was skeptical that she had really made the dress in the drawings. Then Sheila opened her bag and brought out the most delicate lace dress that anyone had ever seen.

Sheila hung the dress on a hook near the chalkboard. She stepped back and faced the class. Taking a deep breath, she began. "This dress is made from different colored lace." Pointing to the collar, she continued, "The collar is an empire design of white velvet. I put a small ring of lace sticking out of the top. This will make it look like the lady's head is cradled in a bed of lace. The sleeves are a large lace pattern and hug the arms of the wearer and disappear into the same white velvet trim at the cuff with a white cloth button. The underskirt from the high-waisted bodice to the floor is pale rose silk. Over the rose silk underskirt are layers upon layers of fine white and rose lace. As you can see"—she turned the dress over—"down the back of the dress is a row of white cloth buttons. At the waistline where the buttons close the white velvet covering that part of the skirt is a large, white, velvet bow. Here on the top of the loops of the bow is a small button on the underside, so when the dress is buttoned up, the bow will stretch from hip to hip and cascade down the back of the dress."

The room went absolutely silent as Sheila turned the magnificent dress around and hung it back on the hook for everyone to see. Sheila was afraid that something was wrong. All of a sudden, the classroom erupted into hoots and hollering about how wonderful the dress was. Everyone left their seat to get a closer look. The teacher came over and took the dress from the hook and took a closer look at the fine workmanship. She was astonished.

"This is just lovely, Sheila. For whom did you make this dress?"

"For my mother. She has a charity party that she is going to in a couple of weeks, and I would like her to wear this. I have talked to my father about it, and he has kept her busy so she cannot get another dress made. I feared she would get another made and would not want to wear this."

"It is by far the most complex garment anyone in this class has ever made. An A-plus for your dress. I believe your mother will love it and look glorious in it."

"Thank you."

When school was over, Shirley and Sheila gathered their garments and carefully placed them in the bags. They didn't want them to be ruined before they presented them to their mothers that evening.

~~~

When they got home, both were grinning from ear to ear, and Sarah knew something was up. Neither girl said a word, just put their stuff away and helped with dinner.

When at last it was dinnertime, they could hardly sit still. They arrived at the table late, after running into the other room with packages behind their backs, and rushed to take their place at the table. Neither girl said much, despite everyone's best effort to get them to talk. They just smiled and giggled at each other.

When dinner was done and the dishes cleared off the table, Sarah was surprised when Shirley grabbed her hand and pulled her into the living room. Sheila did the same and the family had no choice but to follow.

"All right, we are all here. Now what is going on with you two? You both look like you are about to burst," Wesley said.

"Sheila and I have something we want to show you. Mother, please accept this gift from me. I made it in school for my final project and got an A on it. I made it for you," Shirley said as she handed her mother the wrapped package.

Sarah slowly opened the package and, with tears in her eyes, carefully lifted the skirt from the paper. She sat there with tears streaming down her face, staring at the skirt. Looking up at Shirley she said, "Thank you so much. This is just the prettiest skirt I have ever owned. I will wear it with pride."

Shirley ran to her mother's outstretched arms and fell into her embrace. A silence fell on the room as everyone watched mother and daughter hug, with a squirming Tyler caught in-between. When Sarah and Shirley separated, everyone could see that both mother and daughter had been crying, but the smiles were ear to ear. Shirley sat down and they all looked toward Sheila.

Slowly Sheila rose from her chair and picked up a bigger brown package from behind her chair. She walked to her mother and handed her the package.

"I know you have a big charity dinner next weekend, and I know you have been fretting about what to wear. I apologize, I asked Dad to keep you busy so you would not have time to get another dress, and I know that it has made you crazy wondering what you will be wearing. I would be honored if you would wear this dress I made you in school." With that she handed the package to her mother.

Eloise opened the package slowly, and her eyes got wide and her mouth dropped open as she lifted the delicate dress from the package. She stood up to get the whole view, and the brown wrapping fell to the floor. Ohhs and ahhs could be heard from the rest of the group, but Eloise just stood there with a look of disbelief on her face.

"Do you like it, Mother?" Sheila asked.

"It is the most beautiful dress I have ever seen. Words cannot describe how beautiful this dress is. I am speechless. Thank you, sweetie!"

Eloise put the dress on the couch and held her arms for Sheila. Mother and daughter embraced until Thomas decided he didn't want to be left out and wiggled in between them. Laughing, they separated, and Eloise picked up Thomas and kissed him noisily on the cheek. Thomas squirmed, and Eloise put him down. Turning to Sarah, she said, "Let's go try these on and model them for our families!"

"We will be right back for the fashion show," Sarah said as she picked up her skirt and followed Eloise upstairs to change.

A short time later, Sarah and Eloise returned. Each swept in and paraded around the room. Everyone clapped and cheered.

Eloise stopped and said, "Sheila, this is the most elegant dress I have ever seen. I feel like a fairy princess in it. I am glad I waited to get a dress, and I will wear this with pride."

Sarah looked down at the skirt and said, "Shirley, this skirt is more beautiful on than off. I will want to wear it always but will save it for special times. We should bring these to the lake, and we will be the envy of everyone there!"

"I agree. You ladies have never looked lovelier! Walter, we have such talented daughters and such beautiful wives. How did we ever get so lucky?" Wesley said as he rose from his chair to embrace Eloise.

"Can't say that I know how we got lucky, just that you are correct, we are the luckiest men on the planet. Shirley, Sheila, you are both very talented and lovely. We are all so proud of you, and we want you to know it. As a celebration of your talent and of our lovely wives, Saturday we will all go on a picnic in the park. An entire day for just family, how does that sound?"

Thomas and Tyler were the first to whoop it up, dancing and jumping around the room. It was seldom that they got to spend an entire day with their dads, unless it was at the lake, and then there were other kids to play with and their fathers had the other adults. Shirley and Sheila chimed in that it would be fun, but slid each other a sly sideways look, knowing that there was a possibility of seeing Darryl at the park with his friends.

"I will pack us a feast for Saturday. It will be a grand day!" Sarah exclaimed.

Sarah and Eloise changed from their new outfits and carefully folded them and put them back in their wrapping.

Sarah and Walter got up and called to Tyler, "Let's go, we need to be going home. Almost time for bed. We will see you all in the morning."

"Good night," Walter and Eloise said. "Thomas, time for you to go upstairs too. Say good night to Tyler, and let's go."

A chorus of "Oh, Mom," "Not now," and "A little longer" raised in the quiet room, but both boys knew that they needed to go to their rooms to get ready for bed. It was the same each night.

The Greens left through the kitchen, and as they walked back to their apartment, Sarah put her arm around Shirley and said, "Thank you again. I love my skirt. It is perfect."

"I am glad you like it. I knew you would, since blue is your favorite color, and you have said you need a new one. This is a bit dressier than the others, but for the dances at the lake or other parties, you can wear it."

"This is true, and I will wear it with pride! Handmade by you! You are so talented."

By the time they reached the apartment, Shirley kissed her father and mother good night and went to her room. She felt great that she had made her mother happy. She loved to see her smile. She could hear her father wrestling with Tyler to get him into the bathtub and then into bed. She loved her life, and as she settled to go to sleep, she had a smile on her face.

Chapter Thirteen

Saturday dawned brightly and Sarah was up early, making sure that the picnic basket was packed with all the goodies the families liked. She also made a large breakfast of pancakes and bacon.

When Walter finished his breakfast, he went to the stables to hitch up the team while everyone else was getting ready. He brought the carriage around to the front of the house and then went to the kitchen to get the picnic basket. Once it was secured and blankets were found, Walter went back inside and started hollering for everyone.

"Let's not waste this beautiful day! Hurry up, everyone! Time is a wasting!"

He heard the clatter of Thomas's feet as he ran down the stairs. Soon after, Sheila, Eloise, and Wesley came down. Walter went outside to help Thomas into the carriage and saw that his family was already in the carriage waiting. He climbed up on the wagon seat and took hold of the reins. Wesley ushered his family out of the house and closed the door. Climbing up into the carriage, Wesley settled next to Eloise.

Walter guided the team to a corner of the park that was off the beaten path. The family got out of the carriage, and Walter secured the horses under the trees. Everyone walked to the edge of the pond to take in the view. The pond was surrounded by weeping willow trees and tall grasses that were dotted with cattails. There was a small beach-type area where you could walk to the water and wade in a few feet without it getting too deep. To the right of the wading area was an area filled with lily pads, more cattails, and beautiful flowers. Farther out was a deep hole for swimming, and the water looked cool and clear. Walter was busy getting the basket and blankets out while the families checked out the pond.

"Wonderful, isn't it?" Walter called to his family.

"Oh my, what an adorable pond. Imagine, I have lived here all my life and did not know that this place existed," Eloise said.

"My parents found this when they were dating, and this is where they, and Walter and I, held our receptions after getting married. We thought it was the perfect time to share our secret spot with you," Sarah said as she hugged Eloise.

"Thank you for thinking enough of us to share such an important and meaningful spot. It is just lovely."

"You are most welcome. We are a family, and I love you like a sister. I didn't think that was possible, but each day we grow closer. Everyone does. I don't think that the children could be any closer."

"Let's get the food unpacked and see if we can find some tadpoles," Walter said to Tyler and Thomas.

"Are there really tadpoles? And fish in there, Dad?" Tyler asked.

"You bet. That is why I brought these with us," Walter said as he pulled two fishing poles out of the back of the carriage. "One for you, and one for you." He handed a pole to each of the boys.

"Ohhhh," they exclaimed together. "This is just the best. Thank you." They both dropped the fishing poles on the ground and launched themselves at Walter. Surprised, Walter caught them, one in each arm, just before tumbling to the ground in a big heap.

"I made them especially for this day. Why don't we go and try them out while your mothers get the food laid out on the blanket?" Walter said as he untangled himself from the two squirming boys. They all scrambled to their feet, and as Walter was brushing himself off, he felt Tyler grab his hand and start toward the pond.

"Come on, Dad!" Thomas said as he went to Wesley and grabbed his hand, furiously pulling him toward the pond.

"Okay, son, let's go. Let's see if we can catch the first fish."

"Race ya!" Thomas hollered as he let go of Wesley's hand and took off toward the pond.

Walter and Wesley ran to keep up with the two excited boys, and soon they were sitting side-by-side, fishing.

Sarah and Eloise laid out the basket on the blanket and walked over to watch their sons fishing. Tyler got up and pulled in his line.

He walked toward the lily pads and cast his rod, as his dad taught him, toward the edge of the lily pads. Sarah walked over to stand with him as Walter watched from where he was sitting. All at once, Tyler's line went under and his pole bent over.

"*Dad!* I got a fish. It's a big one!" Tyler turned toward his father and yelled. Just as he was turning back, the fish jumped and dove straight for the bottom. Tyler lost his footing and fell into the pond, still clinging to his brand-new fishing pole. Sarah reached for him and grabbed his shirt as he was going in, but the momentum pulled Sarah into the water also. Tyler tread water, all the while holding on to the fishing pole. The water was too deep for Sarah to swim. She let go of Tyler's shirt and managed to call for help before going under.

Walter was on his feet as soon as he saw Tyler and Sarah go into the water and jumped in just as Sarah started to panic. Walter grabbed Tyler and turned to hand him to Wesley, who was on the bank calling with outstretched arms. With Tyler safely in Wesley's arms and being pulled to the shore, fishing pole and all, Walter turned and grabbed his wife's blouse. Finally, Walter grabbed Sarah's flailing hands and pulled her tightly against his chest. With one arm around Sarah and the other swimming toward the shore, they slowly made their way. Wesley was there to grab Sarah's outstretched hands and pull her onto the bank. Walter climbed up after her, and they both lay panting on the shore.

Tyler, who had been fighting the fish the entire time, finally landed the largemouth bass. He picked it up and went to where his mother and father lay on the grass.

"See what I caught? I didn't lose my fishing pole, Dad. I kept a good hold on it so the fish wouldn't take it away."

"I see that, son. That is a big fish! Congratulations!" Walter said.

Tyler proceeded to show everyone and told the story over and over about his dip in the pond and how he kept a hold of the rod and caught the fish. He was so excited that Sarah had a hard time getting mad at him for being so close to the edge. She started laughing, and Walter looked at her with a quizzical expression.

"Why are you laughing? Are you all right?" Walter asked.

"I am laughing with relief, that we were not hurt, and how Tyler cannot see anything but his fish and the way he held onto the rod."

By this time, Eloise and the girls had seen what had happened and come over to where a soaking wet Walter and Sarah lay laughing on the ground. With their assistance, Walter and Sarah got up, and they all walked back to the blanket. They sat down and relaxed while their clothes dried in the sun.

After a couple hours of relaxing and chasing the boys around, the families sat down to a cold fried chicken dinner, complete with potato salad, tossed salad, and sweet tea. After lunch, when the dishes were put back in the picnic basket, Sheila and Shirley decided to go for a walk around the park. After assuring their parents they would be back soon, they set off to see if Darryl was in the park with his friends.

They strolled around for almost an hour with no sign of Darryl. They sat in the park square, feeding the pigeons and talking before heading back to their families. As they were getting up and brushing the crumbs off their skirts, they heard a familiar voice.

"Got any crumbs for me?"

Turning, they saw a very dirty, sweaty Darryl approaching. He had a huge grin on his face and a ball in his arms. "Hello, pretty ladies! I was hoping to see you today. Were you by chance looking for me?"

Sheila smiled. "We are here with our parents and decided to take a walk to see if you and your friends were here. I have been thinking about you since the last time we saw you and was wondering when I would see you again."

"I was here with my friends playing ball this morning. Most of them just left. Todd and I were on our way when I saw you sitting there. It was like a picture from my dreams. I couldn't believe you were here. I apologize for my appearance. I would also like to introduce you to Todd Stevens. Todd, this lovely lady is Sheila Danvers and the equally lovely lady next to her is Shirley Green. Ladies, Todd Stevens."

Shirley had noticed Todd standing behind Darryl, blushed slightly when Todd turned to look at her.

"Nice to meet you, Todd," Sheila said. "Would you two like to come see our families? They are over by the pond."

"I would like that very much, although I am not sure what kind of impression I will make, being all sweaty and dirty," Darryl said as he started to brush off as much dirt as possible from his trousers and shirt.

Shirley giggled. "My father, mother, and little brother took an unexpected swim in the pond, so they are not looking their best either, so you should be in good company."

The walk back to the pond took less time than Sheila would have hoped, and before she knew it, they were at the pond and she was introducing Darryl to her family.

"Father, Mother, this is Darryl Powell and his friend, Todd Stevens. Remember I told you that I saw him in the park a few weeks ago? We met him and his parents at the lake."

"Pleased to see you again, Darryl, and nice to meet you, Todd," Wesley said.

"Likewise. It is nice to see you again. I can see where Sheila gets her loveliness," Darryl said as he kissed Eloise's hand.

Eloise blushed as did Sheila, and as they were about to speak, Thomas came over and tugged on Darryl's trousers. Darryl looked down to see what was happening and looked into the grinning face of young Thomas. Getting down on one knee, he held his hand out to Thomas.

"I am Darryl, a friend of your sister's. Who may you be?"

"I am Thomas, Sheila's sister. Do you want to come fishing with me and Tyler? We got new fishing poles, and Tyler caught a big fish in the pond, and it was so cool."

"I would love to fish with you and Tyler. Is Tyler your brother?"

"No, silly. He is my best friend. We practically live together, and things are the best when he is around."

Darryl looked up at Sheila, who had placed a hand on his shoulder.

"I wanted you to say hi to Shirley's parents, also."

Walter shook the hand of each boy. "Nice to see you again, Darryl. Nice to meet you, Todd."

"Likewise."

"My advice to you: do not keep Tyler and Thomas waiting, or you may find your arm dislocated when they come to get you," Walter said with a smile.

At that moment, Tyler grabbed a hold of Darryl's arm and Thomas grabbed Todd's arm and started dragging them toward the pond.

Laughing, Darryl yelled back to Walter as he tripped behind Tyler, "I see what you mean. Nice to see you again! I guess I will be fishing if anyone needs me."

Shirley trailed behind her brother and Todd, watching him intently.

Eloise looked at Sheila and could see the smile on her face as her eyes followed Darryl to the pond. Nudging her husband, they all looked a Sheila, and when she realized that they were staring at her, she got all flustered.

"What are you all looking at?" she said as she started to blush.

"Just wondering what is going on in that pretty head of yours," Eloise said.

"He is cute and nice. That is all." And with that, she stormed off in the direction of the pond.

Eloise started laughing. "Guess our baby girl is growing up. Get the shotgun ready to ward off all the suitors!"

With a loud, comical sigh, Wesley said, "I guess it was inevitable!"

Sarah watched Shirley follow Todd to the pond, and a frown appeared on her face.

Walter looked to where Shirley was standing by the pond talking to Sheila and turned to Wesley. "Can I borrow the shotgun when you are done?"

When Walter was done laughing, he sat down next to Sarah and noticed the frown on her face. "Why the frown, darling? We are all just joking around."

Sarah did not respond to Walter and continued to look toward the pond. Walter followed Sarah's gaze and saw Shirley and Todd laughing and talking.

Walter stood up, reached for Sarah, and said, "Come, my love. Let's take a walk."

Startled, Sarah looked up and saw Walter's outstretched hand, reached up, and let Walter pull her from her spot on the blanket. Walter put his arm around Sarah, and they started off in the opposite direction from the pond.

"I know that look, my love. What is troubling you? We were all having such fun."

"My fears are coming true, Walter."

"How do you mean? We have seen our friends from the lake, and things were as Eloise predicted."

"No, I do not mean that. Shirley. Todd Stevens, do you know who his parents are? Dora and Larry! He is not of our class, and I saw the look on Shirley's face when they walked to the pond. I just hope that she will not get her heart broken."

Walter stopped under the large oak tree and turned to face Sarah. "Shirley is a smart young lady. She is just overwhelmed with attention from an older, good-looking boy. She will not let it get out of hand."

"I hope so. But you know as well as I do that where your heart leads, you follow. I had hoped she would find someone of her own class."

Walter put his arm around Sarah and led her back toward their family. "I think things will be fine. Please do not let this bring you down. Now, before we reach them, please put a smile on your face. We can talk to Shirley about this later. Let's have a nice afternoon, with no worries."

Sarah smiled up at Walter. Walter was right; Shirley was a smart girl. Things would be all right.

The rest of the day passed without incident, and as it was getting late, Eloise and Sarah started to pack up the blankets and glasses. They called to the kids, who were still at the pond to come and help. Tyler and Thomas raced back with their prize fishing poles in tow, each chattering about how many fish they caught or how big they were or the frogs they saw. Shirley had said good-bye to Todd and Darryl and followed the boys back to the carriage. Sheila and Darryl stood a little ways away and talked quietly. Sarah saw Sheila blush and look down. She looked back up and said good-bye to Darryl. When she reached her mother, she turned and waved one last time.

"He is a nice man, Sheila. Quite handsome too," Sarah said.

"He is nice. He said he would be going to the lake this summer with his family, instead of staying in town and working. I can't wait. I so wanted you all to like him," Sheila said.

"It will be nice to get to know him in the relaxed atmosphere of the lake this summer. We only met him for a brief time last year. Don't forget your father will be watching you closely, and you know how intimidating he can be. I hope he doesn't scare Darryl off," Eloise teased.

"You don't think he would? Oh, I would be so embarrassed if he did that. Mother, you have to talk to him. Please?"

Laughing, Eloise replied, "I will handle your father. Don't worry."

By that time, Walter had the team hitched and the blankets and picnic basket stowed. He called to everyone to get in. Once settled, Walter turned the horses home, and they set off.

"What a great day," Wesley said.

He looked over at Tyler and Thomas and noticed they were fast asleep, still clutching their beloved fishing poles. Shirley and Sheila were quiet for once, and each watched the scenery as it went past.

At the house, Walter stopped the horses and came back to help everyone from the carriage. He took Tyler from Wesley and carried him into the apartment. Walter pried the fishing pole from his son's sleeping hand and put it in the corner, where he would see it when he woke up. After putting him to bed, he went back to unhitch the horses, rub them down, and feed them. Then he climbed the stairs and sat down for some quiet time with Sarah before turning in. Shirley said good night, and soon Sarah and he were alone.

Summer of Gold and Water

As they sat and watched the sun set out their window, they each nodded off in each other's arms. It was well into the night when Walter stirred and realized that Sarah was lying in his arms on the couch, where they had fallen asleep. He watched her sleep and marveled at how beautiful she was. Shifting slightly to free his arm, he accidently stirred Sarah. Sarah bolted up, eyes wide open, screaming at the top of her lungs. Her arms flailed and caught Walter in the chest with a closed fist.

Walter pinned her arms to her side and tried to calm her. When that didn't work, he shook her and called to her.

"Sarah! Sarah! Wake up, honey. It's me, Sarah!"

From behind him, Walter heard Tyler and Shirley running down the hall. They both came around the corner and stopped to look at their parents. Sarah was thrashing and swinging at Walter, her hair wild and eyes wide open. Walter had a hold of her arms and was trying to calm her down.

Tyler started to cry, not knowing his mother was having a nightmare, and Shirley held him.

Finally, after only a few minutes, Sarah calmed down and slowly blinked her eyes. When she focused on Walter and slowly looked to where Tyler was crying in his sister's arms, she got a puzzled look on her face.

"What's going on? Why is Tyler crying? Come here, baby."

As Tyler crossed to his mother's arms, his crying subsided. Sarah wrapped him in her arms and drew him into her lap. "Walter, what happened? Why is everyone looking at me like that?"

"You were having a nightmare, crying and screaming for help. I couldn't wake you up, and the children heard and got worried. Do you remember anything of the dream you had?"

"We were at the park, in our favorite spot. Tyler was catching monster-sized fish, and all of a sudden, I was in a raging river, feeling like I was drowning. I was being pushed along with the current. I couldn't see anyone and couldn't hold on to anything. Someone kept yelling, '*Swim!*' I tried and tried and couldn't get my hands and feet working in the right direction. All I seemed to be doing was pushing myself underwater. I kept yelling for help, and the people on the banks and in boats just went past me, like they couldn't see me or hear me. It was very scary."

"I remember you had a few nightmares after our swimming lessons, none so violent, but maybe the fall in the pond reawakened them and that is what caused it."

"Possibly."

Tyler had grown quiet as Sarah held him and stroked his hair. She looked down and realized he was sleeping. She nodded to Walter, who picked him up and took him back to bed.

"Shirley, honey, please go back to bed. I am sorry I frightened you." Sarah held her arms out, and Shirley crossed and gave her mother a hug. Straightening up, she turned and slowly went back to her bedroom. She left her door open a crack this time, just in case.

Walter came out of Tyler's room, and Sarah got up from the couch. He walked over and gave her a hug, blew out the lamp that was still burning, and walked toward their bedroom.

"Just remember, I am always here to save you. Just dream me into your dream, and I will save you. You will always be safe with me in your life. I love you, Sarah."

"I love you too, Walter."

〜〜〜

A couple weeks passed, and Sarah did not have any recurring nightmares. Walter hoped they were over. It had happened frequently after the first summer, and they scared everyone. Every night he lay down and prayed that there would be no nightmares and that Sarah would sleep well. It seemed every time he relaxed, she had another. This time he hoped they were done for good.

Sarah kept to her duties at the house and worked hard. Eloise asked Sarah to come over and help her get ready for the charity ball that she and Wesley were attending. Sarah was delighted to help and met Eloise in her dressing room. Sarah had become quite skilled at styling Eloise's golden hair and often came up with new, elegant hairstyles for Eloise. The end results of Sarah's creations were normally quite breathtaking. They laughed over the few that did not look as they should or the ones that fell hopelessly flat. But they tried and tried, and out of the repetition, came perfection.

Perfection was what Eloise wanted tonight. She wanted a hairstyle that would be worthy of the lace dress that Sheila had sewn for her. They talked as Sarah worked her fingers through Eloise's golden hair, pinning it here, making curls there. When she was done and turned Eloise around to face the mirror on the vanity, she held her breath and waited to see what Eloise thought.

Eloise stared at her reflection in the mirror. Her golden hair hung in soft ringlets and wisps of hair that hung in tendrils down the side of her face, framing it in gold. Sarah had woven pink ribbon with roses attached into the creation, and it looked as if Eloise had a pink halo. It set off her face and looked so magnificent that Eloise was speechless. She sat there staring at her reflection, not able to speak.

"What do you think, Eloise?" Sarah said very quietly.

Softly and slowly, Eloise replied, "It is the most gorgeous hairstyle yet. I feel like a queen."

"And you will look like a queen when you get into the dress Sheila made. We must hurry! Wesley will be waiting. This hairstyle took longer than anticipated."

Sarah went to the wardrobe and took out the dress. While Sarah was buttoning the back, Eloise buttoned the cuffs of the dress. When all the buttons were buttoned, Eloise turned to the full-length mirror hanging on the wall. Her breath caught in her throat, and at the same time, she could hear Sarah's gasp when she looked at Eloise. She was gorgeous.

Breaking the spell, they heard Wesley at the bottom of the stairs calling for Eloise. Eloise smoothed down the dress and looked for her small purse.

Sarah handed it to her. "Let me go downstairs first. I want to see their faces." Giving her friend a hug, she walked out of the room.

Eloise could hear Sarah tell Wesley that she was coming. As Eloise was walking toward the door, Shirley and Sheila poked their heads into her room.

"Can we see, Mom?"

"Of course, my darlings. Come in and tell me how I look."

The girls walked into the room and stopped in their tracks. Eloise did a slow turn for them, showing off all sides, and when she was facing front again, asked, "Well, how do I look?"

"Wow, Mom. You have never looked more beautiful. I mean it. Like a queen."

"You sure do, Mrs. Danvers. Mr. Danvers will be speechless when he sees you."

"Then let us not keep him waiting any longer."

The girls raced ahead of Eloise, and she smiled as she heard them thunder down the stairs. Eloise walked to the top of the stairs and, looking down, saw her whole family, which included the Greens. They were all standing back, near the door, and at the bottom of the stairs was Wesley. He had put on his tuxedo, and his left foot was on the bottom stair. They stopped and stared at each other for a few minutes, and then Eloise started down the curving staircase. When she reached the bottom, Wesley found his voice.

"You are lovely, my darling. You will be the belle of the ball."

"Thank you. You are very handsome yourself."

"I have a present that I want you to wear tonight." He reached in his pocket and pulled out a small blue velvet box and handed it to Eloise. She took the box and opened it. Inside lay a pair of ruby and diamond drop earrings. Unable to find her voice, she looked up at Wesley and, with tears in her eyes, leaned over and kissed him.

"They are acceptable?"

"Wesley, they are lovely. Please hold the box while I put them on."

After they were fastened to her earlobes, she walked to the hall mirror to examine them. "They match perfectly. They are so lovely. Thank you." She walked back to where Wesley was standing and threw her arms around him. Wesley drew his wife closer and kissed her.

"Let us go or we shall be late."

Wesley put on his gloves and hat and held his arm out for Eloise. Sarah opened the door to see Ryan waiting with the carriage in the driveway. As they climbed in, they waved good-bye and set off for the charity event.

The children scattered to their rooms, and Walter and Sarah went into the kitchen to have some tea and start dinner. When they were alone, Sarah turned to Walter. "Living here has been a lot different than I would have ever imagined. We are treated as one of the family, but when it comes to things like this, it kind of puts us back in our place, as servants here."

Walter crossed to Sarah and could see tears shimmering in her eyes. "My love, do not be sad. We have a blessed life, with two wonderful children and wonderful friends in the Danverses. It does not matter to me that we live in the servants' quarters and work for the Danverses. Or that I cannot give you ruby earrings to adorn your ears or diamond necklaces to drape from your neck. All that matters is that I have you, Shirley, and Tyler, that everyone is healthy and happy, and that we are together. My life is perfect because you are in it." With that he wrapped Sarah into a bear hug and kissed her soundly.

At that moment, Tyler and Thomas walked into the kitchen.

"Eww," they said in unison. Tyler tugged on his mother's apron. "We're hungry. Isn't it supper time? Quit the mushy stuff."

Walter released Sarah. He promptly picked each boy up, one under each arm, and twirled them around the kitchen. Squeals of delight resounded, and when Walter set them down, they were so dizzy they could barely stand. They fell into a heap on the kitchen floor, giggling hysterically.

Soon after, Shirley and Sheila entered and saw their brothers on the floor laughing.

"So you complained about supper again, eh Thomas?" Sheila said to her younger brother. "That's what you get, twirled around. But I suppose you do it on purpose to get a free twirling!"

"Maybe, but it's fun."

"A tradition," said Walter.

They all got up and went to help Sarah with dinner. It was informal since the Danverses were not there, so the boys usually got their favorite meal, chicken strips, and the girls groaned about it, but enjoyed dinner anyway.

Chapter Fourteen

The spring of 1886 was fast approaching, and the families were starting to talk about going to the club for the summer. Shirley and Sheila had read everything they could find at the library about sailing and were anxious to try out some of the things they learned. Sailing was all they could talk about. When one girl started a sentence, it seemed the other finished it. Shirley and Sheila were closer than natural-born sisters, and likewise with the boys. They were three and a half, and they moved as one. They were always content to play games, each complimenting the other with their vivid imaginations. They could often be seen running through the house playing cops and robbers or cowboys and Indians. Hooting and hollering to beat the band.

Spring finally arrived. All the plans had gone as smoothly as before, and the ride to Johnstown was as uneventful as ever, although for Wesley, he could not keep still. The whole family thought it was funny that for this year, Wesley was the one who was most excited about the trip. This was very hard to imagine. Sheila also secretly hoped that Darryl would keep his word and come to the lake this year. She had a tinge of regret, since she had a beau and Shirley didn't. She wanted them both to have someone to dance with and was hopeful that Todd would be at the lake. She had seen Shirley's face when they met him in the park, and although Shirley didn't talk very much about him, she knew her friend would like to see him again.

As they disembarked from the train in Johnstown, the family went to the carriages sent from the lake and started to climb up. Wesley went to the driver and talked in earnest with him for a few minutes and then went to the second driver that would be bringing the Greens to the club and did the same thing. When they parted, the drivers were richer, and both were smiling. As

Wesley walked toward his family to get in the carriage, Eloise asked him, "What was that all about? Why did you give our driver extra money? You know they are paid by the club."

"Just a small bonus for him, my dear. Nothing to concern yourself with. Now, into the carriage! We don't want to keep the driver waiting." With that he helped Eloise into the carriage, climbed up after her, and shut the door firmly. "We are ready, driver!" Wesley shouted out the window, and the driver flicked the reins, and off they went.

Settling back in the seat, Wesley had a smile on his face. He looked at Eloise, and she gave him a quizzical look. He patted her hand and looked out the window.

As the carriages approached the clubhouse, everyone started to move about to get ready to disembark. When the carriages passed the clubhouse, Wesley heard shouts to stop. The drivers went directly up the access road toward the Browns' store and stopped at the last house. When the carriages came to a halt, the drivers opened up the doors to help everyone down. Wesley could hear grumblings at how far they would have to walk and what a mess it was. It was then that Wesley gathered the families together and said, "Quiet! Please! I know you think there has been some sort of mistake, but guess what. You are all wrong. I have a surprise for all of you."

He went over to where Eloise was standing and took her by the arm. "Come this way, all of you."

Wesley took them around to the front of the cottage and walked up the stairs to the porch. On the door to the cottage was a large, red bow with a ribbon strung from the door handle to the banister railing. Mr. Daniels stood at the door with a pair of scissors. Joseph and Betty Stamper, who designed the cottage, were on the porch, along with their sons, Michael and Steven. Even Mr. Timmons was on hand for the cutting of the ribbon.

Wesley turned to Eloise and took her hands in his. "Eloise, my love. I have kept a secret from you for the last year. This wonderful cottage is ours. I asked Joseph to oversee the building of it, and his lovely wife, Betty, has furnished the inside, I hope to your liking. Now, if you would do the honors of cutting the ribbon, I can carry you across the threshold and we can see our wonderful new cottage."

With tears in her eyes, Eloise gingerly took the scissors that Mr. Daniels had and cut the ribbon. A loud cheer went up from all assembled as Wesley opened the door, scooped up Eloise, and walked inside. The kids ran in next. Walter looked at Sarah, scooped her up as well, and carried her in. Mr. Daniels and Mr. Timmons walked together down the boardwalk to the clubhouse. The Stampers followed the families into the house to see if everything met with the specifications and if there was anything that needed fixing or changing.

The cottage was one of the last to be built by a member. It was the farthest from the clubhouse, but it was closest to the Browns' store. In fact, the store was right around the bend, and Wesley believed that he would be able to smell the bread that Mrs. Brown baked in her store from his front porch. As with all the cottages, their cottage had a large, sweeping front porch that wrapped around two sides. The cottage was three stories tall and had six bedrooms on the second floor and a large playroom on the top floor. There was also a staircase leading to the widows walk, which Wesley made sure was large enough to hold a dozen chairs.

They stood in the great room and slowly turned around, taking it all in. Wesley could hear the children running up the stairs to check out the bedrooms, and then heard them shouting as they found the playroom Wesley had built on the top floor. "Do you like it?" Wesley asked as Eloise slowly pivoted in the room.

"It is marvelous!" Eloise exclaimed, and as she turned, she saw Betty Stamper standing with her family by the door. Eloise walked over to her and took her hands in hers. "Thank you, thank you all for the wonderful work you have done. This cottage is magnificent. You are all so talented, and I am honored to be living here."

Blushing, Betty replied, "It was fun and a privilege to do this for you. I am glad you like it and will be happy here during your summers."

Joseph stepped forward and said, "If there is anything you do not like, or wish to add or change, please feel free to let us know."

"No, nothing will change. It is perfect! You and your family are very talented, and I would not dream of changing a thing!" Wesley replied as he looked toward Eloise. Eloise was nodding in agreement. Betty visibly relaxed.

"We will let you get settled. I will have Michael and Steven bring your bags in, and we will leave you to explore your new cottage. We hope to see you around this summer. Thank you, Mr. Danvers. It was an honor to do this for you," Joseph said as he and his family left.

An excited Wesley gave them a tour. The fireplace encompassed most of the back wall and separated the living room from the dining room. On the right side of the fireplace was a door to the kitchen. This was the most modern kitchen to be had. A wonderful six-burner wood stove and a brand-new, full-sized icebox. Behind the living room, next to the kitchen, was a dining room. The table held ten chairs and had a matching sideboard. The back wall had a large picture window, which faced the woods that surrounded the lake.

Climbing the stairs to the second floor, they emerged into a hallway that cut the upper floor almost in half and then halfway down the hall made a sharp right turn. Everyone had their own rooms. This would be a change from previous years, when everyone was in two rooms and there was very little privacy. Sheila's room would be in the first room on the right. And on the left was Eloise and Wesley's room. The next room on the left was Sarah and Walter's room. Both of these rooms looked out over the front porch and over the lake. At the junction where the hall took a hard right was Tyler's room and next to it was Thomas's. At the end of the hall was Shirley's room. Wesley had arranged for adjoining doors to be put in Tyler's and Thomas's rooms as well as Shirley's and Sheila's. This would cut down on the traffic in the hall.

His room and Walter and Sarah's room would have a large wardrobe, a queen-sized bed, and a vanity for the ladies. The children's rooms would each have a double bed and a large wardrobe. Tyler's and Thomas's rooms would have a table with chairs for drawing or playing, and the girls' rooms would have two identical vanities. As much as Wesley did not want to admit it, the girls were growing up, and their interests now were starting to turn to hairstyles and bows instead of dolls and tea parties. He was not sure what colors the curtains and bed linens would be, as he had given Betty Stamper free reign over what was appropriate.

The local merchants in the surrounding area made beautiful furniture, and he ordered the couch, chairs, tables, beds, and other furniture, all to be made locally. The playroom on the third floor was also stocked with desks, tables, chairs, and all the toys he could find. The stairs to the playroom were right above the first-floor staircase and opened up to a room that was the entire length and width of the cottage. There were windows on all sides of the room, so you could get a panoramic view of Lake Conemaugh and the woods behind the cottage. In the corner were the stairs to the widow's walk, which could hold a dozen chairs and provide a nice place to watch the lake and relax.

When they had all gathered on the widow's walk, taking in the view, Wesley asked, "Well, what do you think?"

Everyone started talking at once, and Wesley had to clap his hands to get their attention.

"So, one at a time. Eloise, what do you think?"

"It is absolutely perfect. I love it," Eloise gushed.

"Walter? Sarah?"

"We agree. It is perfect," Walter said while Sarah nodded, still speechless from the view and the cottage.

"Kids? What do you think?"

"Great!"

"Terrific!"

"Wonderful!"

"Really great!"

"I guess it is unanimous! We will keep it! Now let's go unpack and get the summer started!" Wesley said.

The kids all rushed down the stairs and into their rooms to start unpacking with the adults trailing behind with smiles on their faces. Wesley was happy that the cottage was everything he dreamt it would be. It was a perfect gift to his perfect family.

When the clothes were unpacked, everyone met on the porch. Wesley and Eloise had agreed to take the boys horseback riding, Walter and Sarah wanted to stroll the hills and down by the spillway, and the girls, naturally, wanted to go sailing. After securing the money necessary to rent the sail boats, Shirley and Sheila ran upstairs to get their towels and put their bathing outfits on. Walter and Sarah strolled off in search of a quiet trail and some alone time, and Wesley gathered the boys, and off they went to the stables.

~~~

May turned into June, and June would flow into July. Soon it would be time for the Fourth of July party, and Sheila had not seen Darryl or his family. This party was the third largest the club threw. The first was the welcoming party and then the last party. The July party ranked right up there as a wild shindig. There would be dancing, food, and of course, fireworks over the lake.

She was constantly looking at all the faces at dinner and at the parties in the clubhouse. She was beginning to wonder if he would make it at all. Shirley knew of her disappointment, they would talk late into the night about everything, and Darryl was brought up more than once. The summer was going well and both girls were becoming quite good at sailing, and when the races started, you could usually find the boat the girls were in out in front. They felt so alive when the wind was whipping through their hair and the boat was skimming along the water.

Over the summer, Sheila had talked her father into buying a sailboat so they wouldn't have to wait for one to become available, and Wesley, unable to say no, consented. The boat was delivered in June, and Sheila wasted no time in getting it ready and taking it out for a spin. Because this was a new boat, it was sleeker and faster than the boats the club had for the visitors, and the girls were unbeatable.

It was on a partly cloudy day in late June that Sheila got her wish. Shortly after lunch, the girls went to the docks and were getting the boat ready to take out. They had promised to take their parents out for a ride, and they needed to make sure all the life vests were there. Just as they finished their inspection of the boat, vests, and sail, they heard a shout from the clubhouse. Sheila looked up and saw her parents and the Greens coming toward them.

"Here they come, Shirley. Is everything ready?"

"Of course, it is all set. This will be fun."

Their parents arrived, and like good captains of their sailboat, they handed them each a life vest. Shirley held the boat as Sheila helped everyone in. Sarah was the last to board and was reluctant to step off the dock. Sarah had made progress. She wasn't as terrified of the pier as she was when they first arrived many years ago, but she was unsure if she wanted to get off the safety of the pier and into the boat that seemed to bob with every wave and movement.

"Mom, it will be all right. I have a line rigged for you to tie yourself to the boat just so you will be confident, and hopefully you will be able to relax and enjoy the ride. Sheila and I are the best captains on the lake, and you will be perfectly safe," Shirley said.

Slowly, Sarah put on the life vest and allowed Sheila to help her into the boat. Sheila climbed in right after her and showed her where the lifeline was tied and helped Sarah tie her life vest to the lifeline. As Sheila got to the helm of the boat, Shirley untied the moorings and pushed away from the dock, jumping nimbly onto the boat.

Sheila guided the boat away from the dock as Shirley put up the sail. Everyone settled back and took in the sights as the girls expertly maneuvered the boat around the lake.

"Everyone, look, there is our house!" Shirley said as they skimmed up the lake.

The scenery was flying past, and before anyone realized it, Shirley and Sheila were changing places and Shirley was piloting the boat from the end of the lake back to the docks. As the boat was swinging around, the sail boom swung and caught Walter and Sarah, and they fell backward into the lake.

Walter had been holding Sarah's hand when they went over, and he found he was still holding her hand. Walter hung on as they found themselves being dragged alongside the boat. Even with their life vests on, Walter found that the wake of the boat was rushing over them, pushing them under.

Sheila and Shirley scrambled to lower the sail. They had to wait for the boat to glide to a stop.

Walter pulled himself around and with his free hand grabbed the lifeline that was tied to Sarah's life vest. He pulled himself up out of the water and let go of Sarah's hand. Sarah reached out to reconnect with Walter when she felt his arm go around her and pull her up so her head was out of the water.

Walter pulled Sarah close and held them up as far as he was able. They noticed the boat was slowing, and they looked up to see Wesley pulling the lifeline up and reaching for them. As the boat slowed, the rushing water slowed down, and Walter was able to help hoist Sarah into Wesley's outstretched arms. As soon as he let go of Sarah, Walter grabbed the side of the boat and pulled himself in. Flopping like a fish on deck, Walter lay there and caught his breath. He looked around and saw that Sarah was sitting on the bench, pushing her wet hair out of her eyes.

"I am so sorry, Mrs. Green. Are you okay? The rope slipped out of my hand, and the boom got away. I am so sorry," Sheila cried.

"I am all right. It is okay, Sheila, accidents happen. I am glad you girls had the foresight to make us wear vests and tie this line on me. I feel very safe with you both sailing this boat."

Seeing the relieved look on Sheila and Shirley's faces, Sarah put on a smile and settled back on the bench. The girls went about getting the sail up and the boat moving again, but when Walter looked at Sarah, he saw the strained look on her face. As he looked at her with a question on his lips, Sarah shook her head and then smiled and looked as though she was relaxed and ready to continue her trip.

Walter got up, shook his head like a wet dog, which made everyone laugh, and settled in next to her. He could tell by the look on her face and the tightness of the grip she had on his hand that she was putting on a brave front for the girls, but was scared to death inside.

Shirley looked around again, and seeing smiles on everyone's faces, she shouted, "Ready to get going?"

"Let's go!" Walter said.

Sheila tightened the sail, and a gust of wind caught it and propelled the boat forward.

Once the boat was underway, Walter leaned over and whispered to Sarah, "Are you all right? You look as though you are in pain."

"My shoulder hurts from being pulled beside the boat, and the boom caught me in my side. I fear I will have some bruises before the night is over."

"My side hurts a bit too. Guess we both got hit pretty hard. We will take it easy the rest of the day, and later if we are still hurting, we can go see the club doctor, just to make sure nothing is broken."

"I will be fine, Walter, just banged up a bit. I would like to take it easy the rest of the day. Come, we mustn't look so worried, or the girls will suspect something is wrong. Give me a kiss and put a smile on your handsome face."

Walter leaned over and kissed Sarah. Putting his arm back around her, he turned his face to the wind.

They sailed around the lake a couple more times, and by the time they got to the docks, Walter and Sarah were dry and the mishap had been forgotten by everyone, but Sarah. The adults climbed out of the boat and thanked the girls and proceeded to go back to the cabin to get ready for afternoon tea. Shirley and Sheila stayed behind to clean up and put the sails away properly. As Sheila stood to tie the sail to the boom, she happened to look up, and at the end of the dock was Darryl. He looked so good standing there that Sheila shook her head because she thought it was a dream. He smiled and started down the dock toward her.

"Shirley, look who is coming down the dock! Oh dear, do I look all right? My hair must be a fright." Sheila tried to capture the wayward curls that had blown free while sailing.

Shirley turned to see Darryl walking toward them. He was smiling and looked relaxed and happy.

"Hi. Nice day for sailing," Darryl said. "That is a very nice boat. Is it yours?"

"Hi. Yes, my father bought it for us this year. We just came back from taking our parents out, to show them what great captains we are. The trip didn't turn out like we planned, but we had fun," Sheila said as she continued to tie the sail to the boom.

"I was hoping that you would take me out sailing sometime. I love to sail, although I must admit I am a bit rusty. I have been cooped up in an office for far too long. I forgot what a joy this place is and how much I love to sail."

"How about now? What do you say, Shirley, want to take a quick run up the lake?"

"Sure, why not. Come on, Darryl, we'll show you the sights." Shirley started to untie the boat from the dock. She looked up, and Sheila was grinning and untying the sail from the boom.

"Great! Toss me one of those life vests, and let's get going!" Darryl said as he hopped into the boat. He settled back in the seat, put on his vest, and watched the girls get the boat ready and then push off.

Just as they were about to leave the pier, Tyler yelled from the beach.

"Hey, we want to come too!"

"Yeah, it's our turn!" Thomas joined in.

Sheila was about to protest when Darryl waved his arms and said, "Let's get a move on if you want to come."

The boys ran down the pier, and when they approached, Darryl got up and lifted each onto the boat. He handed them each a life vest and proceeded to help them into it. When the vests were secured, they all sat down, Darryl in the middle, and turned their eyes to Sheila, who was at the helm.

"We're ready, Skipper!" Darryl said as he winked at Sheila. He put his arms around the boys and settled in for the ride.

Just as Shirley was about to untie the boat, she heard a shout. She looked up and saw Todd walking down the pier. "Do you have room for one more?"

"Sure," Shirley said.

"Great! Look out below, here I come," Todd said as he made a pretense of jumping on the boat where Tyler and Thomas were sitting.

"No, don't jump!" Thomas yelled. "You have to get in easy so it doesn't tip over. Don't you know anything?"

"I guess I don't. Could you teach me, squirt?" Todd said as he climbed aboard and ruffled Thomas's hair.

"Sure, just watch me and I will show you how!"

The boat left the dock, and Sheila and Shirley took their places for a quick run up the lake. Shirley took the helm and allowed Sheila to sit next to Darryl and man the boom. Shirley could see them talking and Sheila laughing and blushing. She strained to hear what they were saying, but the wind took their words away as they sped down the lake.

Todd got up and moved next to Shirley as she piloted the boat. "Hi. Glad I caught you at the dock. We just arrived this morning, and I wasn't sure where to find you."

"Most of the time this is where you will find us. How long are you staying at the lake? Will you be here until the end of the summer?"

"I think I just might. The scenery has improved one hundred percent since I arrived."

Shirley smiled and blushed slightly.

As they reached the far end and were circling to return to the dock, Shirley noticed a herd of deer had come down from the woods and were drinking at the lake. She hollered to Sheila, and she, Darryl, and the boys got up to look at the deer. Shirley slowed the boat and edged it closer to the shore to get a better look. Darryl grabbed the backs of Tyler's and Thomas's life vests for fear they would fall overboard in their zest to see the deer.

There was a loud snort from the buck standing on the side of the hill, and all the deer quickly became alert. In an instant, the once peaceful herd of drinking deer became a mass of legs and white tails as they ran into the woods. They watched them go, and then Shirley engaged the sail and they were off toward the docks.

As they approached, they saw a group of friends getting ready to take one of the club's sailboats out. Greetings were called, and Darryl helped Tyler and Thomas out of the boat and went to help tie the boat to the dock. Immediately Tyler and Thomas tore down the dock and into the clubhouse. No doubt they were going to tell their parents about the deer and the boat ride. Shirley smiled as she watched them go. Sheila turned and handed the two life vests to Shirley, who quickly stowed them under the seats along with Darryl's and their own.

Darryl hopped off the boat and turned to help Sheila, and when she was safely on the pier, he turned and helped Shirley off. Todd hopped off and watched as both girls checked the moorings, and when they were certain they were secure, the four of them started down the pier. When they reached the beach, Todd heard his name being called. He looked up and saw his mother standing on the clubhouse porch. He turned to Shirley and said, "I must go. I had a wonderful time on the lake with you. Maybe we can do it again sometime."

"I would like that also."

"I will see you later. Good-bye, Darryl, Sheila." With that he turned and started toward the clubhouse.

Shirley turned around just in time to see Sheila shudder. "He gives me the creeps. He is always hanging around, and he can't get close enough to you. His father is the one who ran us off the road that time, and I just would rather not even stir up that hornets' nest."

"Oh, he's okay. He isn't like his father. But you're right, he is always there. Why don't we all go and have tea anyway?"

Darryl held out his arms and said, "It would be my pleasure to escort you to tea."

With Shirley on one side and Sheila on the other, they went up the lawn and into the clubhouse.

Chapter Fifteen

It was the last full day of summer. Shirley was in Brown's General Store to get some hard candy and licorice for everyone, and she bumped into someone coming around the corner of the isle, dropping the bag of candy she had just purchased. He had dark hair with long eyelashes that framed his deep green eyes. He was a bit taller than Shirley, and when Shirley got a look at who she bumped into, she was star struck. It was on the tip of her tongue to say, "I'm sorry," but as she looked into those intense green eyes, she was lost.

The two stared at one another for, what Shirley later would describe to Sheila, "an eternity."

As he regained his composure, he smiled at the enchanting creature before him and said, "Are you all right?"

"I am fine, thank you."

He stuck out a hand. Shirley nearly missed it for staring at his smile.

"My name is Justin Brown. The Browns who own the store are my parents. I come up every year to help them move their things back to Johnstown. Who are you?"

"Shirley Green. My mother and father work for the Danverses." Shirley gasped. "Although I am not supposed to tell you that!"

Justin winked at her. "It is nice to meet you, Shirley Green. I am glad I ran into you. Will I see you later?"

"We are leaving tomorrow to go back to Pittsburgh." Shirley abruptly turned on her heel and raced out of the store, forgetting the bag of candy she had dropped.

Shirley ran all the way back to the cottage and up the stairs without pausing to say anything to her mother, who was sitting on the front porch.

She ran into the bedroom where Sheila was reading a book. Sheila looked up, expecting Shirley to be carrying candy, and when she saw the look on her friend's face and her empty hands, she jumped up off the bed. "Where is the candy? Were they out of the cinnamon sticks I love?"

"I met the most handsome boy in the whole world!" Shirley said as she plopped down on the bed next to Sheila. "I ran into him at Brown's. His name is Justin Brown, and he had dark hair and green eyes and is tall and strong and really cute."

"I have seen him around. The Browns' son, right? Did you talk to him?"

"Only to introduce myself, then I made a fool out of myself by rambling on, sounding so childish, and telling him that my parents worked for your parents. Then I ran out." With a groan, she dropped her head into her hands.

Sheila patted Shirley on the back. "I think it will be okay. Justin is of the working class, and it is probably good you told him. That way if he likes you, he can show it and not worry about whether you are in his class or not. The people here do not allow members of their class to marry beneath them. That is how they see it, like they are subhuman. I think it is silly, but that is how they think. And it is ok for you and Justin to get to be friends, because you are not one of us."

Seeing the stricken look on Shirley's face, Sheila hurriedly continued, "But you are one of us, I didn't mean it that way. We don't see you as anything less than wonderful!" She hugged Shirley.

As she let go, Sheila said, "So was he really, really cute? Was he nice? Tell me all about him, and then maybe we can go up to Brown's and just look around and get the candy you dropped. Then I can get a look at him and see if he is good enough for you!"

When the girls were done talking, they devised a plan for returning to Brown's. Sheila insisted on plaiting Shirley's hair and practicing what she was going to say to Justin. And then it was time to go. Shirley couldn't wipe the grin off her face, and as the pair jogged the path to Brown's, they would lapse into conspiratorial giggles. Several times they had to stop to catch their breaths.

Sheila and Shirley slowed to a walk as they approached Brown's General Store. They did not want to seem to be in a hurry, so they sauntered up the stairs and paused at the entrance. Shirley quickly scanned the room and did not see Justin. She motioned to Sheila, and they entered the store. They tried to appear to be browsing, so they went to the hats, and started trying them on. Shirley chose a straw bonnet with yellow and white daisies.

"That hat is definitely you, Shirley Green."

Shirley froze, and she stared at Sheila, who subtly motioned her to turn around. Shirley spun, nearly running into Justin for the second time that day. He steadied her with a hand and, with the other, held out a bag of candy.

"I believe you dropped this the last time you were in the store. I added a few more pieces for you."

"Th-thank you," Shirley stammered.

Sheila thrust out a hand, all business. "I am Sheila Danvers, Shirley's best friend."

Justin shook Sheila's hand while continuing to stare at Shirley. "Justin Brown. Nice to meet you. I'm sorry I did not come up this summer to help in the store. We would have met earlier."

"I am too," Shirley mumbled.

"I was only asked to help my parents pack up the store. My sister came up and stayed with them and helped out this summer. I didn't know there was such beauty here or I would have volunteered. I usually work with my father, helping out on the train. I shovel coal or clean up the coaches. My father is teaching me how to become a conductor, like he is."

Shirley's face lit up. "Then you travel to Pittsburgh also?"

"My father goes at least twice a week. I go sometimes but not every run."

"I live in Pittsburgh. Maybe I will see you there. We will be coming to the lake every summer. I hope that you will come back to help your parents again. I should like to see you."

"I will do that. I hope you have a nice winter, Shirley Green, and I hope we will run into each other in Pittsburgh. Would it be all right if I wrote you a letter or two this winter? I would not want you to find another beau before I have had the chance to court you next summer."

Shirley's face, if possible, turned a shade redder. "I would like that very much. I will write back, and you can tell me all about the train ride and the sights and sounds. That would make me very happy."

Justin turned and went to the counter and found a pad of paper and a pencil. As he was walking back to where the girls were standing, he wrote his name and address on the pad. He ripped the page off and handed it to Shirley along with the pad of paper. As Shirley wrote her name and address on the paper, Justin said, "Me too. Please have a safe trip home tomorrow. Just think, I may be in the engine that takes you home. So keep a look out, I may be just around the corner."

Shirley handed the pad back to Justin and turned to go. "Good-bye Justin. It was a pleasure meeting you."

Shirley reluctantly walked out of the store, sending longing glances behind her as she did so. Suddenly, Shirley stopped short and turned around, causing Sheila, who was right behind her, to bump into her. She went back into the store and called to Justin.

"There is a farewell party at the clubhouse tonight. Will you be going?"

"No, I am not a member."

"But you could go with us, if we invited you, couldn't he?" Shirley asked Sheila.

"I am sure it will be fine. Will you come with us? We could meet at the clubhouse at seven."

"I would be honored to escort two lovely ladies to the party. Farewell until seven tonight, Shirley Green." With a smile that would melt ice, Justin smiled at Shirley and then turned to go into the storeroom.

Shirley literally ran from the store, and when Sheila caught up to her, she saw the stricken look on her friend's face.

"What is wrong? Why are you so upset?"

"I was such a fool, blurting out the invitation. I just didn't want him to think I wasn't interested, and oh, I am such a fool. He will think I am such a child and will go just to humor me. I am so embarrassed."

"Nonsense! He is about our age, and I think he was quite taken with you. He couldn't stop looking at you the entire time, even when he was talking to me. And besides, he wouldn't have asked for your address if he was just humoring you, now would he? Now, get those silly notions out of your head. We have those lovely dresses your mother made us for tonight. We will ask your mother to do your hair special tonight. We want to make sure his eyes stay glued to you!"

Shirley smiled gratefully at her friend and linked her arm through the crook in Sheila's elbow. "Sounds good to me. Let's go!"

They raced back to the cottage and found Sarah still on the porch. They were out of breath when they plopped down in the porch swing and told Sarah all about Justin. Sarah agreed to do a special hairstyle for Shirley and was happy to see her interested in someone. She had seen Justin when she was at the store and thought he was a polite, handsome boy. Her daughter had good taste. Sarah was also happy that she had fallen for a boy that was of the working class. She was very afraid she would find one of the wealthy sons interesting and would have her heart broken when she realized that she would never be allowed to wed.

There had been many boys that were taken with her, she was a beautiful young lady, but her head had not been turned by any of them. Sarah knew that Todd Stevens had been hanging around all summer, squiring Shirley here and there, although it was hard to tell if he was interested in Shirley or just part of the large group of friends they had. Sarah watched Todd, and he always seemed to be close to Shirley, watching her. She hoped it was her imagination, for Todd was a nice enough boy, but his parents would never allow a match with her daughter.

Sarah was not happy about the class distinction that was such a big part of their lives, but this time she was glad. Todd Stevens's father did not like Wesley very much and seemed to be a very unhappy man. It showed in everything he did, from the way he talked to the way he looked down on others. Todd did not appear to be like his father, but Sarah would guess he knew that he would not be able to court a servant's daughter. Marrying into that family was not something that Sarah wished on any young lady.

Sarah sat on the porch watching the people walking around and the boats sailing on the lake. Walter had walked up quietly and stood at the foot of the stairs, looking up at his wife. He never could get enough of her, and she looked so peaceful and happy. As he walked up the stairs, Sarah snapped out of her daydream. Walter sat next to her and kissed her on the cheek.

"You look happy, my love. Are you thinking, perhaps, about me?"

Sarah chuckled. "No, my darling, but about our daughter. She is taken with a boy, and I have never seen her so nervous and happy."

"Shirley nervous? She is never nervous or shy. Must be true love. Who is this boy?"

"The Browns' son, Justin. She met him today at the store, and she has invited him to the dance at the clubhouse tonight. The girls are upstairs fussing about dresses and hairstyles now."

"What time is the dance?"

"Seven."

"It is only a little after two. Must be a lot of fussing going on!"

"It is good to see her interested in a boy that is not one of the club members' sons. I was worried that she would be taken with someone not of our class and would have her heart broken."

Walter nodded. "I noticed Todd Stevens hanging around also. His father is a most unpleasant sort. I believe Todd is taken with Shirley, although she never really gives him any special look, which is a good thing. Justin would be good for our daughter. His father is a good man. I have had many occasions to talk to them, and they are quite knowledgeable and friendly. I believe the winter will be a long one for our dear Shirley."

"Not as long as you think, dear. Justin told Shirley that he makes the run with his father to Pittsburgh once in a while. I have a feeling we will see him more than you expect."

"We will have to invite Richard and Justin over for supper when he is in town. That will make Shirley very happy."

Sarah beamed at her husband. "Wonderful idea. But we must wait until we see if they hit it off. If not, it will be a very uncomfortable supper!"

Laughing, he said, "We will wait. I am sure that Shirley will bring up the idea way before we would ever suggest it."

Sarah leaned back against Walter's arm and nestled her head on his shoulder. Together they watched the boats on the lake.

〜

Time passed slowly that day, much too slowly for Shirley's taste. She was so anxious about going to the dance with Justin, she could not concentrate on anything else. Sheila suggested they go sailing to pass the time. Shirley reluctantly agreed. Once on the water, Shirley relaxed and got caught up in the joy of skimming along the lake. They saw many of their friends and had a few races. Shirley found the day flew by, and before she knew it, they were tying the boat up to go and get ready for the dance.

As they were tying the boat up, Todd approached them.

"You both were pretty quick out there. Would you like to go again? I am sure I will beat you."

Laughing, Shirley said, "You haven't beaten us all summer, Todd. What makes you think you could if we went out now?"

"Luck. It would be on my side. The summer is over, and I just feel lucky. How about it? One more race."

"We can't, Todd. We are going to the dance at the clubhouse and have to get ready," Sheila said emphatically.

"May I escort you to the dance tonight, Shirley?"

Sheila stepped between her friend and Todd. "Shirley invited Justin to escort us, and he said yes."

"Justin *Brown*? Will he be able to get the coal dust off his hands so he doesn't get it all over your dress?" Todd sneered.

"You are such a snob, Todd. Come on, Shirley. Don't pay any attention to him." Sheila pushed past Todd, almost knocking him over.

"Wait, Shirley, I am sorry."

Todd reached for Shirley as she was turning around. When he saw the look on her face, his hand dropped. "I didn't mean to sound like a snob. I just was looking forward to having dinner with you one last time this summer."

"Sorry, Todd. We will be at the dance. I will see you later." With one last look at Todd, Shirley walked away.

When they were out of hearing distance, Sheila whispered, "I think he is smitten with you."

"I don't think so. He's just a friend. Anyway, he knows I don't like him like that. Now let's forget about Todd and focus on Justin. Just please, don't be too charming, or he may like you instead of me!"

"Never. He couldn't take his eyes off of you in the store."

"Really? I thought so but didn't want to stare at him. He is just so cute."

With a shout of laughter, Sheila dashed toward the cottage with Shirley hot on her heels. Sarah was waiting for them when they returned. She had brought two fresh pitchers of water for them to wash up in, and as each girl washed the day from their skin, Sarah got the brushes and ribbons ready for their hair.

After an hour of fussing with dresses, bows, and hairstyles, both girls were ready for the dance. Sarah stood back and looked at the two girls. They both looked so grown up and excited. Shirley had on a dress of lavender with lilacs in her hair. Sheila's dress was rose, and Sarah put small roses in her hair.

As they walked to the clubhouse, Shirley said, "Is Darryl meeting us at the clubhouse, or is he coming later?"

"I think he said he had a few things to do and would meet us there later. I hope he isn't too late. I want to be able to have a lot of dances with him."

"His family only came up a few weeks ago, and we really haven't had much time to spend together. He told me that he was working, and he just couldn't get away. But he is here tonight, and he has promised me a couple dances, so that is a good sign."

Justin was waiting at the bottom of the stairs when the girls walked up. As they neared, he fell into a deep bow.

"You both look lovely. Shall we go in?" Justin offered his arms to the girls, and together they mounted the stairs.

Shirley introduced Justin to all their friends. Some of them had met Justin at the store, and as the night wore on, no one could tell that Justin had just joined their group. Everyone got along great and found they all had a lot in common. Jokes and conversation flowed as the night wore on. Justin and Shirley danced every dance together. Some of the other girls looked at Justin, but he had eyes only for Shirley.

Darryl and he became fast friends and spent most of the night joking and talking. It was toward the end of the evening when Shirley realized that she had barely talked to Sheila all night. They all sat at the same table, but she and Justin found they had a great deal in common and never ran out of subjects to discuss. Shirley looked around for Sheila and saw that her friend was just as occupied with Darryl as she was with Justin and was relieved that she had not neglected her.

After the dance, Justin asked to walk the girls back to their cottage, and they found they had an extra person with them. Darryl had asked to escort Sheila home, and they all walked back together. It was a beautiful evening and the stars were out in full force. None of them wanted the night to end, so they lingered on the porch, enjoying the night air. When the evening came to a close, Darryl and Justin walked toward the general store, talking and laughing.

The girls watched until Justin and Darryl turned the corner and were out of sight. They turned and went to sit on the front porch swing before going in for the evening. They heard the door open and saw their mothers peek their heads out of the door with wide smiles on their faces. Eloise and Sarah came out onto the porch and sat down.

Sarah said, "Well? How was the dance?"

Sheila and Shirley glanced at each other. Their smiles got broader until they were unable to contain them selves.

Shirley started. "It was so wonderful. Justin met us at the lodge, he was standing there at the bottom of the stairs, and he was so handsome, and he was such a gentleman, offered us both arms, and walked in with us."

Sheila broke in, "And we went in and the music was playing, and all our friends were there, we went to the table and a little while later Darryl came in. All the girls were watching him and he came over to me—me, Mom! And we all sat and talked and danced…"

Shirley sighed. "And Justin is such a good dancer. He guided me around the floor, like an expert, and I felt like a fairy princess. All our friends knew Justin, and we all talked and ate and danced all night long. Then at the end of the dance, when the music stopped, Justin offered me his arm to walk me home. I was walking down the stairs of the club and stumbled, and Justin caught me, saved me from getting hurt. He is so strong."

"Darryl held the door for me, and we came out as Justin was holding Shirley. I thought he was fishing for a kiss." Sheila wiggled her eyebrows at her friend. "But then we saw where her heel was caught in her dress and knew he saved her. Then they walked us home, and they both took our hands and gave us a kiss."

"It was such a nice evening."

Sarah smiled at the girls. "We are both glad you had such a great time. I shouldn't tell you this," she said with a wink, "but both your fathers could not sit still tonight. After dinner we all played pick-up-sticks, and they both kept looking at the clock. Then occasionally they would go to the window and look out, or walk on the porch and comment on the stars."

"They even wanted us to sit on the porch to watch the stars. It was quite a comedy show this evening." Eloise giggled.

"I think we should all go in so you can tell your fathers all about your evening, and then we should turn in."

"Good idea," Eloise said.

They all rose and walked inside, where the girls saw their fathers trying to be nonchalant about things.

The next morning, the trip back to Pittsburgh was quiet. Everyone was thinking about the time at the lake, where there was fun and sun and fresh air. But the air had grown cooler, and they wanted to make it back to Pittsburgh before it got any colder.

The winter storms could come upon them quickly, and it was not uncommon that they would have a snowstorm in late August or early September. As promised, Shirley kept her eyes on the engine, and to her delight, Justin was in the cab with his father. He waved to her and went about his job. Shirley felt very safe in the train as they journeyed back to Pittsburgh.

Chapter Sixteen

The fall and winter crawled for Shirley. She looked forward to the weekly letters that Justin wrote. When Justin wrote he was going to be in town with his parents on an overnight trip, Shirley begged her parents to invite them to dinner. Sarah and Walter consented and plans were made. Walter picked up Richard, Frances, and Justin at the train depot and brought them to the Danverses estate.

As they rode up the driveway, Frances exclaimed, "You live here?"

"We live in the servants' quarters, although I must admit they are far more lavish than we had ever dreamed of living in." When he saw the shocked look on their faces, he quickly continued, "I know we are listed as members of the club, but that was Mr. Danvers's idea. He bought our membership as a bonus so we could accompany them to the lake and not have to work. I don't think it matters much when we are at the club, but here in town, we know our place. The Danverses are very generous as well as down to earth. You will not find a better couple. In fact, they insisted we have dinner at their house. Shirley has become like a daughter to them, and we are all as close or closer than family. They wanted you to come and dine with them so they can get to know you better, away from the club. I must confess that Shirley has been a bundle of nerves at the prospect of seeing Justin again."

"Justin has done nothing but talk about Shirley since he got back from the lake."

"Mother!" Justin cried.

"It is all right, young man." Walter chuckled. "Shirley has done nothing but talk about you, too."

Walter pulled the carriage up to the stable, and one of the hands appeared and helped everyone down.

"Let's go inside. We will go to our home and get everyone, and then we will go over to the main house for dinner."

As they entered the apartment, Sarah came out of the kitchen.

"Welcome to our home. Nice to see you again. Tyler, get up and say hello to the Browns."

"Nice to see you again," he said, rising, shaking Richard's hand and bending over Frances's hand and kissing it lightly.

Frances smiled. "Nice to see you too, Tyler."

"Justin, it is nice to see you again." Shirley stood shyly regarding Justin from the edge of the living room.

Justin cleared his throat and said, "It is nice to see you, too."

After a quick tour of the apartment, Walter said, "Why don't we head over to the Danverses'? They are expecting us."

Walter pointed out the stables and the gardens on the short walk to the mansion. He held the door and everyone filed in. As they went through the kitchen into the dining room, they were met by Eloise, Wesley, and Sheila. Thomas came running down the stairs behind them.

"Welcome! So nice to see you again. I trust your ride in was pleasant?" Wesley said as he shook Richard's hand.

"Yes, it was very nice. It is such a treat to ride in the passenger car of the train and not have to steer. But don't get me wrong, I love being a conductor."

"It must be fascinating having that much power," Walter said.

They all filed in and sat at the lavishly decorated table. Walter helped Sarah bring in the meal, and they all sat down and Wesley said grace. "Dear Lord, bless this food and the company that we have. May you look on us with kindness and keep us all in the palm of your hand. Amen."

"It is a wonderful job. I love the freedom of the open road, so to speak. I have been fascinated with trains ever since I was a young boy. When Justin was very young, he would come to the train yard with me. I have watched his love of trains grow, so when he became of age, I started to train Justin on all aspects of working at the rail yard. I started at the lowest jobs and learned all I could, and worked my way to the position I am in now. I believe that is the way to learn a job, from the bottom up, learn everything you can and you will be successful. He is such a natural at it, and I couldn't be more proud."

"I agree. I came up the same way, and it has made me a better manager at the bank, at least I hope so." Wesley laughed.

"Is it dangerous?" Shirley asked.

Justin shrugged. "It can be if you do not follow procedures and keep your wits about you. My father is the best there is, everyone says so, and I know I can be as good as he is, with time and hard work."

"An honest day's work is all anyone should expect of themselves. Congratulations, Justin. Looks like you have a good support system and a good teacher!" Sarah said.

After dinner was finished, Sarah started to clear the dishes. Frances got up to help, and Sarah said, "Please sit, you are our guests. Shirley and I will get these cleared away quickly, and we can all enjoy the rest of the evening."

"Let's all go into the library to get a bit more comfortable," Wesley suggested.

Tyler and Thomas said in unison, "Can we be excused?"

Thomas appealed to his mother. "We want to go to our room and play."

"Run along then. I will come up later to get you ready for bed," Eloise said as she picked up her wine glass and led the way to the library.

The conversation continued as they moved to the parlor for sherry and cigars. Finally, Mr. Danvers looked at the time and found it was well past midnight.

"It seems we have talked half the night away. Would you like to spend the night here, instead of trying to find a room this late?" Seeing the worried look on their faces at the prospect of staying in the mansion, Wesley added, "We have an empty apartment across from Sarah's apartment, if you would like to stay there. It is quite comfortable."

The Browns were relieved. "Thank you, that would be most kind."

"I have not heard a peep from the boys upstairs. I believe they have fallen asleep. Would it be all right if Tyler spent the night?" Sarah asked Eloise.

"Yes, that is fine. I will check on them when we go upstairs."

"Good night. We will see you in the morning for breakfast," Wesley said as he put his arm around Eloise and started for the stairs.

"Bye! See you in the morning," Sheila said as she followed her parents.

Sarah and Walter showed the Browns to the apartment. Shirley and Justin trailed behind their parents, not wanting the night to end.

"The apartments are very comfortable, and if you need more heat, we can stoke the stove up before you turn in."

Richard nodded, a thoughtful look on his face. "That would be nice. Thank you, Walter, Sarah, for a lovely evening. We feared it would be quite uncomfortable, dining with the Danverses. We know them from the lake, but here is the real world, and we were not sure what to expect. But as you said, they are wonderful, down to earth people."

"It was an enjoyable evening, one we hope we can repeat often," Sarah said.

Before they climbed the stairs to the apartment, Walter grabbed some logs and carried them to the empty apartment while Sarah checked the bedrooms to make sure there were linens and covers. By the time Sarah made up the beds, Walter had a nice fire going in the stove. The apartment was warming up nicely.

Justin came in carrying the bags they had left in Walter and Sarah's living room and put them in the bedroom for his parents. They all said good night and closed the door. Sarah, Walter, and Shirley went across the hall to their apartment.

"What a wonderful evening. Don't you think, Shirley?"

Shirley was walking slowly down the hall to her room, and they could hear her say, "Just wonderful!"

Laughing, Walter put out the light, and he and Sarah turned in.

～

The next morning, Shirley knocked on the apartment door, and Justin opened it.

"Did you sleep well?"

"Yes, we all did. This place is amazing. I dreamt about you, and when I opened the door, here you are, like you stepped out of my dreams."

Shirley blushed. "You are very kind. If you and your family are ready, we are going to the Danverses for breakfast, and then my father will take you to the train depot."

"Sounds wonderful."

They all walked over to the house for breakfast.

Elosie greeted them. "Did you sleep well? Did you find the accommodations to your liking?"

"They were wonderful. Thank you so much. You have such a nice place here," Frances replied.

"We try and make it as comfortable as possible. By doing this our employees are happy and will want to stay and do a good job. They then have a vested interest in doing their best, and that benefits all of us," Wesley explained.

"It would be nice if the rest of the world thought that way. We have heard so many tales of people who are not treated well, but they have nowhere else to go. So they endure. We are fortunate that we have our own home and store, but some of our customers could treat people a bit nicer," Frances said.

"Please, sit down. Breakfast is getting cold," Sarah scolded everyone.

Justin held the chair for Shirley as Richard held the chair for Frances. Walter looked at Sarah and smiled. This was a good man for Shirley.

Shirley blushed and said thank you as she sat down, and when Justin looked around, he saw Sheila standing by her chair. He went over and held her chair too.

"Thank you. Just because you are sweet on Shirley, doesn't mean you can ignore *me*!" Sheila laughed.

"Of course not. Who could forget Shirley's best friend? I will do my best to stand in until Darryl can be here to hold your chair, my lady!"

Sheila blushed and sat quickly.

Everyone laughed as they sat down for a hearty meal of eggs, bacon, sausage, hash brown potatoes, toast, and hot coffee. When everyone was full, the Browns said their farewells.

"Thank you, Mr. Danvers. It was a most enjoyable time," Richard said as he held his hand out to shake Wesley's.

"It is Wesley, not Mr. Danvers. You make me sound so old and stodgy!" He laughed.

"Wesley it is then. Thank you. I look forward to doing this again, maybe at our house next time you are in Johnstown."

"Absolutely!"

"Good-bye, Shirley," Justin said. "I shall write to you and will see you the next time I come to Pittsburgh!"

"I hope to see you again soon."

As they left the house they saw that Ryan had brought the carriage around. Walter helped the Browns into the carriage and climbed up.

"What a nice evening! I hope they come visit again soon," Sarah said to Shirley as they watched the carriage pull away.

"Me too! Isn't Justin dreamy?" And with that, Shirley dashed off to find Sheila.

Sarah chuckled as she watched Shirley run. "Yes, he is dear."

～

Around Christmas time, one of the stable hands from town brought a package to Walter. Walter looked at the address and smiled. He called for Shirley.

"Yes, Father?"

"You have a package. It was just delivered."

"A package? For me? Who could it be from?"

"Justin, I suppose."

Shirley squealed with delight and snatched the package from his hands. She brushed her lips across his cheek in a quick kiss and ran to her room.

Sarah came out of her bedroom. "What is all the commotion?"

"Shirley just got a package from Justin. Christmas present, I believe."

Shirley came dashing out of her room. "Look what Justin sent me. A sterling silver hair comb with butterflies carved on it. Isn't it lovely?"

"Oh dear, it's gorgeous."

"I have to go find Sheila. She will be green with envy. Be back soon."

The door slammed shut as Shirley dashed out of the apartment.

"Our baby is growing up, Sarah."

"We may be planning a wedding soon, but that is okay with me. Justin is a fine man, and he comes from a good family. I am glad that she did not fall for Todd. That would have been our worst fears come true. I believe that Todd is out of the picture now."

Chapter Seventeen

Neither could believe that it was finally May. The snow had melted, and the flowers were blooming. Shirley was so excited. Tomorrow they would be going to the lake. Justin had promised to go and help his parents this year. Except for the occasional trip with his father on the train, he would be relatively free this summer. Shirley could not wait to spend the summer with him, swimming and sailing.

Sheila was equally excited, even though she saw Darryl on a weekly basis, since he lived in Pittsburgh, she wanted his undivided attention. During the winter months, he was preoccupied with work and school, and the time he could spend with Sheila was limited. He came around at night and often brought her flowers, but he was studying to become a lawyer, and the work was taking up a lot of his time. In the summer, he would have more time to relax since school was out. He had been to the house several times for dinner, and their parents knew each other well.

Darryl's father, Robert Powell was a prominent lawyer in Pittsburgh. He and his wife, Dorothy, lived closer to town than the Danverses, but when the weather was nice, the girls would meet Darryl in the park to go horseback riding or stroll by the fountain. Shirley was usually sent along as a chaperone, so they were all very well acquainted. Darryl and Justin had become friends the last year at the lake, and Darryl often asked about Justin and what the news was from Johnstown. Whenever Justin came to Pittsburgh with his father, the four of them would get together, even if it was for a brief time while the train was loaded, and talked about the fun they would have at the lake.

Sheila and Shirley were on the bed giggling about Sheila's conjecture that Justin was in love with Shirley already. It came to an abrupt halt when they saw Eloise in the doorway.

"Mother! This is girl talk," Sheila whined.

"But I'm a girl, aren't I?" Eloise answered.

"No, you are Mother! That's different."

Eloise sighed dramatically. "I understand. Please make sure that you and Shirley have your stuff packed. Please help your brothers get packed also. We don't want them to arrive at the lake with no clothes and just toys in the suitcases."

"Yes, Mrs. Danvers," Shirley answered.

"Sure, Mother," Sheila responded.

Sarah called the teaming masses to dinner, and Eloise descended the stairs into the waiting arms of her husband.

"How was your day, dear?" Eloise asked as she gave Wesley a kiss.

"Fine, but is that a proper greeting for your returning warrior?" teased Wesley. He pulled her close and began waltzing her around the foyer, gave her a deep dip, and ended with a long kiss. As he set her on her feet again, Eloise blushed like a schoolgirl and started toward the kitchen with Wesley close behind.

They all took their places at the table and bowed their heads to give thanks. "Bless this food we are about to receive. Bless those less fortunate and the hungry; may they be granted your blessings. In his name we pray. Amen."

Dinner was a noisy affair as always. The two families ate in the dining room together. All the children were firing questions about the lake, asking what time they were leaving.

"So, are you all ready to go to the lake for the summer?" Wesley asked.

A cheer erupted from the family. Everyone started talking at once about the things that they would do at the lake, the clothes they needed to pack, and the friends they would see again. Sarah sat back and watched the families interact as one. She watched Shirley and Sheila giggle about seeing Justin and Darryl again and having all summer to swim and go sailing. Thomas and Tyler were discussing which toys to bring with them. There were so many other boys to play with, and they wanted to make sure they had enough toys to keep them busy. Walter and Wesley were deep in discussion about an acquisition of a thoroughbred horse that Wesley had his eye on.

He was considering buying a racehorse. Since Walter was an expert on horses, they often had discussions on the best lineage and lines.

Eloise exchanged looks with Sarah. She had the same satisfied smile on her face as Eloise.

"It looks like one big happy family, don't you think?"

Eloise nodded. "I was thinking the same thing. I am so glad that you came to work for us, Sarah. I could not have asked for a better worker, friend, confidant. Have I said thank you lately?"

Blushing, Sarah replied, "No, it is I who should thank you. You changed my life and the lives of my family."

Seeing how uncomfortable Sarah had become, Eloise quickly changed the subject. She chuckled to herself that Sarah was still so humble and loved her even more for that. "So, are you ready to go to the lake? What play do you think we should put on this year? It is so much fun rehearsing and then playing another character, don't you think?"

"I don't know. When I was in town last week, I heard some people at the market talking about vaudeville, and how they went to see a show when they were in New York City. They said it is a show of different acts, like juggling, reading poetry, or whatever talents people had. It might be fun to see what kinds of things everyone comes up with."

"Yes, I heard the Powells talking about that at the dinner we went to last month. I think that would be a splendid idea. There are quite a few people who play instruments, and others are quite knowledgeable and love poetry. What would you do, if we were to do that this year?"

Sarah sat back and thought about it. "Well, maybe I could play the piano. I have been practicing here, and some of my songs are good enough to play. At least I think people will recognize the tune if I played it." Sarah laughed.

"That would be lovely. You have become accomplished on the piano lately."

"I wouldn't say accomplished, just average. But I love to sit down and hear music coming from my fingertips. What will you perform?"

"Oh, I don't think I will perform. I will be content to sit and watch everyone else."

"Nonsense, Eloise! You have a wonderful speaking voice, why don't you read one of your favorite poems? I think you could do them justice by reading them out loud."

"Do you think so? I don't know. I am not much for public speaking."

"What?" Sarah leaned back in her chair and let out a loud laugh, so much so the entire family fell silent and turned to stare at Sarah. When Sarah finally stopped laughing, she wiped her eyes and realized the dining room had suddenly gotten very quiet. When she opened her eyes, she looked around at the startled faces of her family. "What is wrong? Why is everyone staring at me?"

"You were laughing pretty loud, Mom," Tyler said.

"Eloise said she was not much for public speaking. It just struck me as funny."

The whole family started giggling and laughing.

"Okay, okay, everyone. I get the point," Eloise said as she joined in their laughter.

Sarah looked around and marveled at the similarities and loved feeling like part of a large family.

Chapter Eighteen

Monday morning dawned brightly. It was the first full day for the families at the lake, having arrived late yesterday afternoon. Sheila slept very little the night before, despite the long ride yesterday from Pittsburgh. She stretched and got out of bed and went to the window. The light glistened off the lake in the early morning sun, as if diamonds were sprinkled over the top and floated on the surface. Soon, the lake would be dotted with sailboats, and cries of joy would be heard from the beach as swimmers braved the cool lake waters.

Not everyone was at the lake this early in the year. Sheila knew that Darryl and his family would be arriving later that day, and since Darryl was officially Sheila's beau, they looked forward to spending the summer together. They had talked about getting married, and Sheila hoped that Darryl would ask her father for her hand in marriage this summer.

She watched the early morning activities from her window. The road leading to the clubhouse was filled with horses and wagons piled high with boxes and crates. Numerous men guided the wagons up the road toward the clubhouse, where they would unload the food and drink the members would be served the first few weeks of the summer. Wagons would come and go the rest of the summer, restocking the depleted supplies.

Along with all the supplies that were being delivered to the clubhouse, Sheila would occasionally see a wagon pass the clubhouse and go around her house. She knew it was heading to Brown's General Store, which was around the bend from their cottage. Richard and Frances Brown had arrived on Saturday to open the store so they were ready for the goods that were going to be delivered. Richard's brother, Floyd, often came up on the initial run to the lake to help bring supplies and to help his brother unload the numerous crates. This year, only Justin and Derrick, one of Floyd's sons and Justin's cousin, wanted to go to the lake for most of the summer.

The wagons Sheila watched were bringing the party decorations and the special food that would be served at the big welcome party for all the members of the club that was being held on May 31, Decoration Day. This would be the first big party of the season, and it usually lasted from noon well into the night and would end with a spectacular display of fireworks. Most of the people coming to the lake for the summer would be arriving between now and May 31, and they all expected a big welcome and kickoff to the summer. The Danverses were one of about a half dozen families that came to the lake early. There would be few cookouts and parties no matter when people arrived. The club made sure there were plenty of activities going on every day, because that is what the members expected.

As she watched the workers, she could hear the rest of the family starting to move about. She tore her eyes away from the activity below. She dressed quickly and went downstairs to see who was up.

Sarah and Shirley were already getting breakfast ready for the family in the kitchen. As Sheila descended the stairs, she could smell bacon and fresh-baked bread. Mornings were her favorite time, the warmth of the kitchen and the wonderful smells. The family was slowly trickling into the kitchen this morning, worn out due to the anticipation of the summer, packing and getting ready all last week, and the trip up. It also had to do with the fresh mountain air, Sheila suspected, and the fact that they all slept very well here in their comfortable cottage.

Mornings were the only time that the family would eat together on a regular basis during the summer, and even that was not guaranteed. There were many parties and picnics, so time around the table would be limited to the mornings and occasionally the evenings when they would all gather on the porch and watch the stars.

"Good morning, Sheila! How did you sleep last night?" Sarah asked.

"Very well, thank you, and you?"

"Very well, I always do up here. Are you hungry? Shirley made some wonderful flapjacks."

"Great, I am starved. This place always makes me eat twice as much!" Sheila giggled.

As Sheila was sitting down and putting butter on her flapjacks, the boys rushed in.

"Oh, flapjacks. Can I have some, Mom?" Tyler asked.

"Of course, sit down, and Shirley will get you some. You too, Thomas."

Shirley heaped three large flapjacks on each of the boys' plates. She set the plate down and reached for the maple sugar syrup. She spread it liberally and stood back to watch her two brothers, as she thought of them, attack their food. She picked up the plate with the bacon on it. "Would you boys like some bacon too?"

"Yes, ma'am! We surely would," Thomas said with his mouth full of flapjack.

Eloise breezed into the kitchen. "Don't talk with your mouth full, Thomas. Good morning, everyone. I trust you all slept well?"

"Very well, and you? Coffee, Eloise?" Sarah asked.

"Very well, and yes, coffee would be divine. Thank you, Sarah."

Wesley walked in. He went up behind Eloise, kissed her on the cheek, walked over to the boys, and ruffled their hair. "Good morning, all. Isn't it a glorious morning! This will be a great summer, one we will all remember! Has Walter come down yet?"

"Walter was up rather early and took a walk. He promised to be back for breakfast. Please, everyone, eat up while it is still hot."

Wesley sat down and they all proceeded to fill their plates.

"So what does everyone have planned for today?" Wesley asked.

"Sailing."

"Playing trucks and cops and robbers."

"Planning plays, strolling, and needlepoint."

"Whoa, everyone! One at a time. Tyler, you and Thomas first."

Beaming, Thomas said, "We are going to see who is here, but we are going to take our new trucks to the beach and build a sand castle, Mom said we could, because she will be at the clubhouse watching us. And later, Mom said she would take us swimming."

"Terrific, tiger! Sheila and Shirley?"

"Of course we are going sailing and swimming. And maybe we will go strolling down to the spillway. Just walk around and see who is here. Hang out."

"Yeah, hang out," Shirley piped in. The girls looked at each other and started giggling.

"This 'seeing who is here' wouldn't happen to have anything to do with the fact that I saw Justin at his mom's store and heard that the Powells will be arriving today, now would it?" Wesley teased.

Blushing, Sheila said, "Maybe. Is that all right with you?"

"Of course, just wanted to see if you would tell us, that's all." Wesley winked at his daughter.

"And my lovely wife, what will occupy you today? Me?" Wesley said hopefully.

"Sarah and I are going to see the other ladies, watch the boys on the beach, work on some needlepoint, and see what plays they want to perform this year. You are welcome to join us if you like." Eloise smiled at Wesley. Seeing his wince, she said, "If this is not to your liking, we hope you will meet us for lunch at the clubhouse."

"Walter and I will be there!"

"We will be where?" Walter said as he entered the kitchen. "Something smells wonderful."

"At the clubhouse for lunch with our lovely wives. I talked to Mr. Daniels, and there is a hunting party going out in about an hour, if you are up for it."

"Absolutely. Let me get some of this wonderful breakfast in me, and we'll be ready to go," Walter said as he sat down.

When breakfast was done and the dishes washed and dried, everyone took off in their own directions. Shirley and Sheila went down to the docks to see if their boat was there. They were pleased to see it was, and set about readying it for the summer. On the porch at the clubhouse, Sarah could see the girls as they cleaned the boat. Their eyes constantly looked toward the clubhouse as they chattered and scrubbed. Sarah guessed what they were looking for, and as she looked around at the people who were arriving, she spotted Darryl and his family. Dorothy spotted Sarah and came over.

"Sarah! How wonderful to see you. It has been a long time."

"Yes, it has, Dorothy! I see you brought Darryl and Susan with you this summer."

"Susan always comes. She is far too young to be left home alone, and Darryl, well we couldn't keep him home if we had rope! He is so anxious to see Sheila. He was jittery the whole way up."

Sarah shared a knowing smile with Dorothy. "Sheila has been anxious to see him too. Shirley is waiting for Justin also. Between the two of them, I don't know who was more excited. They are down at the docks, and from the smile on Sheila's face, I'd guess she has seen that Darryl has arrived."

"I see Justin coming down the boardwalk. Do you mind if I sit next to you and watch the show?"

"Not at all," Sarah said.

"What show are we watching?" Eloise asked as she walked toward Sarah. "Hello, Dorothy! Nice to see you."

"We are waiting to watch the fireworks when Darryl and Justin make it to the docks where the girls are readying the sailboat," Dorothy said as she sat in the rocker next to Sarah. "Do sit, we'll all get a kick out of this." She indicated the chair next to her for Eloise to sit in.

Eloise sat down and the three mothers watched as Justin and Darryl shook hands and greeted each other, each trying not to look in the girls' direction. Finally, they started to walk slowly toward the docks, with neither of them acting like it was his decision. Sarah looked at Shirley. She and Sheila were straightening their wayward curls and smoothing down their dresses. The boys approached and they all acted as if they were meeting for the first time. It was awkward and stilted.

They saw the girls say something and the boys smile and hop aboard the sailboat. Justin untied the line from the front while Darryl untied the line from the rear. They pushed off, and with Sheila at the helm, they drifted off toward the center of the lake. As they went around the bend, Sarah saw Shirley put the sail up and the wind took the boat and soon had it racing across the lake.

"I wonder if they know how silly they all looked?" Dorothy asked. "They have known each other for years, and they acted like it was a first meeting. Young love."

"Very true," Sarah said, "but I have a feeling that we will all be related soon. I have it on good authority that Justin is going to ask Walter for Shirley's hand this summer. Frances mentioned it to me this morning that Justin is petrified of approaching Walter to ask for Shirley's hand. Darryl came up to lend Justin support, so Justin was nervous when he didn't see Darryl yesterday. He thought his friend had backed out."

"And I heard Darryl asking his father if he could ask Wesley for Sheila's hand this summer also," Dorothy said. "But you didn't hear it from me, if Sheila asks."

"Heavens no! I know that is what she wants, so we will see if these young men have it in them to brave the asking of the fathers!" Eloise laughed. "I sincerely hope that Wesley doesn't give Darryl too hard a time, or he may turn tail and run for the hills. Sheila would definitely not take that well."

"It will be a summer to remember, that is for sure!" Dorothy said. "I am glad we are all here, and I look forward to us all being family before too long. Although I wouldn't technically be part of your family, Sarah, but with the girls as close as they are, I think I will consider us one big, happy family!"

"I'll drink to that!" Eloise said as she lifted her lemonade to clink glasses with Sarah and Dorothy.

Chapter Nineteen

May 31 dawned gray and dreary. It had been raining all night, and it continued to come down, heavily at times. Justin put his oilskin on and pulled his hat low over his eyes and started toward the clubhouse. His friends Steven and Michael Stamper were on the porch. Their father was there, too, speaking with Mr. Timmons, the club owner.

"What is going on?"

"Mr. Timmons has just noticed that the lake is rising and the dam doesn't have the proper drainage on the spillway. I think Dad, and he are discussing what needs to be done," Michael explained.

"Didn't your dad say something the other day about that."

"He sure did, but Mr. Timmons would not hear anything other than getting the cottages ready. So now we have to scramble in the rain."

"Do you need help?" Justin asked.

"All the help we can get, once they figure out what to do." Michael walked up the stairs to stand next to his father.

"We need to get a spillway cleared and flowing so the lake doesn't overflow and flood the houses and the boardwalk. I will get twenty men started on it right away. We should have done this last week, like I told you. Now we are racing the clock." Turning toward his sons, he said, "Steven, Michael, Justin get over to the laborers camp and round up as many men as you can. Start clearing out the spillway on the west end of the dam. Mr. Timmons said there are large branches and debris caught in the netting. They must have fallen over the winter and during the heavy rains. I don't remember the last time we cleared it. There is probably more debris than we know blocking the spillway opening. Try and clear it as quickly as possible. More water should be flowing through the spillway and I want it cleared! Quickly, we have no time to lose."

Steven, Michael, and Justin dashed off into the rain. Joseph gave a last look at Mr. Timmons and raced after his sons.

~~~

From her bedroom window, where Sheila started each morning, she could see the lake and the main road. There were not a lot of people out because of the rain, and the lake took on a hazy almost mystical look. A strange feeling came over Sheila as she watched the rain. A quick movement caught her attention. She turned and saw Michael, Steven, and Justin race off toward the laborers' camp. Sheila looked toward the lake and could see nothing but the rain. She continued to watch and then saw Mr. Stamper race off after his sons.

She shivered and pulled her robe closer. As she felt the warmth of her robe slowly seep into her body, she walked to her wardrobe, where her new dress was hanging. This dress was made by Sarah especially for the party today. Sheila wanted to look perfect. She ran her fingers over the satin and lace. The dress was a pale yellow satin, with a simple design. The bodice was a scoop neck with ivory trim, and the arms were entirely made of ivory lace. The skirt was of the same pale yellow satin and went all the way to the floor. It was simple and yet so elegant. When she turned away from the wardrobe, she noticed Shirley in the doorway.

"You looked so happy staring at that dress. My mom did a great job making it, didn't she?" Shirley asked as she crossed to the bed and sat down.

"She did. I can't wait to see Darryl's face when he sees me. I feel like a princess in it, and I hope he likes it."

"Likes it? Are you kidding? He will love it. He won't let you out of his sight for fear someone else will tempt you away from him."

"He knows better." Sheila plopped on the bed next to Shirley. "I can't wait until this afternoon for the party. I heard Mr. Daniels telling someone that this party would be one of the biggest that the club has ever put on."

"Well, with this rain, the day will not be as exciting since we won't be able to sail, but I am sure we will find something to do."

Sheila paused and looked at her friend's face. There was something different this morning. "What is on your mind? You look…different, today. Happier. What secret are you keeping from me? I thought we were best friends?"

"We are," Shirley said. "Last night, after you and Darryl walked over to the clubhouse to get an ice cream, Justin and I stayed on the porch, watching the moonlight. He told me that he asked my dad earlier in the day to marry me. And my dad said yes!"

Sheila jumped off the bed and embraced her best friend. They danced around the bedroom squealing and carrying on.

"I knew he would! I told you he would. This is so terrific! I am so happy for you!"

"Let's get dressed and go and tell the rest of the family." When they were dressed they raced to the kitchen and pulled Sarah into the dance.

Eloise came running into the kitchen, wondering what all the commotion was about. When she saw the girls dancing, and Shirley told her the good news, Eloise joined in the dancing and singing.

When the singing calmed down, Sheila asked her mother, "Mom, after Darryl asks Dad if we can be married, can we have a double wedding? *Please?*"

"We will see what your father says, but I do not think that will be out of the question."

Sheila and Shirley launched into more dancing and ran from the room chatting and giggling to discuss the wedding.

After the girls left, Sarah looked at Eloise. In a quiet, embarrassed voice, Sarah said, "Please do not mind the girls. We can give Shirley a fine wedding. I do not want you to think you need to pay for my daughter's wedding. I would never ask such a thing."

"Nonsense." Eloise walked over and gave Sarah a hug. "It would be my pleasure to have a double wedding. The girls have grown up together, and I know that this has been a dream of theirs forever. In fact, if it is okay with you, I insist!"

"Thank you. I will make them, and us, the prettiest gowns in all of Pittsburgh. I know Walter will be thrilled and a bit overwhelmed by this generous offer, but he is wrapped around Shirley's little finger and he will give in quickly."

"Now we just have to pray that Darryl isn't too intimidated by Wesley and asks for Sheila's hand, otherwise I hate to think what Sheila will do to that poor boy."

～

At precisely twelve o'clock, Sheila and Shirley walked regally down the stairs as if they were princesses, dressed in their new dresses. Sarah, who was waiting downstairs, felt her breath catch when she saw how beautiful the girls looked. As they reached the bottom of the stairs, each girl twirled to show off her dress. As they donned their coats and hats to shield them from the rain, they called to the rest of the family to hurry.

"Mother, Father, Thomas," hollered Sheila, "we don't want to be late."

"Coming, coming," Wesley called from the top of the stairs. "Hold your horses, ladies. We will not be late. I promised you, didn't I?"

Wesley, Eloise, and Thomas came down with amused looks on their faces. Sarah and Walter were waiting downstairs, helping Tyler with his coat.

"You just want to see the *boys*," Thomas joked.

Blushing, Sheila turned and fussed with her hat. Eloise and Wesley exchanged smiles and hurried to get the coats on. When all were ready, they donned umbrellas, and the families stepped into the rain and walked the short distance to the clubhouse.

As his family was entering, Wesley approached Mr. Timmons, who was standing on the porch off to the side, looking toward the dam. "Everything all right, Mr. Timmons? You look tired."

A startled Mr. Timmons turned and smiled. "Everything is fine. Going to be a wonderful party! I hear the band starting up.

Going to be great, just great." Mr. Timmons was already looking toward the lake and mumbling to himself as he walked away from Wesley.

A puzzled look came across Wesley's face. Mr. Timmons's tone was distracted. Wesley shot a quick look at the lake, and seeing nothing but the rain, he turned to go into the party.

Just inside the door was a small room to hang up coats or leave their umbrellas. The members only had to turn their backs to the waiting staff, and they would be helped out of their coats. In the far corner, a small band was set up, playing jigs and waltzes. There was a section of floor that was cleared to be used as a dance floor. Scattered around the rest of the room were tables covered in the finest white linens with a large gold *C* insignia in the center, edged with gold brocade. The silverware, china plates, and crystal glasses all had a *C* insignia on them and shone in the lamplight. The oil lamps on the wall gave off a soft, yellow glow that made the room shimmer.

Sheila looked around and her eyes alighted on Darryl. He was standing next to a table with the rest of their friends gathered around. He was wearing a new suit with a white shirt and dark blue cummerbund and matching tie. He always took Sheila's breath away when she saw him. He seemed to be in a heated discussion with Todd about something, and knowing Todd, it was about horses. Todd was a passionate horseman and was constantly talking about horses.

Darryl looked up and saw Sheila in the doorway, taking off her coat. He excused himself from the conversation with Todd and hurried over to greet her.

"Sheila, you look lovely! That dress really makes you look like a princess, my princess," Darryl said as he put his arm around Sheila and kissed her on the cheek.

"Thank you, my prince. You look very handsome yourself."

Darryl held his arm out to lead her to the table and then turned and offered the other arm to Shirley, who was standing behind them. Shirley smiled and took his arm, and together they all went to the table. Darryl pulled out her chair, and when Sheila was comfortable turned to offer the same to Shirley. But Todd had beaten him to it.

"You look lovely today, Shirley. May I offer you a chair?" Todd said as he held the chair for Shirley to sit down.

"Thank you, Todd."

As they all sat down, Darryl leaned over to whisper in Sheila's ear. Then he got up and walked to the other side of the room. Shirley looked at her friend and saw that she was blushing and watching Darryl.

"What is going on? What did he say to you?" Shirley asked her friend.

"He is going to ask father for my hand in marriage. He figures if it is in public, my father won't say no and won't give him a hard time."

Shirley giggled. "Boy, is he in for a surprise."

Both girls watched Darryl approach Wesley. They could see them talking and were shocked to see a frown appear on Wesley's face. Just then, Eloise, who was standing next to them, playfully nudged Wesley, and he started to smile. They could see Darryl visibly relax as Wesley reached to shake his hand. Eloise kissed Darryl on the cheek, and he turned back toward the table. Darryl had a huge smile on his face, and as he approached the table, all eyes were on him.

"I have an announcement to make," Darryl said as he walked up behind Sheila's chair and put his hands on her shoulders. "Please, everyone, quiet down."

A hush fell over the crowd.

Darryl turned Sheila's chair sideways and proceeded to kneel on the floor in front of her. He took her hand in his. "Sheila, would you do me the honor of becoming my wife? Your father has given us permission to marry, and I would be pleased if you would say yes."

Sheila looked at Darryl, and with tears streaming down her face, she said, "Yes, I would be most honored to become your bride."

Darryl leaned over and kissed Sheila as their friends cheered. Soon the entire room was cheering, and they heard the band strike up "Here Comes the Bride." Even though there were only seven or eight families at the lake at this time, there was quite a crowd, due to the staff at the club along with any servants or nannies that the guests brought with them. The band transitioned into a soothing waltz.

Darryl got up and with her hand still in his and asked, "May I have this dance?"

"Of course, I would be honored."

Darryl led Sheila to the dance floor and glided gracefully around the floor to the waltz the band was playing. As Shirley watched her best friend dancing, she silently wished that Justin could be there to hold her close and dance with her, but she knew that they were not part of the genteel class, that they were working class and that was what Justin was doing. She was one of the lucky ones that got to attend with the members of the club.

When the song ended and everyone returned to the table, there was a lot of backslapping and congratulatory hugs and kisses going on. Darryl turned to his friends and, grabbing Shirley's hand, pulled her closer. "It seems that I am not the only one to ask for a lovely woman's hand in marriage. I am told that last night, Justin Brown asked for Shirley's hand, and she too has consented. So let's all congratulate Shirley and Justin!"

Cheers went up around the table. Shirley felt her face get hot with all the congratulations that were cast her way. She wished Justin was with her, but she would tell him about the entire dance later. She would see him that night, and they would sit on the porch and talk about their day. She looked forward to those quiet times with him, when they could be alone.

She was startled when she was tapped on the shoulder. She turned to see Todd standing next to her.

"I know you would rather have Justin asking, but he will have a lifetime to dance with you. Would you like to dance?"

"Yes, Todd, I would. Thank you."

Todd had a crush on Shirley from the first summer he saw her. He spent every summer with her and all their friends. He knew she was fun and full of life, not to mention beautiful. But she was not of his class, and his parents would not tolerate him courting or marrying anyone outside of his social circle. When he was home, Todd heard his father rant and rave over how he felt about people intruding into the upper class, and felt that Mr. Danvers was one of those people. Although the Stevens were technically part of the working class, they got their membership from Dora's parents, who were very well off. Mr. Stevens always considered himself better than most, even though he worked for a living in the bank, under Wesley.

Todd knew how his father felt about the Danverses and knew that his feelings spilled over to the Greens. Todd didn't dare ask his father if he could court Shirley. He didn't think he could handle the lectures, so he just enjoyed the summers when he could be near her. He was very jealous of Justin, but he resolved to be happy for them and never let Shirley know of his true feelings. To her, he was just a good friend, and that was the way it would always be. For now, he was content to have Shirley in his arms.

When the dance ended, Todd led Shirley back to the table. When everyone was seated, lunch was served. Talk started about what they would all do that summer and how many races they would win. Eventually, the ladies decided to talk about wedding plans. Shirley and Sheila said they would like to have a double wedding, and Darryl got up abruptly.

Sheila looked at him with a horrified look on her face.

"Where are you going?"

"I am going to find Justin. I think he and I can still catch the train to Johnstown!" he joked as he looked at his watch and started for the door.

Sheila grabbed his coat tails and pulled him back. "Sorry, mister. You cannot go anywhere just yet. You are stuck with me for life!"

As he sat down again, Darryl said, "A pleasure I am looking forward to." He kissed Sheila.

Shirley was a little quiet, and when Sheila looked at her friend, she saw sadness.

She leaned over to her and whispered, "What is the matter? Don't you feel well?"

"I miss Justin. He would have enjoyed this so much, and I saw him with Michael out in the rain, doing who knows what. I always miss him at these dances."

"I know, but soon he will be at your side all the time, and you will be looking for ways to get rid of him."

"I don't think so, but you never know. I am fine, thank you."

The two friends hugged and continued eating lunch.

Chapter Twenty

Outside, Steven, Justin, and Michael had been pulling branches and logs from the heavy screens that covered the overflows on either side of the dam that were put in place to keep the fish in and let the overflow out. When they had pulled all the branches they could reach, they decided that they needed to heighten the breast of the dam, and maybe that would push the water to the sides to drain that way, alleviating the pressure.

They started to haul dirt from the sides in buckets and wheelbarrows to try and heighten the breast of the dam. The work was difficult, and the water cresting the dam was washing away the added dirt. After a half hour, Steven told the men to stop.

"This is futile. The water is rushing too quickly over the dam and taking our hard work with it."

Justin looked at the dam and the drenched men. "Let's try just rocks. If we can get enough rocks lined up, and if they are wedged together, we can fill the cracks with tree limbs and dirt, and hopefully that will hold better than just dirt."

"It's worth a shot. Okay, we need rocks. Lots and lots of rocks to try and build a foundation."

The men ran to the sides of the dam and filled the wheelbarrows with rocks of all sizes. Another group went into the brush on the side of the dam and brought back tree limbs. Piles of rocks and tree limbs were dumped on the breast of the dam, and Steven and Justin set to arranging them. It was slow work as they fought the water that was pushing over the dam and taking the smaller rocks with it. As they started to make headway with their rock wall, Steven told half of the workers to bring mud. It seemed that Justin's plan was working. The men worked faster, and when they had stemmed the flow over the dam, Steven took the men to find Michael and to help him clear the spillway.

What was once the most beautiful spot at the club, was now a tangle of branches, logs, and broken trees. Most of the debris was tangled in the net that was strung across the spillway, just under the water's surface to keep the fish in the lake.

Steven waded to where his father was and, shouting above the rain, said, "We put rocks, limbs, and mud on the breast of the dam. It seems to be holding. I have brought my crew to help. Where would you like them?"

"Have them work on the spillway, wherever they can. We must get it cleared."

Steven turned back to his men, and instead of finding them waiting for him, they were already hard at work trying to clear the spillway. Steven smiled and went over to help. The work was going slowly, and they could see they were not making much progress, but they didn't give up.

Joseph went to the breast of the dam to see what work Steven and Justin had done. He could see the height extension of the dam they had built, but also noticed that the mud that was packed between the rocks was slowly being washed away. Mud wasn't holding well under the torrential downpour and the constant lapping of the lake on the breast of the dam.

Joseph continued to the south side of the dam, hoping to find a spot where they could dig to allow water to flow out of the dam. He knew that the club had started to build another spillway on the south side of the dam, but was unsure of the progress that had been made. He hoped that they had gotten far enough that they could finish it and get the water flowing. Joseph walked into the brush and saw the beginnings of a spillway. Hope flared as he raced back over the dam, slipping and sliding the whole way. He yelled to Michael.

"The club has started another spillway on the south side. They did not get very far, but I think we can open it up if we hurry. It may relieve the stress and save the dam. Grab some men, and let's see what we can do."

Joseph raced back to the south side as Michael went to the workers and explained. The men, energized by the hope that they would succeed, ran across the dam to the south side to help Joseph clear the other spillway. As they approached, they could hear Joseph thrashing through the bushes and raced to help. The woods were teeming with men tearing limbs, moving rocks, and digging ditches. After what seemed like hours of digging, a trickle of water started down the trench they had dug, and a cheer went up. Energized, they dug harder and faster.

Joseph saw how hard the men were working and yelled over the roaring storm, "I know you are cold, tired, and wet, and I want you to know that I appreciate all the work you have done so far. We are making progress, so let's keep going!"

Joseph climbed back to the breast of the dam, and as he looked across, he saw Mr. Timmons standing near the dam watching the men. Joseph started toward Mr. Timmons, but before Joseph could reach him, he turned and walked quickly back toward the clubhouse. Joseph called to him, but he kept walking. Joseph continued to the other side of the dam to see if Steven and Justin had made any progress with the choked spillway. There wasn't much progress, but the men were still hard at it.

Joseph ran around the spillway and dam, examining everything, looking for places that they could alleviate the stress on the dam. He saw the lake was rising and water was sloshing over the top of the dam. He watched the immigrants working and saw his sons and Justin working alongside them. For a moment, he was filled with a tremendous sense of pride.

"Justin, Justin!"

Justin emerged from the brush and came slip sliding in the mud toward his father. "What is it? Where are you going?"

"Mr. Timmons has asked that I take the train to the nearest telegraph office to warn Johnstown and the other towns down river about the amount of water that is coming their way. He is afraid that the water is going to continue to rise and the dam could possibly break." Richard held up a hand to stall his son's words. Time was of the essence. "I know you and the others are working on getting the spillway open and the pressure relieved, but even if you succeed, there will be more water than Johnstown can handle. I want to make sure they are properly warned, so I need you to come with me. Go and let Joseph know you are going with me so he doesn't look for you, and then we need to get going."

"Okay, I'll be right back."

Justin ran to Joseph and exchanged words, motioning to where his father. Joseph waved and went back to work.

Richard and Justin ran to where a few horses were tied in front of the clubhouse, untied the reins, and raced toward the train depot. When they got to the depot, they climbed aboard and Richard fired up the engine. Justin shoveled coal into the fire. Richard pushed the engine as hard as it would go, and as they picked up speed, Richard looked outside and noticed the river that ran next to the train tracks was flowing faster and with more water than he had ever seen.

Richard went from town to town, blowing the whistle and warning each of the villages and anyone he saw on the way. Justin jumped from the train at each town or village to make sure the people knew what was happening. He asked each of the towns to telegraph the operator in Johnstown. They hoped that at least one of the towns would get through to Johnstown, but to be on the safe side, they went all the way to Johnstown, not relying on the telegraph.

At four p.m., Justin and Richard pulled into the Johnstown depot, blowing the train whistle in one steady sound, not the short blasts he usually used when pulling into the station. The residents of Johnstown were used to the streets flooding from all the rain, and most had moved what they could to the second floor and settled in with the thought that they would be stranded through the night. Some of the other residents heard the whistle and knew that something was seriously wrong. They grabbed their families and ran for the hills.

When Richard and Justin were just about to turn back, Richard heard a roar unlike any he had ever heard before. He grabbed Justin and pulled him into the train. "Shovel, son, shovel! The dam has broken. Our only hope is to outrun the water."

Justin shoveled the coal faster than he ever had in his life, and Richard pushed that engine and prayed they would make it to higher ground.

~~~

Joseph stood on the edge of the dam watching Michael try to replace the rocks and mud as quickly as the water was washing it away, when he saw the center of the dam start to give way. Slowly at first, and with the full force of the lake behind it, the center of the dam collapsed.

"Watch out!" Joseph grabbed Michael by the back of the shirt and pulled him off the crumbling dam. Both landed on the ground with a hard thud but were safely out of the way. Joseph watched as the other laborers scrambled to get out of the way, and when they were all safely on solid ground, they stood there, watching Lake Conemaugh drain and begin its race toward Johnstown. A feeling of helplessness and despair fell over the men. Some openly wept; others sat down and shook their heads in disbelief.

Joseph, Steven, and Michael sat in stunned silence. It took thirty-six minutes to drain the lake, and as the last of the water rushed over the broken dam and started to subside, Michael stood up and walked slowly back to the clubhouse. The rest of the workers followed, unsure of what the next step was.

~~~

As Shirley was returning to her seat from a dance with Todd, she heard a loud noise, so loud that she stopped in her tracks and Todd ran into the back of her. "What was that?" Shirley started for the door with Todd right behind her. As she stepped onto the porch, she looked around and didn't see anything unusual. It was still raining very hard, and it was difficult to see the lake. She heard a noise and looked to the left and saw Michael and a large group of men walking slowly toward the clubhouse. They looked like ghosts coming out of the mist with all the rain. As he got closer, she was shocked at the condition of his clothes. He was covered from head to toe in mud and soaked to the skin from the rain. She peered into his grimy face, the question in her eyes.

"It's gone. The dam is gone. I can't believe it."

"What happened?" Shirley whispered.

"It just broke, and all that water…" Michael sat down heavily on the steps and started to cry.

Stephen sat next to his brother and put his hand on his shoulder. Slowly, he looked up at Shirley. "The dam broke."

"What are you talking about?"

"The dam broke. We tried so hard to fix it, to get the sticks and branches out of the way so all that water would run off safely, but we failed. And now all that water is rushing toward Johnstown. It is too terrible to imagine."

Shirley looked toward the lake and couldn't see their sailboat. Confused, she blinked her eyes and rubbed them and looked again. All she could see was the tops of the sails. She pushed past Stephen, down the stairs, and walked toward the pier. Stephen was right! The water was gone. As she got closer, she saw the sailboats all sitting in the mud on the bottom along with the swimming platform and dock. Heedless of the rain soaking her, she continued as in a trance to the edge of the lake. Todd walked up behind her and touched her shoulder.

"Shirley, you mustn't stand here in the rain. You will get sick. Come back to the clubhouse."

Shirley let herself be led back to the porch.

As Stephen related the events of the morning to other concerned partygoers, Larry Stevens burst onto the porch. "What are you filthy men doing here? Clear out immediately or I will call Mr. Timmons and he will order you away from here."

"Mr. Stevens," Stephen said, "we filthy men, as you call us, have just come from the dam that holds the water and fish in your precious lake. We have tried to save your summer by working in this pouring rain to help keep this club as nice as it has been—"

Mr. Stevens advanced, shaking his fist at Stephen. "Get off this porch! You have no right to be here!"

Wesley had been watching the exchange and was growing increasingly agitated.

Summer of Gold and Water

"Larry! Please do not interrupt again. We are trying to find out what has happened, and your outbursts are not getting us anywhere. Stephen, please continue."

"Thank you, Mr. Danvers. Early this morning, Mr. Timmons came to us and told us that the lake was rising at an alarming rate with the storm and the wet spring we have had so far. He asked us to check out the dam to make sure that things were solid. We found the overflow screens were clogged with trees and branches, making it difficult for the water to flow normally and keep the level of the lake at a manageable level. We attempted to clear it and could not. About a half hour ago, the dam broke. We were in the process of shoring up the top, and it just crumbled."

Sheila had been watching in silence, as were the rest of the members of the club. Finally snapped out of the trance that she was in, she asked her father, "What are we going to do? What will happen now?"

Suddenly, Shirley grabbed Michael's arm. "Where's Justin? He went with you to the dam. Where is he?"

"He went with his father in the train to warn Johnstown. They were only going to the nearest town to get a telegraph off. They should be back soon."

Shirley ran to her father, throwing herself against his chest. "Father, Justin…" Her chin trembled so, she could barely speak. "I have to go find him. He could be hurt."

Wesley looked at Shirley crying hysterically on her father's shoulder. He had come to love her as a daughter, and seeing how torn up she was with grief, turned his attention to the group of his rich friends. He was appalled at what he saw. Most of the people were discussing packing up and going home; since there was no lake, there was no reason to stay. Some people had drifted away to start the chore of packing and getting back to Pittsburgh.

"What is wrong with all of you people?"

Everyone on the porch stopped and turned to face Wesley.

"I hear you talking about going home, that your summer was ruined and you have no reason to stay here. What about the people who live downriver from us? The lake is now rushing toward Johnstown, winding through the narrow gorge. Do you know how much water is racing its way to the town? All the water you spend your summers swimming in, fishing in, and boating in. The fish you all took pride in catching and eating, and the water you watch your children play in and sail in, it is all gone! Every drop is right now picking up speed and will destroy everything in its way. You are all thankful that you don't live in Johnstown, that you live in Pittsburgh, high above the lake and any problems that the lake emptying will cause. Don't you have any compassion?"

Sheila and her mother walked up to her dad and stood with him, watching the disbelief filter over the faces of their friends.

"What can we do? It isn't our town. Why should we care? We are going home," Larry Stevens said and grabbed his wife's and son's arms, turned his back, and started toward his house. Others followed suit, but a few of the people were moved by Wesley.

Todd wrenched his arm free from the hold his father had. "Father, what is wrong with you? I am ashamed to be called your son. You don't care about anyone but yourself."

Larry slapped him across the face. "Don't you ever talk to me like that again. Do you understand me?"

Todd stood there, a red welt rising on his face. He stared down his father and said, "I understand all too well. I agree with Mr. Danvers, and I, for one, think we should do something. When I am done, I will pack my things and move out of your house. You will never have to lay your eyes on me again. I am ashamed of you and your beliefs." Todd turned to Mr. Danvers. "I want to help, if you will have me."

Larry turned and, with his head held high, grabbed his wife's arm, and pushed his way through the crowd toward his cottage.

"Yes, Todd, you are most welcome. We will need all the hands we can get. We must help with whatever we can, blankets, food, medicine, muscle. None of us know what condition Johnstown is in right now or what horrors her people are suffering."

Turning to the other members of the club who were still on the porch or starting to walk away, Wesley continued, "How can you be so unfeeling and turn your back on them? Are you that afraid of getting your hands dirty or mud in your shoes?" Wesley walked to the door to the clubhouse and blocked the way. "We are going to help, because it is the decent, Christian thing to do. You can go home to your snug mansions and forget about this place, or you can step up and help. I am getting together anyone who wishes to help, and we are going to Johnstown."

Wesley walked back to where his family was waiting. "Everyone, go and get some work clothes on, put on some pants, pack a small bag, get all the medicine, bandages, and food and water you can carry, and meet me at the wagon."

Wesley turned and searched the crowd for Frances Brown. She was standing near the railing behind all the members.

"Frances, we need to get supplies from the store. Will that be all right? I will pay for everything we take."

"Absolutely, I will give you whatever you require. Payment is not necessary, my friend. My home is in Johnstown, along with our sons and grandchildren. I have lived through many floods, and some people do not pay attention and will lose everything. Most are smart about the floods, but with the dam bursting, who knows what Johnstown is like now?"

Wesley placed his hand on Frances's shoulder. "You're welcome to join us. Thank you for your generosity and willingness. I will pay for the supplies we take. I don't want you to suffer along with the rest of Johnstown. I will pull up the wagon, and we can load it there. Walter, we will meet you in twenty minutes in front of the store. Anyone who wishes to come with us to Johnstown, meet in front of the store in twenty minutes. We are going to go see what is left and if we can help out. *Move!*"

Turning, he spotted Mr. Daniels near the door to the clubhouse. "Mr. Daniels, would it be possible to get supplies from the club to take with us? I know there are linen closets and pantries filled that after today will not be used. May we take them with us and help the people of Johnstown?"

"Yes, of course, Mr. Danvers. What you are doing is commendable. I would like to come and help, but my place is here until all the guests have left. Godspeed, Mr. Danvers. And God bless you and what you are doing. I pray you will not have need of all the supplies you are bringing, but I know in my heart that you will."

Shirley turned to go back to the cottage to get ready to go to Johnstown when she saw Todd standing by the railing watching his father and mother walk away. She walked up and put her hand on his arm. "That must have been hard, to stand up to your father like that."

"It was. I have done what he has said all my life. I guess it is time to stand on my own two feet." Todd smiled.

Smiling up at him, Shirley said, "It was the right thing to do. We should get ready, or we will be left behind."

Todd took Shirley's hand and bent over it and kissed her. "Yes, let us get ready. Thank you."

People were spurred into action, and some raced back to their houses to gather their supplies, change clothes, and get the teams hitched up. Others went home to pack up to go back to Pittsburgh.

Twenty minutes later, a caravan of six covered wagons, all filled to the brim with food, water, clothes, blankets, and medicine, were lined up in front of the store. As Wesley looked over the group assembled, he heard a shout. Looking down the road toward the laborers camps, he saw a parade of people walking up to join the caravan. Most were on foot, but they carried shovels, picks, and whatever meager belongings they had to go to help the people of Johnstown.

With all the food, medicine, and muscle he could round up from the club and its members, Wesley started the caravan on the journey to Johnstown, knowing it would be morning before they reached their destination.

Chapter Twenty-One

The road was very muddy and slippery in most places, which was understandable as it had been raining on and off for almost a week. The group was unusually quiet, each lost in their own thoughts as to what they would find when they reached Johnstown. As the group of six wagons rounded the bend, they came upon the town of South Fork. They brought the wagon train to a stop near a pile of rubble. As Walter climbed down from the wagon, a small group of people emerged from a damaged barn nearby.

"Hello! Is everyone all right?" Walter asked.

"We are still a bit shaken up, but we are all right. Where is your caravan going in this horrible weather?"

"We were at the lake when the dam broke. We're on our way to Johnstown to see what the damage is and see if they need help of any kind."

"It is very admirable what you are doing, but you may not get the reception you expect. The townspeople may be angry and feel it is your fault that they are in the predicament they are in."

"Nonetheless, we are going to help. It is the Christian thing to do. How did your town fare?"

"We lost about twenty homes and four people are unaccounted for at this time. We were very lucky. We heard the train whistle and headed for the hills. The four who are unaccounted for were downstream, and we were unable to warn them."

"Is there anything you need right now? We can offer blankets, water, and food."

"Thank you kindly. Most of our supplies are dry. We all have many friends and family in Johnstown, so please, take some supplies with you to help them."

"Thank you, we accept. There can never be enough blankets and water."

Walter called to the waiting group, and they all followed Mr. Walsh to the nearby barn. Mr. Walsh pointed to a stall full of supplies. "Please take these with you. Give whatever help and comfort you can with them. It is not much, but every little bit can help."

"Thank you kindly, Mr. Walsh. God bless you."

When the supplies were loaded into the wagons, Walter thanked Tom again and climbed back on the wagon. With a wave of his hand, he cracked the reins, and the horse caravan was once again on its way.

Slowly, through the muddy trail, the group continued. The road they were traveling followed the river, and time and again, the railroad tracks would come into view, for they too followed the valley toward Johnstown. The scenery was much different than the first time Sarah had come this way. It seemed so long ago that they followed this road toward the club, that first wonderful summer. All along the shoreline, Sarah could see evidence of the force and magnitude of the water that preceded them down this valley. Trees were ripped up by the roots and tossed aside, mud covered everything, and the road was almost washed away completely in some places.

As the wagon train approached the Valley of Little Conemaugh, the road became almost impassible. Steven, Michael, Darryl, and Todd got out of the wagons and walked ahead of the caravan, moving trees, limbs, rocks, and other debris that blocked their path. When the immigrant workers saw what they were doing, they exited the wagons and helped clear the way for the wagons. Their pace slowed considerably, but they were moving forward, and that was what counted.

Shirley climbed up to the front of the wagon to sit with her father. As they slowly made their way, she could see the train tracks and railroad ties that had been torn up and tossed aside like kindling.

"Father, do you see the railroad tracks in the rubble?"

"Yes, dear. But do not fret. I am sure Richard and Justin made it to Johnstown and are probably miles away from here, safe and sound. They probably could not get back to the lake because the tracks are torn up."

Stifling a sob, Shirley just nodded.

As the group rounded the bend, they looked for the Viaduct that rose over the river. They only saw trees that were knocked down and rocks and mud. The Viaduct was gone! In its place was a hole where the pilings had been dug. The mud was especially thick on the road, and the horses had to be led, so as not to slip. When they passed the area, they decided to make camp for the night. The sun was dipping low over the horizon, and with the roads extremely muddy and debris filled, it was not safe to continue. They found a large, open area and pulled the wagons close. Steven and Todd made a makeshift corral for the horses. After the horses were fed and watered and secured for the night, Steven and Todd joined the group. Sarah had made a wonderful-smelling stew, and they all sat down to give thanks for their journey.

Wesley did the honors. "Dear Lord, thank you for the safe journey so far. Help to give us strength to continue on and help your people who are in need. Please watch over us and our friends and family in this difficult time. In your name we pray, amen."

A chorus of amens could be heard, and they all started to eat, each lost in their own thoughts. After the meal was eaten and cleaned up, everyone drifted off to find a dry place to sleep. Walter and Wesley took a large tarp and made a lean to, just in case it started to rain again. The night sky was clearing and stars could be seen twinkling. Shirley lay on the blankets and stared at the stars. She wondered if Justin was looking at the same stars and thinking about her. Her mind wandered to all the horrible things that could have happened to Justin, and as she lay there staring at the stars, she started to cry. Sheila, who was sleeping near Shirley, heard her and reached over and held her hand.

"Shirley? Are you okay?"

"I am fine."

"Why are you crying? Are you cold or hurt?"

"No, I am fine. I was just lying here thinking about Justin and if he was looking at the same stars and thinking about me. Then all these horrible thoughts came into my head… Oh Sheila, what will I do if he dies? I will be lost."

"He will be all right. He is a strong, smart man, and he loves you very much. There won't be anything that stands in the way of him getting to you so you can be married. Just wait, you will see."

"I hope so, but I'll try not think of bad things, just of our wedding and getting married. Thank you. I think we should get some sleep. It will be a long day, and we will be getting into Johnstown early tomorrow morning. Who knows what we will find? Good night, Sheila."

"Good night, Shirley."

Sheila rolled over and snuggled into her blankets. She looked over to where her mother and father were lying. She could see them talking quietly so as not to disturb the others. As she lay there, she thought about Darryl. He was sleeping on the other side of the fire. She had seen him in many different settings, at dinner parties, or playing with his friends, but today she got a look at another side of him. He was out there working to clear the trail, guiding the horses, and doing whatever needed to be done. This was as far away from a lawyer's office that you could get, but he looked so natural helping everyone. She was so happy that they would be married. She sighed and closed her eyes to get some sleep.

~~

The new day dawned bright and clear. The rains had moved out, and the sky was a clear blue as the group packed up to get moving. Todd, Steven, and Michael took turns with the immigrant workers clearing the brush and trees away from the path. Darryl and Derrick helped guide the horses of the other wagons so the men could clear the path. The mud started to dry up, so the road was not as slippery, but there was still a considerable amount of debris left in the water's wake.

There was not much left of Woodvale, or any of the other towns that they passed on their treacherous journey to Johnstown. At each stop they were able to lend a little comfort, but as they saw what the condition of the smaller towns were, each of them envisioned Johnstown, a town that many of them had close ties to. The mood of the group got more and more somber the closer they got to Johnstown.

Chapter Twenty-Two

When they left the last town they would reach before Johnstown, Walter walked back to the wagon and climbed aboard. Sarah said nothing as he pulled her close and kissed her on the cheek. No words needed to be spoken, they were both thinking of Shirley and what they would find in Johnstown and if Justin was alive.

As soon as everyone had remounted the wagons, they started off on the final leg of the journey. Everyone was quiet, and all Walter could hear was the snorting of the horses and the creaking of the wagons and harnesses. They were approaching Prospect Hill, and from there they would be able to see Johnstown. Each hoped the damage would not be as bad as it had been in the towns they had recently passed, but knew that it could be as bad or worse. Johnstown was a larger, more concentrated town, and they were sitting in the middle of a valley, with mountains on all sides. Everyone knew that Johnstown had survived floods before and probably would again, but the question ran through everyone's mind: how did they fare this time?

In the early morning light they stood on Prospect Hill, and a silence fell over the group as they looked toward where Johnstown should have been. The only sounds that could be heard were the horses, who were puffing and foaming after the ride from the lake to Johnstown.

It was gone! Everything that was familiar was flattened. No one spoke as they looked out over the town.

They searched for familiar landmarks. Only a few were visible from the view on the hill. The stone church still stood along with some of the houses around it. The houses along the river were gone, and many of the houses that still stood were leaning or severely damaged. Some of the buildings they could see had large trees sticking out of the sides. There were piles of trees, wagons, furniture, and whole houses and parts of houses lining the streets. Men, women, and children could be seen standing on the piles that were once their homes. The iron works and the lumber mill still stood.

They saw people moving around, searching for loved ones in the devastation. From where she was standing, Shirley could hear names being called and the anguished cries of those finding dead loved ones. As the group stood there and watched, more and more people could be seen moving about. Sheila and Todd walked to where Shirley was standing. Sheila knew she was looking for the train in the hopes of finding Justin and Richard in the town below. When she couldn't find the train, Shirley started to cry.

Todd put his arm around her. "We will find him. Maybe they made it out of Johnstown, on the other side, and back up the hill. Do not think the worst. They could be anywhere. They even could be some of the voices that you hear. Isn't his family from Johnstown? He could be searching for them. Do not give up hope."

"I know, I was just hoping to see the train, you know?"

"You are a good man, Todd Stevens. No matter what anyone says." Shirley reached over and kissed Todd lightly on the cheek.

Todd blushed and mumbled something Shirley could not hear.

Wesley called to everyone to mount up, that there was work to be done. When the wagon convoy reached the bottom of the hill, the group agreed that the church on Franklin and Main would be the best place to set up a refuge for the survivors. Once the plan was set, they realized they would have to cross the river to get to the church. The river was high and moving swiftly. Wesley got down and went to talk to Walter.

"We have to find a place to cross the river. The water is way too deep here. These wagons will never make it. Let's look down this way."

Walter and Wesley walked a few hundred yards up the river, scouting for the best location.

Wesley nodded toward where the river widened. "Here is a good place. The water is only to the bottom of the wagons. Our supplies should stay dry enough, and the wagons should stay solidly on the ground, I hope."

Walter picked up a stick and threw it into the middle of the river. The two men watched as it raced downstream. "The water is moving very rapidly, but I think the wagons are heavy enough not to be pushed downriver in this current."

"The best way would be to go one at a time, with the first wagon bringing a rope across the river to be set up as a guideline for all the other men to hold on to while they guide the wagons. We can tie the rope to the back of my wagon, and you can feed the rope out until I get across the river. I will guide the horses, for I fear they will not want to go into the river and they may bolt. We will tie the rope on this large rock, it seems pretty solid, and once I am across, I will tie the rope onto that large tree. Wait until I have the rope secure, then we can start the rest of the wagons, one at a time."

"That is a good idea. I will go tell the others."

Walter went back and explained how they would cross the river. The group followed Walter back down to where Wesley waited.

Wesley handed Eloise the reins. He tied the rope to the back of the wagon and handed the rest of the coil to Walter, who went to the rock and tied it securely. As Wesley started across the river, Walter slowly fed the rope out. Finally, a loud sigh of relief and a cheer went up; Wesley had made it across the river. He tied the rope onto the large, uprooted tree and motioned for Walter to start across.

Walter handed the reins to Sarah and gave the same warning to the passengers of his wagon. Halfway across, a log floating down the river startled the horses. They shied, and Walter had to struggle to keep the horses under control. The people in the wagon gave a scream as the wagon started moving side to side behind the frightened horses. He reached for a better hold on the horses' bridles and ran his hand down their necks to soothe them. He moved closer to the horses, and the horses focused their attention on him and finally calmed down.

When the horses were calm, he turned to smile at Sarah and let her know that they would be finishing the journey across the river. But she was not on the bench of the wagon. He looked in the back of the wagon, thinking she had climbed in the back to calm the children, and when he didn't see her, panic filled him. Frantically, he searched the muddy water. Nothing broke the monotonous brown of the river. He pulled the team to the shore and thrust the reins of the horses at Wesley and then scrambled to the back of the wagon to see if she was in the back. When he did not see her, he waded as quickly as he could out into the river, holding onto the guide rope. Frantically he searched and searched. Some of the men on shore heard Walter yelling for Sarah and came rushing into the river to help.

A shout went up. Walter spun to locate its source, hoping against hope that it was Sarah. Michael was racing toward a lone tree. Walter made it to the shore and started running after Michael. In the tree, down the river, was a clump of clothing. When Michael reached the shore parallel to the tree, the clump materialized into Sarah, clinging to a branch. She was covered in mud, and her eyes were closed.

"Sarah? Are you all right? Sarah?"

Slowly, Sarah opened her eyes. She looked round and saw Michael's face and realized she wasn't dead. A group of people arrived at the spot behind Michael and tied a rope around Michael's waist. He slowly walked into the raging river toward Sarah. Sarah saw Michael slip and let out a scream. He regained his footing and continued toward Sarah. When he reached the tree, Sarah reached for him, and he took her in his arms and gave her support as together they made their way slowly back to the bank.

Just as Sarah was getting out of the rushing water and onto safe ground, Walter arrived and grabbed his wife. "Thank God you are all right. One moment you were there and the next gone!"

"The horses started to dance, and the wagon got caught up in the water and started to sway side to side. I lost the reins, and when I reached for them, the wagon lurched and I went over the side. I tried to swim or stand, but the water was just too strong. I thought I was going to die. It swirled me around, and I didn't know which way was up. It seemed like such a long time, but then I was thrown up against something hard. I grabbed and held on."

As Michael was untying the rope from his waist, Walter reached out and grabbed Michael into a bear hug. "Thank you, my friend. Your quick thinking saved the most important person in my life. I am forever in your debt."

As Walter let Michael go, Michael's eyes misted over as he looked at his friend. "No, it is I who am in your debt. My family and friends are in Johnstown. Without you, I would have made the trip myself and would not have been as effective as I think we all will be." Walter smiled and said, "Why don't we call it even? Now let's get moving and get these supplies to the people in Johnstown."

"Agreed."

Smiling, everyone started back to where the others were waiting. Sarah waved to the children to let them know she was all right. Walter helped her into Michael's wagon, and the group started to cross the river, slowly and much more carefully. When the last wagon was across, the group made its way to the church.

Chapter Twenty-Three

They arrived at the church without another incident, and they all breathed a sigh of relief. As they dismounted the wagons, they were not surprised to be standing in mud and ankle-deep water. They were looking around at the people gathered near the church for a leader when the pastor approached them.

Wesley shook his hand. "Pastor, we are here to help. We have brought food, water, and medicine for the people of Johnstown."

"Bless you, my son!" Pastor Smith cried.

Walter looked around at the flattened town and could see the layout much better with no buildings in the way. "Johnstown was the basin the torrent emptied into."

"Yes, it was," Pastor Smith said. "If you look to the north where the Little Conemaugh comes into Johnstown, you can see that before it turns toward the Stone Bridge, it comes straight into the center of town, facing that mountain over there." He pointed behind them to emphasize the point. "But with the dam bursting as it did, and the angle of the river entering Johnstown, it was sure to run right over us. And when the water hit the side of the mountain, it had nowhere to go but to wash back into the town. Many people who were climbing the mountain on the west side of the town to escape the water got washed back when the water hit. As the water flowed back into town, it collided with more water coming in, and it caused quite a riptide. Eventually the water found the only outlet, which went past the Stone Bridge. I am told the bridge did not give way, so a lot of the debris probably got caught there. Then, when there was too much debris built up, it created a dam and the water could not get through, so that started a pool or lake in front of the bridge. People have come back from there and said it is quite a whirlpool."

Walter looked around as the pastor was talking, imagining the horror as the wall of water descended on the tiny town in the valley. A shudder ran through his body as he felt the terror of the people climbing the hillside to escape, only to be dragged back down.

"The one thing that saved the people of this town was the train whistle. A lot of people took the warning seriously, they knew something was just not right. Richard is well known and well liked in town. We all knew that if he was blowing the whistle in a steady sound that something was wrong. The mass hysteria that followed was a sight I will never forget. Nor will I forget looking out and seeing the hillside teeming with people, and then a short time later, the hillside was empty." Pastor Smith bent his head and removed his glasses. As he rubbed his eyes, he said, "The best idea is to leave the supplies in the wagons, that way they will stay dry. We can get what we need as we need it."

"Good idea." Wesley turned to the group and saw that they were all staring in disbelief. The town was a pile of rubble in most places, missing in others, and broken in the rest. The buildings that were directly in the path of the water were gone, but other parts of the town were just flooded. Everywhere you looked was debris of some kind and the ground was thick with mud. For many people in the wagons, this was not their first time in Johnstown, and even for them, they were hard pressed to find any familiar landmarks in the rubble.

Frances snapped out of her shock first. She jumped down from the wagon, and mud splashed everywhere. With a determined look on her face, she started clapping her hands and shouting, "Let's go everyone, there is work to be done and people to help. We won't get it done standing around like statues. Sheila, Shirley, please see to getting one of the wagons ready to hand out food. There will be many hungry people coming here, and we need to be ready. Eloise, Sarah, use the last wagon as a first aid wagon. Get Steven and Todd to help clean out the wagon and set up some beds for the injured. Michael, help Tyler and Thomas get one of the wagons ready to use as a playroom for the children. Tyler, Thomas, get your toys that you brought and put them in the wagon. You will stay there and play with the kids. Get some blankets also, just in case the children are cold or want to sleep. Okay, move! We have work to do and people to help."

Everyone jumped into action, and soon the front of the church was teeming with people hurrying here and there.

Frances had Darryl and Derrick start a fire and was able to put on a pot of water for stew. She helped Shirley and Sheila get the food. Derrick found a table in the debris and brought it over for his aunt. She placed a tablecloth on the muddy table and set about getting the food ready for anyone who was hungry.

Sarah and Eloise tended to cuts and other injuries out of the back of one of the other wagons. There were quite a few people that needed medical attention, and they were happy to help. Walter walked into the church and saw that it was mud strewn like the rest of the town. The pews had been moved into a position to hold caskets or boards with people on them. It was a makeshift morgue and, unfortunately, a very busy place.

Tyler and Thomas, being too young to help out in the city, followed Michael to one of the wagons to set up an area in the back of one of the wagons for the kids. Children came and played with the toys the boys had brought and were watched after while their parents searched for survivors. If there were no parents around, Pastor Smith consoled the children and made sure they were looked after until permanent arrangements could be made. Some of the children wandered in looking for their parents, and some of the children were brought by their families and were glad to see that they could leave them in good company while they looked for relatives or helped their neighbors. Tyler and Thomas took care of them, with a little help from Pastor Smith, and made them forget the horrors they endured for a while.

When the wagons were set up for the ladies to work from, Wesley and Walter said good-bye to the women and joined the other men from the lake in the courtyard in front of the church.

Pastor Smith called to all the volunteers. "You will need to search each house, barn, and pile of rubble for survivors. Some people who were swept away by the water grabbed onto whatever they could find, so you may find people in trees or on top of buildings. Most of the debris collected at the stone bridge. I have to warn you, along with the houses and other buildings, the wire works building did not withstand the waters. There is a great deal of barbed wire that was swept away and is tangled in the debris. People may be caught up in that as well. Early this morning we heard a loud explosion. I was told that the oil that was mixed in the water has caught fire, and the rubble is burning at the Stone Bridge."

"Wouldn't the water have put the fire out?" asked Darryl.

"One would hope so, but we cannot be sure. The water receded some overnight, so the buildings and other debris would be out of the water, and if that has caught fire, there would not be water nearby to put it out. I ask that you all be very careful and direct people back to the church. Good luck and Godspeed to you all."

Walter motioned to Wesley. "Why don't we take our group this way, and the workers from the club can go the other way. We can meet up at Stone Bridge. On our way we can check buildings and see if anyone is trapped."

"Good idea." Wesley turned and addressed the workers from the club. "Thank you all for coming to help. You have all worked so tirelessly and are still ready to go. I applaud your resilience. We will split into two groups. Walter and I will take this half of the group this way, Steven and Michael will take the rest of you the other way, and we will meet up at Stone Bridge."

Shirley raced over to where her dad was getting shovels and pick axes out of the back of the wagon. She grabbed Walter by the jacket. "Please find Justin! Please!"

"We will do our best. He is strong and smart, and we will do what we can to find him and bring him back safely. Be strong, dear." He bent over and kissed Shirley on the head.

As the group moved out of sight, Pastor Smith put his arm around Shirley and led her back toward the wagons. "There are many people who need your help, child. Please have faith in the Lord, and He will return your family to you."

The front of the church was a flurry of activity. Shirley went over to where her mother was helping the injured. When it slowed down, she went over to help Frances feed everyone and found Sheila already there handing out bread and bowls of stew.

Pastor Smith walked from group to group, helping where he could and directing people when he couldn't help. The tone was subdued, and there were many residents who were crying because they had lost loved ones. When Shirley or Sheila came by to give them a blanket or a cup of stew or coffee, a slow smile crept across their faces, warmed by the caring. Both girls, dressed in men's trousers and work shirts, moved from person to person, alternating helping the doctors that had generously given their services to the injured. The other would give out blankets or a cup of hot stew and a smile.

Chapter Twenty-Four

The ground was thick with mud and debris. As Walter started to pick his way down the road, he scanned the buildings for visible signs of life. Glancing down to make sure of his footing, he thought he saw a shoe. He stopped suddenly, and Wesley, who was following him, bumped into him.

"Sorry, I wasn't paying attention. Why did you stop? Do you see something?" Wesley asked.

When Walter did not reply, Wesley looked at his friend's face. Walter was staring at the side of the road, horrified. Wesley followed Walter's stare, and soon he saw what had shocked his friend.

Wesley carefully made his way to the pile of tree limbs and began to move them aside. In the mud below the limbs was a hand sticking out holding a shoe. No other part of the person was visible. Walter turned and rushed to the other side of the wagon. Wesley came up behind Walter and saw that Walter had emptied his stomach in the mud. Walter stood up and, wiping his mouth, turned to Wesley.

"It took me by surprise. I will be all right."

Wesley reached his hand out to his friend, and together they returned to dig the body out so he could be given a proper burial. Slowly the hand gave way to an arm and finally the rest of the body was revealed. The rest of the search party arrived as they were lifting the man out of the mud. They watched in horror as Walter and Wesley carried him to the wagon.

The rest of their search party gathered around and bowed their heads in silent prayer. Walter had tears streaming down his face, and Joseph came over and put his arm around his friend's shoulders. He turned to everyone and said, "I don't think any of us were prepared for this. But this is what we are going to find, more than survivors, and we must prepare ourselves, mentally, for more bodies. The survivors are going to be few and far between, and we will celebrate each one, and pray for the fallen. Let's continue on."

Slowly they all gathered their tools, wiped the tears from their faces, and continued down the road. All the familiar buildings were gone, and in their place were thick rivers of mud, broken homes, trees, and occasionally a person who did not survive. Wesley had tasked two wagons that the groundsmen from the lake had brought to load up the dead people that were found so they could be identified and given a proper burial. When the wagon was full, they would return to the iron works building, which was now being used as a temporary morgue along with the church.

Darryl made sure that each building and pile of rubble was searched, top to bottom. Each time a body was discovered, Darryl dreaded that it would be his friend, and each time it wasn't, Darryl was hopeful that he would be found alive.

As Darryl was searching a pile of debris that had once been a few houses, he heard weak cries for help.

"Over here! Wesley, Walter, everyone, I found some survivors that are trapped. Bring all the tools you can. *Hurry!*"

Walter and Wesley raced as fast as they could in the thick mud to the place where Darryl heard the cries. Working quickly, and carefully, the men removed the debris, piece by piece. Pieces of furniture, wood that looked like kindling that had once been the outside of the house, and parts of carriages were pulled away. Finally, they reached the source of the cries. A father, mother, and two small children were huddled inside the fireplace of the house. The stones had withstood the flood, and the debris had piled around it. They were banged up and very wet and scared. Darryl carried the children to a waiting wagon.

Walter helped the mother and father. "We are going to take you to the church. Pastor Smith has set up a refuge there. There is hot soup and blankets. Medical care can be received there also. Do you know if anyone else survived around here?

The mother said, "I heard some cries from the Jones's house."

"Where is the Jones's house, ma'am?"

"It was directly behind ours. The cries stopped some time ago. I fear they did not make it."

"How many people would be there?"

"The husband is a widower, and there are three children. They are all in their teens."

"Thank you, we will search for them. Go with these men and they will take you to the church."

"Thank you, sir. I don't know how we would have gotten out if not for you. God bless you."

After putting the children into the wagon, Darryl grabbed a few of the men standing nearby, and said, "We need to go to the Jones's house. There were cries heard from there."

Darryl led the men around the rubble and started searching and shouting for the Jones family. Darryl and the others pulled up boards and looked under the rubble. All of a sudden, Todd yelled, "Quiet! Everyone, quiet down. I think I hear something."

The other men stopped what they were doing and listened for any sound. After a few seconds, Todd called to the others, "Over here! I hear them."

He furiously tossed aside wood, tree limbs, and rubble. The other men reached him in no time and dug in. As Todd reached for a broken chair, he noticed a hand reaching through, the fingers moving. Spurred on, Todd called, "Hold on, Mr. Jones! we are coming!"

The other men came to where Todd was, and just as Todd was pulling a piece of table out of the way, Mr. Jones crawled out of the hole in the rubble. Darryl reached down and took Mr. Jones's hand and helped him climb out of the hole.

"Easy now, there you go. Are you hurt?" Darryl asked Mr. Jones.

"A bit bruised up, but my sons are down there. You must help them. Patrick wasn't moving. Aaron and Seth are with him."

Just as Darryl started back to the pile that was Mr. Jones's house, he saw Todd helping one of the sons out. As he reached the rubble, he saw a body being handed out. Darryl watched as Todd and one of Mr. Jones's sons carried Patrick to the wagon. The other son crawled out of the hole and followed his brothers. Mr. Jones went to the wagon where they were loading Patrick's body and embraced his sons. He turned and faced Darryl. "Thank you. These are my sons, Aaron and Seth."

"I am glad you are both all right. I am sorry about your brother," Darryl said. "This wagon will take you to the church, where you can lay Patrick out. We also have food and blankets to warm you."

"Thank you for saving me and my sons. Patrick is with his mother now and is watching us from above. He is at peace."

Todd walked up behind Darryl and clapped him on the back. "Come, we have other people to save."

Darryl looked around and saw a small group of men walking slowly down the street, calling for other survivors. He could hear Wesley's and Walter's strong voices ringing out over the destroyed town. Darryl and Todd turned and started after Wesley. They saw other members of their group also making their way down the street, stopping occasionally to dig in the rubble.

Along the way, they helped rescue people from trees. They also removed bodies of people who had been caught in the branches. The work was tedious and it was getting dark. As they approached the corner of Walnut Street, they realized that it had taken them eight hours of searching to go two blocks. Night was falling, but the glow from the direction of Stone Bridge lit up the night sky. The fire at Stone Bridge was still burning.

The rescue party continued down Main Street, stopping at all the rubble piles to see if they could help the living. Unfortunately, more dead were found than living. The wagons were piling up fast, and soon there were three wagons coming and going at all times. The weary party kept pushing onward. When they reached the end of Main Street, they had a clear view of the Stone Bridge. It was worse than they ever imagined, and the group stood there in shock and confusion, wondering where to start.

They could not see Stone Bridge, but instead a huge pile of rubble with fires scattered all over, and they could also see glints of steel as the fires burned. In front of Stone Bridge, where Stony Creek and Little Conemaugh met, there was a massive whirlpool. They could see debris being swirled around and around.

Wesley went to where Walter and Joseph were standing. "We need to cross the river to get to the debris at the bridge. I suggest we do that upstream a bit. We will never make it across near that whirlpool. It looks deadly."

"I agree. We can cross like we did on the way into town. We should go back a ways. We may find a less dangerous place to cross."

They went back to where the others were waiting and told them of the plan. Each man grabbed ropes and supplies and they started back along the riverbank to find a less treacherous place to cross. They didn't have to travel far when Steven found a narrow part of the river. As before, Wesley and Walter took the first wagon across and tied a guide rope for the others. Soon they were all on the other side and making their way toward Stone Bridge.

When they reached the bridge, they started pulling rubble aside, looking for the injured or dead. Very few survivors were found, in fact, very few bodies were found at all, but they did not give up. The men worked tirelessly late into the night by the light of the impromptu bonfire, and they only searched a small portion of the pile at the bridge. When they were too tired to go any farther, they climbed on the wagons and headed back to the church for some food and a few hours of sleep. They knew that the next few days or weeks would be filled with more of the bone-numbing tiredness that they were feeling already.

Chapter Twenty-Five

It was well into the night when they got back to the church. A weary Pastor Smith welcomed them back and got them coffee, blankets, and hot soup. Most of the people around the church were asleep. The group tried to be as quiet as possible so as not to wake anyone. Sarah and Eloise were among the few that were not sleeping but watching for more survivors. They came to their husbands with a smile and happy tears, glad that they were not hurt. They put the blankets around their shoulders and sat with them on the stairs of the church as they told the stories of their search.

"We didn't find Justin or Richard," Walter said. "Is Frances sleeping?"

"Yes, she fell asleep a few hours ago. I think we can wait until tomorrow to tell her, let her get some sleep. She has been worrying and working since we arrived. She has more energy than most people her age, but she was exhausted," Sarah said.

"I agree, she does not need to be awakened to be told that they are still missing. Let her have some peace for tonight. We are going to head out in the morning. We didn't see the train, so they may have made it to the other side of Stone Bridge, before the water hit. They could be miles away by now."

No one believed that story. They all knew that if Justin and Richard were alive, they would be in Johnstown right now helping their neighbors. The small, weary group fell silent, and soon, they were all sleeping.

~~~

The next morning, Shirley awoke, ready to continue helping the survivors. She got up and crawled out of the wagon and looked around to see how many had arrived since she collapsed at midnight. She saw her father and Mr. Danvers and raced over to see them.

"Father! You are all right. What time did you get in? Did you find Justin?"

Walter took his daughter into his arms. "No, dear, we did not find him, yet. But we are resuming our search today, and we will not stop until we find him. That is a promise!"

As the group started to stir, Eloise and Sarah brought them food and coffee. After eating a light breakfast, the men once again rose and gathered at the front of the church. Frances approached them.

"I know that if you had found Richard and Justin, they would be here now. I know in my heart they are alive and waiting for you to find them. Bring them home, please."

"We will do everything in our power to bring them back safely."

Armed with renewed energy, they got ready to set out. As the searchers started down the steps of the church, a loud explosion could be heard in the direction of the Stone Bridge. Everyone looked toward the sound and saw a yellow glow on the horizon. Pastor Smith came running out of the church along with some of the other survivors.

"Dear God! No!" he cried.

Sheila came running up. "Pastor, what happened? What exploded?"

When the pastor didn't answer, Joseph explained. "Probably the oil from the houses that got swept away and some hot coals came in contact and ignited. There is no telling how many more explosions will occur. We have to brace ourselves." Walter and Wesley took off running as Michael rounded up the men and told them of the new urgency. The men raced after Walter and Wesley toward Stone Bridge. They ran to where they had left the rope that crossed the raging river. One by one the men took hold of the rope and stepped into the cold water. They made their way slowly across the river, and when everyone, along with the wagons, was across, they raced as fast as they could in the mud toward the bridge.

When they arrived, Michael could see that they were not the only people who had come to help. Many were digging at the rubble and trying to pull people from the large pile of trees, broken houses, barbed wire, and other things that had gotten stuck when the bridge did not give way. As Michael stood searching the burning pile, he saw what he thought looked like the top of the smokestack on the locomotive. Michael kept his eyes on the spot where he believed the train was buried as he stumbled toward it.

Steven and Todd looked at Michael and then at each other. Steven yelled, "Michael, where are you going?"

When Michael didn't answer or slow down, Steven and Todd raced after him, yelling for him to slow down and be careful.

Michael reached the pile of rubble and struggled to climb up. Steven and Todd reached the pile shortly after Michael and raced after him. As Michael reached the top of the pile, he started pulling trees and limbs out of the way, clawing at the mud with his bare hands. Todd and Steven reached Michael and saw what looked like the top of the smokestack of the train. Steven heard men yelling to him and looked down the rubble pile and saw the rest of his search party starting up the pile.

Steven stood up and yelled, "Wesley, Walter, this way! We think the locomotive is here. Hurry!"

The immigrants who worked at the lake raced up the pile, bringing shovels and pickaxes with them. The men reached the top of the pile and started digging through the mud and debris, and slowly the top of the locomotive came into view. They yelled, calling for Richard and Justin. When they did not hear anything, they dug harder and faster. It was hard work and the men made slow progress. When they had uncovered most of the locomotive, they found it was filled with mud and leaves. There was no sign of Richard or Justin.

Not giving up hope, and believing in miracles, they continued to dig. Only when they reached the interior of the locomotive cab did they stop and start to believe that they would not find their friends alive. Exhausted from furious digging, Michael and the men sat down. All of the men looked to Michael for direction, but Michael was in shock. He couldn't believe his friend was gone.

Joseph had arrived at the top of the heap to see the dejected look on his son's face. He was about to ask Michael if he found any sign when they heard the banging noise. It was coming from the coal bin. Michael crawled over to the door and pried the door open. As he did, he heard crying. Michael looked in, and to his surprise, he saw two eyes in the darkness. He reached in and grabbed whatever he could get a hold of, and when he pulled the body out, he was looking at a coal-covered Richard. He helped Richard climb out of the coal bin and onto the debris that surrounded the locomotive. Richard turned to watch Michael, and when Michael saw his tear-streaked face, he feared the worst when he reached in the coal bin one more time.

At first Michael couldn't feel anything else in the bin, so he crawled in the small space, hoping to find Justin. He knew he was in there since Richard said they were together. He searched the bin with his hands, feeling for Justin, but found only pieces of coal. He gave up and turned to crawl out to ask Richard where Justin was, when he felt something soft near the door. He moved his hands over and felt a body.

Michael grabbed Justin's shirt and backed out of the coal bin. As he pulled Justin out, he saw Justin's eyes were closed and he was not moving. Frantically, Michael felt for a pulse and leaned his head down to hear if Justin was breathing. A sigh of relief went up when Michael looked up and smiled at Richard. Joseph and Steven carried Justin to the waiting wagon and put him gently into the wagon. Michael stood up and followed them down the wreckage to the waiting wagon. Joseph covered Justin with a blanket and made sure he was still breathing. Joseph wrapped a blanket around Richard's shoulders as he climbed up next to Justin and sat down. Michael gave Richard some water, and with a weak smile, Richard took a drink.

"The wall of water, a wall of death," he whispered. "My God, I have never seen such a sight." He took another sip of water and as he continued, his voice got stronger. "We were coming around Prospect Hill and going at a fairly good speed. We expected to make it to Johnstown and back before the dam burst. Although we were not sure it was going to break. We prayed it wouldn't, but after Justin told me of your efforts, I had a sinking feeling that the dam would break. Justin was putting coal into the engine as fast as it would burn. I had the whistle on the whole time. We had stopped and gave some boys playing by the tracks a penny each to run around town and warn everyone, when we heard the roar. It was unlike any noise I have ever heard. It was soft and then it grew louder and louder. Then we saw it. A forty-foot high wall of water. It was brown and yellow from the mud and oil. It was churning and roiling like a boiling pot of stew, filled with trees, bushes, houses, and occasionally glints of wire. Everything in its path was being eaten, swallowed by the water. People started screaming and running in all directions. I pushed the engine as fast as it would go, and we tried to outrun the wall of death. We were within minutes of Stone Bridge when we realized that we could not outrun the water.

"Justin grabbed me and pushed me into the coal bin, which by now was pretty empty. We hoped the locomotive was heavy enough to withstand the water. Justin climbed into the coal bin after me and slammed the door closed. It was deathly quiet and it felt like time stood still. Then we heard the water surround the locomotive. At first, the train seemed to hold its place, and we silently rejoiced. Our hopes were dashed when we felt the locomotive being lifted and tossed around like a toy in a bathtub. Justin and I were thrown around and got banged up pretty badly as the train was tossed about. It seemed like an eternity, but I believe it was just a matter of minutes. When the train stopped moving, I reached for Justin. It was pitch black. I tried to wake him. His shirt was wet but I was not sure if it was water or blood because water had seeped in and we got soaked. I tried the door, and it was either stuck or blocked. I feared we would die, and no one would know what happened to us… And like angels from heaven, you opened the door and rescued us." He shook his head, emotion robbing him of speech.

"You will be just fine, and I know that Justin will recover. I know that Shirley will give him the best care, and if that doesn't work, she will threaten him until he does get better!" Michael joked.

Richard smiled. Michael climbed up onto the wagon.

"Walter, Father, I am going to take them back to the church. I will make sure that Shirley sees Justin and assure her that he will get better."

"Thank you, Michael. I know that Shirley will be quite relieved, as will Frances and all the others. Please tell them that we are well and will be returning soon. Tell them not to worry." Walter smiled at his young friend.

"I will. I will see you soon. Godspeed!"

Michael urged the horses back toward the church, his wagon filled with the injured and weary. He looked forward to hot soup and a cup of coffee. He smiled when he imagined the happiness that Shirley would feel, knowing that Justin was alive. She would nurse him back to health.

As the wagon approached the church, Michael was not surprised to see Shirley helping injured people from wagons and finding them a place to sit until the doctor could examine them. She looked up and saw Michael approaching with a wagon full of people. She raced to his wagon and her eyes fell on Justin. Michael and Richard lifted Justin from the wagon. One of the doctors started toward Justin after Richard and Michael set him down. Shirley held Justin's hand and helped the doctor to clean the wounds and make sure that there was nothing broken.

Pastor Smith directed Richard to where he would be able to get a cup of coffee and some soup. As he approached the wagon where food was being served, Frances turned and saw her husband. Slowly she set down the ladle and rushed to his arms. Richard grabbed Frances and hugged her. Their tears of joy streamed down their faces as they held each other. "I was so worried! Are you sure you are all right?"

"Yes, I am fine. Justin saved our lives with his quick thinking."

"Justin, where is he?" Frances looked behind Richard, scanning the faces for her son.

"He is over with the doctor. He is unconscious. Shirley and the doctor are with him. Come, let's go see how he is." Richard put his arm around Frances and started toward the wagon.

Richard asked, "Have you seen Floyd or Margaret?"

"No, I haven't. I have been so busy at the wagon ladling food for everyone. I haven't been able to look around for anyone, but they have not been in the line. They may be searching and helping those around town and might not know that we have set up a place here."

Richard nodded at Frances, gave her a kiss on the cheek, and kept his thoughts to himself.

As they approached the wagon where Justin was being tended to, they saw the doctor was putting the finishing touches on a bandage on his head. They saw his arm was wrapped and had a splint on it.

"He will be fine. He is has a bump on his head and his arm is broken. He is also a bit dehydrated. Other than that, he just needs rest."

Shirley was sitting on the back of the wagon next to Justin. Frances bent down and took his hand.

"I hear you are a hero. I am very glad you are okay. I want you to just rest. You'll be just fine. You have quite a good-looking nurse here," Frances said as she smiled toward Shirley.

Frances reluctantly went back to the wagon, and Richard went to find Michael. He found him standing at the top of the stairs of the church. "Have you heard if there any survivors from the other side of town?"

"I don't know, but we can ask the pastor—he may have heard. Survivors were coming here when we left, and I am sure that more have arrived since. Floyd and Margaret may be around one of the wagons as we speak."

"Yes, good idea. I'll ask the pastor."

As Michael watched Richard walk into the church to find the pastor, he looked in the direction of where the lumber mill would be standing. He could not see the mill from the front of the church, so he decided to take the wagon. When the search parties from the lake started out, they had moved toward the bridge, where the flow of the water had gone, dragging half of the town with it in its wake. The mill was in the other direction. As Michael moved up

Vine Street, he passed the iron works building. He remembered Pastor Smith saying they were using the iron works building as the morgue. He could see many bodies laid out on the large floor and heard the cries of relatives as they found loved ones killed by the flood waters. He stopped the wagon and went inside. He looked around, searching for Floyd and Margaret.

Only a few living mixed with the dead, and of those, most had the bustle of important activity. There were too many dead to mourn one at a time. A solitary figure, moving as if in slow motion, caught his eye. Margaret. She was pulling a sheet over a body, while a young boy stood nearby. Slowly she turned and put her arms around the young boy as he wept.

Michael walked up behind her. "Margaret?"

As she let the young boy go, she turned around and stifled a cry. "Michael! How, what, why?"

"Are you all right? Where are the others?"

Margaret flung her arms around Michael. "It is so good to see you. What are you doing here? Weren't you up at the lake?"

"We were there when the dam broke. We tried to stop it, but we just couldn't. Wesley, uh, Mr. Danvers gathered up some of the people, and we came with supplies to help out. Frances is with us. She is at the church."

"Thank the Lord! She is probably cooking for everyone and mothering them all!" She laughed.

"You are right. Where are Floyd and the rest of your family?"

"The gristmill. You know that Floyd works there, and he thought it was the safest place to be. We frequently go there when the river rises. When the water started to rise, we went there as we usually do and started to settle in. Then we heard the train whistle. Dan went outside and heard people screaming. He watched the train leave the depot and grabbed a boy that was running by. He came running upstairs yelling, 'The dam has burst!' I thought I was going to die from fright long before I drowned. Well, Dan grabbed Anna and ran to the feed bins that are bolted to the floor upstairs. He threw the top off and tossed her in. He turned and grabbed me trying to get me in the bin. Between Dan and Floyd, they managed to get me inside and then Floyd climbed in after me. We made room for Dan, but that's when the water hit."

Margaret's pressed her lips together tightly. Her face had gone pale and her eyes out of focus. Michael had seen the expression on many survivors—reliving the nightmare asleep and awake. He reached for Margaret's clammy hand, and she gave a start, shaken from the memory. She squeezed his hand tightly and continued in a slightly more tremulous voice.

"Dan tried to climb in, but the water came through the window and he was swept away. His hand was on the lid, and it came crashing down. We huddled in the bin until it became very quiet. When we got out, everything had been washed away, even Dan. Floyd climbed out and helped me. As we reached for Anna, we realized she was not moving. In our panic we did not notice that she was so still." Frances reached in her pocket for a handkerchief to wipe her eyes. "Floyd climbed back in and helped her out. He handed her to me. She woke up as we lifted her out and told us that her arm hurt. It was broken when Dan dropped her into the bin. We didn't know where to go, so Floyd and I are taking turns sitting with her at the mill."

By the end of the tale, she was clinging to Michael's hand. He gently pried her fingers away and slipped his arm around her thin shoulders. "All right. Would you like to come with me? I have a wagon outside, and we can go get Anna and Floyd and take them back to the church. There is medicine, food, and the rest of your family there."

"Yes, let us go."

Frances followed Michael outside and let him help her into the wagon. He continued down Vine Street, and as he turned the corner onto Oak Lane, he saw the mill still standing just as Frances said. Some of the smaller outbuildings of the mill were gone, as was the water wheel, but for the most part, the mill stood.

Michael pulled his team to a halt in front of the front door of the mill. The door was gone, and as Michael approached the building, he peered inside. Most of the gristmill was still in one piece. The area where the burlap sacks of grain were once stacked was now empty. The upper floor where some of the mills supplies were kept seemed to be in place.

"Hello! Floyd?"

Michael heard shuffling footsteps coming from upstairs. At the top of the stairs, he saw Floyd peek out from behind the wall. Floyd started down the stairs.

"Michael? Is that you?"

"Yes, sir, Mr. Brown."

"Anna is hurt. Margaret and I have been tending to her. Margaret is at the iron works helping with the dead." Then it dawned on Floyd that Michael had been at the lake. "What are you doing here? Weren't you at the lake with Derrick? Is Derrick all right?" Floyd's voice grew louder as the panic he started to feel surfaced.

"Frances and Derrick are fine. Come, I have a wagon outside. Let's get Anna and take her to the church. There are doctors there, and they can help her. There are also blankets, coffee, and hot food. Wesley is with Derrick helping in the search for survivors, and Frances is at the church serving food and handing out blankets. Margaret is in the wagon."

Floyd started down the stairs helping Anna, whose arm was in a makeshift sling.

"Mr. Danvers? Wesley Danvers? The president of the bank? Here? Searching for survivors with my son? I don't understand."

Michael picked up Anna, wrapped her in the blankets, and carried her to the wagon. He handed Anna up to Margaret and turned to help Floyd. "I saw the dam break. We were trying to clear the spillway when it broke. After the lake was empty, we walked back to the lodge. There was a party inside, and when we got there, the people came out and saw the lake was gone. Wesley wanted to help. The look on his face was one I will never forget. He was angry and appalled at the unfeeling and uncaring attitude of the people, those he called friends. He rallied whoever wanted to go, and we came here with supplies to help. He has been digging in the mud like everyone else, searching. This has hit him very hard."

"Wow. I am impressed."

Michael loaded the Browns into his wagon and started toward the iron works. Floyd rode up front with Michael.

"What about Richard and Justin? Are they searching too?"

"Frances was at the lake when the dam broke. Richard and Justin left when we feared there would be a problem and drove the train to Johnstown to warn everyone of the impending dam break. Richard and Justin tried to outrun the water in the train. The 'wall of death' is what Richard called it. Their train was tossed about like a toothpick. They are at the church, a bit banged up, but otherwise they are fine. Richard was asking for you. He has quite a tale to tell."

"I'm glad they're safe. So many lives were lost today. I am glad the damage to my family was minimal."

"We cleaned out the store at the lake and brought the supplies with us. Pastor Smith has been wonderful. The stone church withstood the floodwaters and has served as a refuge for many. You will see when we get there. I am just glad we found you safe. I am truly sorry about Dan."

"Yes. He was a good boy." Floyd hung his head, and for the first time since the waters had taken his son, he wept.

They rode in silence until they approached the iron works.

"Do you want to go in now or do you want to come back?" Michael asked softly.

"We will come back. I think we need to get into some dry clothes and drink some hot soup. Anna will need to see a doctor as soon as possible. If Dan is here, we will find him when we come back."

They rode to the church in silence. Floyd helped Margaret down from the wagon. Michael reached in and picked up Anna. As they slowly made their way to the church, Derrick spotted them.

"Father, Mother! You are all right." He ran up to his parents and grabbed them in a bear hug. Everyone was crying and talking at once. Derrick spotted his sister in Michael's arms and very gently took her.

Michael could hear Derrick asking about Dan and did not hear the answer. He knew what Derrick's reaction would be at the loss of his brother. Although the brothers were three years apart, they were very close. Derrick would take the loss of his brother very hard.

∿

The group from the lake, as they came to be known, stayed a few weeks. Each day was the same, new horrors, new piles of debris to sift through, and new joys when loved ones were found alive, although this did not happen as much as the group wanted. Mostly there was sorrow and anguish. Many families and friends were never found. The water in the town subsided as it filtered through the debris at Stone Bridge. The town was covered in a thick mud, and everything was brown. All the color and life seemed to have been swept away with the floodwaters.

At the end of the week, Clara Barton and the Red Cross arrived in Johnstown. They brought medicine and all sorts of supplies. She organized the building of a Red Cross hotel for the survivors to live in. They brought furniture and helped get people back on their feet and off the street. It was a welcome sight for the weary residents of Johnstown to see people from the outside world come in and help. Ms. Barton's group came with a renewed energy and determination to help put Johnstown on its feet again. After the success of the first Red Cross hotel, more were built to house survivors.

As Wesley and his family gathered at the church to leave, Pastor Smith approached them.

"You all have been a blessing to this town. We will never forget you nor forget the wonderful work you have done here."

"It looks the same as when we came," Shirley said. "Like we haven't done a thing."

"Ah, my child, you see the town that has been destroyed. I see the spirit of my people arising from the ashes. We will all thrive once again. It will take a while for this town to be free of the mud and debris, but the spirit of the town is what you have helped. That is more important than washing the mud off the streets. There are more important things than material possessions. There are the things you cannot see, the kindness that you have given, a smile here, or a hopeful word, these things are more important than a table or chair."

Shirley smiled. She did feel a sense of pride in the work they had done. It was not the summer she expected, but then again, it was not the summer that Johnstown envisioned either.

~~~

As the weeks went by, reports of the devastation of Johnstown reached Pittsburgh on a regular basis. The newspapers were filled with the stories of death, destruction, and the horrors of not having water and food. The papers reported that over 2,209 people lost their lives and over 99 complete families had been wiped out.

Wesley saw that Ms. Barton stayed for five months helping Johnstown get on its feet, and as a thank you, the town bought her a gold pin and locket set in diamonds and amethysts. Wesley smiled when he read about all the donations to the town, including the ones his customers contributed. Wesley had set up a place to donate money, blankets, clothing, and food at the bank. The town knew of the work he and his family and friends had done in Johnstown, and they wanted to help out. He was quite vocal in the playful bullying he did to his customers to get them to help out.

Once a week he asked Walter to make a trip to Johnstown to deliver all the donations. Walter was pleased to deliver good news and enjoyed seeing Pastor Smith again. The donations continued for many months. Wesley was very pleased with the way his customers stepped up and helped out.

Wesley continued to send supplies and donations to Johnstown for over nine months, until Walter reported back that Johnstown was well on its way to recovery. Only then did he start to slow down. Although Wesley knew that it would be quite a while before Johnstown and the surrounding towns would be fully recovered, he knew it would happen.

Pastor Smith and the Browns kept in touch with Wesley, and when Walter would go to Johnstown to deliver donated supplies, he would bring back an update letter for the people of Pittsburgh from Pastor Smith. Wesley posted the pastor's letters in the bank for all his customers to see and had the newspaper publish them so the people of Pittsburgh and the surrounding towns would know of the progress in Johnstown.

Chapter Twenty-Six

As Sarah sat lost in the past, Walter came out of the bedroom. "Feeling better?" Walter asked as he sat down next to Sarah.

"Yes, finally. The lovely sunrise has chased away all the bad dreams. Today will be a magical day. I can barely believe that this day has arrived. The past year was one of horror and of accomplishment."

"Very true, my love. But we came out on top." Walter folded Sarah into his arms, and together they watched the sun rise. The warmth of the sun and the comfort of Walter's arms lifted Sarah's spirits, and as she closed her eyes to feel the sun on her face, she heard Shirley come out of her room and walk down the hall.

"Mom? Dad? Are you awake?"

Smiling, Sarah turned to her daughter. "Yes, dear, come sit with us. Did you sleep well?"

"Not really." Shirley giggled. "I am so excited and a bit nervous about today."

"Justin is a wonderful man, and he will make a fine husband. Why are you nervous?"

"Oh, I am not nervous about marrying Justin. It is what I have dreamed about for a long time. I am nervous about walking down the aisle in front of all those people. What if I trip? Or make a mistake?"

Sarah smiled and hugged Shirley. "Nothing like that will happen. You hang on to your father as you walk down the aisle, head held high, a big smile, and everything will be okay. Trust me, it will be a day that you will always remember."

They all rose from the couch, and while Water went to wake Tyler, Shirley and Sarah got dressed. Tyler usually took some coaxing to get out of bed, but once he was up, he was a barrel of energy. Sarah could hear the groans as Walter tried to roust Tyler.

The groans turned to squeals of laughter, and Sarah could hear Tyler getting up and getting dressed. Walter came into their room to get dressed with a big smile on his face. He loved the mornings, and waking Tyler was a joy he reserved for himself.

The family walked together to the kitchen in the Danverses' mansion. They had done this for many years, but today was special. Today Shirley and Sheila were getting married in a double ceremony, and Wesley had hired extra help to get everyone ready for the big day. Eloise explained to Wesley the amount of work required to get ready for a wedding, for the brides and their mothers to look just right. Wesley consented, as he did when it involved his family, and hired several of the local ladies to help the ladies of his household get ready for the wedding.

After breakfast, Sarah and her family went back to their house to get dressed. Shirley wanted to stay and get ready with Sheila, but there would not be room for two brides in Sheila's room, so Shirley got ready at her house. Two women were waiting to assist them. Sarah and Shirley were ushered into the living room, which had been transformed in their absence to a hair salon. Off to one side, tubs were set up to wash their hair. Large amounts of fluffy towels sat next to the tubs. On the table in the living room there was laid out all sorts of brushes and hair clips and bows. Being pampered was a great thrill to Sarah and Shirley.

Walter and Tyler went into Walter's room to get ready. They did not need help getting ready. They each had new suits, courtesy of Wesley and Eloise, hanging in their wardrobes.

When Sarah and Shirley's hair creations were completed, they looked in the mirror and marveled at the transformation. Shirley's long brown hair was piled gently on top of her head, held with the silver comb that Justin had given her, surrounded by bows of pale yellow. A pale yellow ribbon was woven through the curls that cascaded down her back.

Sarah's hair, which was considerably shorter than Shirley's waist-long hair, was pulled back into a loose bun and clipped with an ornate silver clip. The clip was a present from Frances Brown for saving her sons and family. Sarah wore the clip with great love and pride.

The dresses that they would wear had been hung from a hook on the wall. They had been ironed and cleaned and were just waiting to be put on. They got dressed one at a time. Sarah's dress was lavender silk with a white lace overlay. The long sleeves were a delicate eyelet lace. Four lengths of narrow lavender ribbon wound its way through the lace on the sleeves and ended up at the lavender ribbon that encircled Sarah's wrist. The sleeve had a small cloth button to hold the cuff together. The dress was high waisted and had a lavender silk sash around the waist. The skirt hung straight to the floor, and the lace covering the skirt was a smaller version of the eyelet lace that the sleeves were made of. The bottom of the dress was in a scalloped pattern that ran around the bottom hem. Sarah felt like a princess. She had never owned a more elegant dress, and at the moment felt very blessed.

Shirley sat on the couch and watched her mother's transformation. "Mother," Shirley gasped. "You are so beautiful!"

"Okay, Shirley, your turn."

Shirley got up and walked to where the townswoman was waiting. She had already put on her stockings and new shoes. They were white and had a small heel. They were the most elegant shoes that she had ever owned. The dress looked like a lace cloud on the floor, and when it was picked up and settled on Shirley's shoulders, the dress fell softly in waves around her slender frame. Like her mother's dress, the neckline was rounded with a high waist. The satin sash that wrapped around the dress ended in a large bow in the back, which hung down to the floor. The skirt was three tiers of fine lace cascading down into a V in the back of a short train.

Walter and Tyler called out, "Is it safe to come in? Is everyone decent?"

"Yes, you may come in," said Sarah.

Walter and Tyler walked into the room. They stopped in the doorway and were speechless. After a moment, they both bowed deeply, and Walter said, "You are both very lovely."

"Pretty terrific for girls," Tyler said.

Everyone laughed.

"Time to go, may I escort you?" Walter said as he approached Sarah.

"Of course, my prince."

Tyler walked up to his sister and, imitating his father, gave Shirley a deep bow and offered his arm to her. Shirley curtsied and accepted his arm. One of the townswomen swept the train up and followed the family out and down the stairs.

In the Danverses' mansion, similar preparations were taking place. The dresses that Sarah had made for the wedding were designed by Shirley and Sheila. The dresses were identical. The girls gave their mothers the option of the color of the dresses, and Eloise picked pale pink, while Sarah picked pale lavender. When all was said and done, the dresses were created perfectly from the drawings, and each lady looked like a princess.

When they arrived in the driveway, Walter turned to see Wesley and Eloise come out the front door. They were followed closely by Sheila and Thomas. Three carriages waited in the drive. Two of the carriages were identical, and the last was the Danverses' private carriage. Tears welled up in Walter's eyes as he looked around at the men standing at attention in their finest livery, ready to serve him. These were the men he worked with on a day-to-day basis.

Ryan helped Sarah into the carriage. She was followed closely by Shirley and Tyler. As Walter neared the door, he stopped and shook Ryan's hand. Ryan smiled back and shut the carriage door after he had climbed in.

With the wedding parties safely in the carriages, the groomsmen climbed aboard and started toward the church. The last carriage carried the rest of the Danveres' staff; all of the stable hands had been given the day off and were invited to the wedding. The caravan of carriages caused the people of Pittsburgh to stop and watch the magnificent teams go by. Wesley had similar carriages pick up the grooms and their families and one honored guest. A total of seven matching carriages carried the wedding party. Their destination, Pittsburgh Catholic Cathedral.

Pittsburgh Catholic Cathedral stood at the top of Main Street overlooking the steel mill and all of the houses and shops that created the thriving community. The cathedral's stone spire housed a symphony of bells that played everyday at high noon.

Today was a special day. The bells in the spire started ringing at ten that morning. They would stop ringing at eleven while the wedding was taking place. After the wedding, they would start ringing the joyous sound again.

This morning, June 1, 1890, a year after the tragedy in Johnstown, the organ music filled the church and the surrounding area. The sun was shining brightly, and there was a slight breeze in the air that carried the smell from the gardenia trees that filled the churches garden. Carriage after carriage arrived at the church for the wedding of Sheila and Darryl and Shirley and Justin. Smartly dressed liverymen were on hand to help the guests down from the carriages and to open the doors of the church. This was the first double wedding in the city, and the entire town had turned out to either attend the wedding or to line the streets to watch as the brides and their families arrived at the church.

The railings leading into the church were decorated with white, yellow, and blue carnations. Some of the guests lingered outside, enjoying the beautiful day when they heard the jingle of the harnesses and the clatter of the horses' hooves. Around the corner came a sight seldom seen in Pittsburgh, a caravan of seven identical carriages, each pulled by four high-stepping, white horses with shining harnesses decorated with yellow and white or blue and white carnations. Four crisp liverymen were atop each of the carriages. The carriages alternated their decorations of yellow and blue, and the last carriage was a mixture of blue, yellow, and white, and held a very special guest.

Wesley had hired the carriages to bring the wedding party to the church, and although each carriage came from a different part of town, they all arrived at the same time. Each carriage came to a halt in front of the church, and the liverymen riding on the back of the carriages jumped down and went to the doors of the carriage. The first carriage door opened, and out climbed Wesley as the liveryman stepped forward to help Eloise. After Eloise, Thomas jumped out and the liveryman closed the door. As soon as the door was clicking shut, the door to the next carriage opened. Walter climbed down, and the liveryman stepped forward to help Sarah, and much like Thomas, Tyler jumped out. They all congregated before the steps and watched as the rest of the carriages were emptied.

The next carriage held Darryl and his family. There was backslapping and jokes as Darryl joined the group. The next carriage opened, and Richard Brown alighted. Frances climbed down next, and went to stand with her husband. Justin jumped from the carriage in a grand flourish. "Tada!" Justin cried. "Here I am, ready to be married. Let's *go*, baby!"

Everyone broke into laughter, and Justin, laughing at himself, walked over to Darryl.

"You sure you want to do this? We can take one of these carriages and be at the train station in twenty minutes."

"Why don't we wait and take Shirley and Sheila with us? I think it would be much more fun than just us!"

"True, I suppose we can wait!"

The next carriage door opened, and Joseph Stamper climbed out. His wife, Betty, was helped out after him, and then came Michael and Steven. The sixth carriage opened, and Floyd Brown climbed down. Margaret, Anna, and Derrick followed. Derrick raced to his friends and was immediately enveloped in their circle. Looking around, Derrick thought everyone was there, but there was one last carriage in the line.

"I wonder who is in the last carriage? It seems the wedding party is here, so who are we missing?" Derrick asked.

The group of friends started to walk slowly down the road to the last carriage.

The liveryman opened the door, and out climbed Pastor Smith. Loud whoops and hollers could be heard as the friends raced to the pastor's side. They had not seen Pastor Smith since the flood, and they were pleased he was attending.

"Will you be officiating, Pastor?" Justin asked.

"No, I am here as a guest. I am just here to enjoy the festivities, see my friends, and celebrate in this happy occasion."

Walter and Wesley had arrived at the fringe of the group gathered around Pastor Smith.

"So glad you could make it, Pastor. I was not sure, so I sent the carriage to the train station just in case. Good to see you, my friend," Wesley said as he grasped Pastor Smith's hand.

"I would not have missed it for the world. Another flood could not have prevented me from attending," he said laughingly.

Pastor Smith turned to Walter and Sarah. He motioned for Justin to come over, and he put his arm around his shoulders. "My friends, as a wedding gift to Justin and Shirley, I want to give them a place to live. My sister has a house that was not damaged by the flood, and it has a small apartment on the second floor. I would like to give it to Justin and Shirley as a wedding present, to live in, free of charge, until they see fit to move."

Sarah's eyes welled up with tears. "That is most generous. I am sure they will appreciate it. Thank you, Pastor."

Justin pumped the pastor's hand. "Thank you, Pastor. This means a great deal to us. I am sure that Mother and Father will be relieved to know that Shirley and I have a place to live. It will give them more room, with my room empty."

"It is the least I can do. My sister's family was saved by the train whistle, and we are forever grateful to Justin and Richard."

"Thank you for the generous wedding gift, and please, thank your sister for us, until we can get there and thank her ourselves."

"I will do that, my son. You are most welcome, and I expect to see you in services on Sunday," he said with a gleam in his eye.

"Absolutely!" Justin chuckled.

Pastor Smith turned and faced Darryl. "Now, Darryl, as for you and your lovely bride, in my congregation I have many talented people. My congregation has paid a local wagon maker to build you a nice buggy for you and Sheila. One of the farmers has donated a fine horse for pulling your carriage. We hope that you will ride in this carriage with pride."

"I am overwhelmed, Pastor Smith. I know Sheila will be too. We will cherish and enjoy your fine gift for many years to come. You may see us in town when we visit Shirley and Justin, because you know that Sheila and Shirley will hate to be separated. And yes, we will come to your services also, when we are in town."

The families started to drift into the church. As the coachmen watched the young men enter, they turned to let the brides out of the carriages.

As Shirley stood looking up at the magnificent church, she listened to the bells play.

"Are you ready?" Shirley asked.

"Definitely. Are you?"

"Definitely. Nervous?"

"Definitely. You?"

"Definitely." With that, they both dissolved into laughter.

"Let's go, my friend. Our grooms are waiting."

Wesley and Walter were waiting at the top of the stairs for their daughters. They watched as they walked hand in hand up the stairs to the church, the liveryman following behind carrying their trains. As they entered the church, the organist started the wedding march. Wesley held his arm for Sheila, and Walter held his arm for Shirley. Side by side, on their fathers' arms, Shirley and Sheila slowly started up the isle.

Behind them, Ryan closed the doors.